MW01615378

The Dowrra Series

THE

WAYSIDE

A NOVEL BY

A.A.GORDON

RUNEFIRE PUBLICATIONS • SOUTHAMPTON

Published by RUNEFIRE PUBLICATIONS
in Southampton, Ontario.
Copyright © 2018 by A.A. Gordon
Previously published in 2017 with Amazon 9781520785523

This book is printed in Montreal, Canada, by Marquis Book Printing.
It is edited by Sigrid MacDonald, Rick Irwin and Sheena Bolton.
The author portrait is by Candice April Photography.
Cover design © is by A.A. Gordon.
Formatting is by We Make Books in Toronto, Canada.
Cover images from Public Domain Pictures and Shutterstock.

ISBN: 9781775311843

www.authoraagordon.com
Third edition: May 2018

Also by

A.A. GORDON

The Dowrra Series:

Bloodline

Redemption

Wolfsbane

Incubus

Contents:

BOOK ONE
The Dowrra Series

THE **WAYSIDE**

A.A.GORDON

RUNEFIRE
PUBLICATIONS

Prologue

In the darkness... a heart beats...

Each steady thud drums more insistently upon my senses as it draws nearer from the night. I breathe in expectantly, and my body, which is as hard as carven stone, stirs for the first time in hours. Along with the pungent scent of cigarettes, wet pavement, car exhaust, and garbage is a wicked lure.

My pupils dilate wide enough to blacken my eyes completely, and my eye teeth lengthen several inches. I taste venom, and it numbs my tongue. I open my eyes, and my prey pulses vibrant orange and yellow in the night. I can sense their fear of the dark.

The dark is where monsters live.

I am absolutely silent as I slide from the rooftop and land on the wet pavement below. Agile as a cat, I strike hard and fast. Fragile bones break under my powerful fingers, and soft skin yields bountifully. The heartbeat grows ever fainter until all warmth is gone and the body is as cold as I was before. It falls heavy and limp from my arms. With my bloodlust finally sated, I can see her.

The street lamps are far away from the alley into which I have dragged her, but I can see her dark skin and lifeless black eyes shining eerily blank; her thick hair has been dyed blonde, and her makeup is smudged from the misting rain. Her necklace suggests she was a big sister, and her wedding ring indicates she was a wife. I can even tell, from her pantsuit, that she probably worked hard and, from her knock-off shoes, that she didn't make enough money for it. I can see she was young and beautiful.

But I will never see her sacredness. I cannot see what has been lost in her, which will be mourned tomorrow.

To me, she is only prey, and I am only her hunter.

PART ONE:

There are those whose teeth are swords,
whose fangs are knives,
to devour the poor from off the earth,
the needy from among mankind.

-Proverbs 30:14

Gwendolyn

Chapter One

Gwendolyn Rhys lowered her head as her face grew uncomfortably warm. She'd caught sight of James leering at her again between the cheap bottles of wine in the mirror behind the bar. He made her want to strike that stupid grin from his face before heading home to take a long shower.

She reached the counter and grudgingly accepted his water from Sonia, who eyed her with a mixture of sympathy and anxiety. Gwen wasn't the first Diner waitress to suffer flirtatious harassment, but James wasn't going to be the first patron to suffer Gwen's wrath for it either.

She braced herself, trying to find it in her to smile patiently, before she turned back toward her customer. She watched his eyes travel up her legs, which were bare under the terrible Diner uniform. He eyed the curves of her hips and then her breasts. She immediately lost the battle with her expression and frowned at him when he finally bothered to meet her eyes with a deliberate grin.

Digging up every ounce of self-preservation she had remaining, which was barely sufficient, Gwen straightened and crossed The Diner to him. She lowered his water to the tabletop next to his plate of untouched breakfast with a little more force than was necessary.

'Anything else?' she demanded briskly.

In the beginning, she'd wondered why he never ate any of the food he ordered. As time went on, it had soon become clear James wasn't there for the food. She was pretty sure, in his own perverted way, that he actually enjoyed pissing her off.

'Aye,' he said huskily in an accent that had once intrigued The Diner waitresses, 'why dinna ye sit, lass?'

'You know I'm very busy,' she growled as calmly as she could. 'Will there be anything else today?' she added with the fake smile she'd perfected long ago.

When he said nothing, Gwen picked up his untouched plate and turned away from him.

'I will get your bill then,' she advised him sharply.

She was shocked when he moved with what seemed like unnatural speed to grab her free wrist. The strength of his fingers yanked her to a sudden stop, and she gasped, dropping the plate in her other hand. The shattering of glass silenced the gentle murmur of The Diner and turned every head their way.

Oblivious to their audience, James yanked Gwen backwards into his waiting lap. His hand felt like cold steel as it wrapped around her arm with an unquestionable power.

x x x

Miguel

I truly dislike meeting in public, but I despise it most when the sun is up. During the day, the human world is loud and bright. Their proximity is always overwhelming to my kind, but today was Friday, so there was an increased sense of urgency among them.

Of course, I understood the concerns of my human contact, Agent Samuel Benet, who had suggested the meeting location. He was new to his role, and this would only be our third meeting. He'd been a field agent before his promotion, so the human's interactions with vampires had mostly been with the misfits of our race.

Nonetheless, the diner he'd chosen to meet at was simply unbearable. It was small and crowded and smelled strongly of burned toast. In addition, the young agent hadn't managed to acquire punctuality after our last two meetings, and he was five minutes late *again*. Patience was not one of my virtues, and I was nearing my limit with him.

Anticipating him to be another five to ten minutes, I went to the bar for a coffee. I don't care for the human diet, but I hoped it would keep the waitress on the floor from pestering me while I waited.

As I turned toward my seat, the door opened, and the scent of another male vampire blew in. I glanced up instinctively and saw it was James McNeil, a rather infamous three-hundred-year-old vampire from the Isle of Barra, Scotland. His stride of self-importance was unmistakable.

Upon catching my scent, he looked up in eager anticipation of a fight, but then he recognized me and immediately lowered his gaze. Keeping his head respectfully inclined, he acknowledged my rank with proper humility. Once I had sat down again, he continued toward the back of the small establishment.

I returned my attention to the front when Agent Benet finally stumbled in. He was sweating and panicked as usual with two coffees, which seemed to have spilled down his knuckles. Under one arm, he was awkwardly trying to balance his briefcase.

He saw me and immediately approached the table.

'I'm so sorry, Sir! The traffic—'

'I already have a coffee,' I interrupted him when he tried to put one of his messy cups in front of me.

'Of course you do. We're in a diner,' he mumbled to himself. He retracted his arm, and the briefcase fell. Just before it could bounce off the table, and spill my coffee all over my Armani suit, I snatched it in one hand.

Irritated, I glanced slowly around to be sure no one had noticed my inhuman speed. Then I looked up into Agent Benet's horrified, unblinking eyes.

'Please sit down,' I invited calmly, and he sighed with

great relief before spilling his unorganized self into the booth across from me.

'Okay...' he said absentmindedly, rubbing coffee stains into dress pants in desperate need of ironing. His bright eyes danced about the table, wondering where to start, and he kept jerking his head to toss back his unkempt hair.

It always amazed me how creatures like him managed to survive in the world. Any vampire disposed to be so utterly idiotic would've been killed off long ago while humans seemed to entertain a sort of fondness for their eccentrics.

I wordlessly handed him his briefcase back, for which he was immensely thankful. Once situated, he retrieved an unevenly stapled booklet from inside it.

'Uh... so, good news!' he exclaimed. 'They have decided to accept your proposal for the transfer of 10056—'

'Her name is Rosie,' I cut in with offence.

'Right, uh... Rosie,' he amended. 'Director Donaldson has agreed to transfer her to your custody, provided she is not allowed to remain in the city and she stays well away from all densely populated areas for at least six months,' Agent Benet explained.

Rosalina Armando was a two-hundred-year-old vampiress from Évora, Portugal. She was a first-time offender after her public display of partaking of a Donor in the middle of a nightclub. He'd later died in the hospital, due to blood loss, but that transgression was a relatively small offence since the exchange had been consensual. Rosie had the paperwork, signed by her Donor, to prove he'd understood the risks of his choice. It was the public nature of the demonstration for which she'd been taken into custody. She wasn't from my coven, but, as Ambassador of Human Affairs, it was still my duty to see to her release.

'Agreed,' I acknowledged. 'What about Alexios?'

Alexios Kokinos, an unruly four-hundred-year-old

Greek vampire, had been a pain in my ass for decades. My father and I had quickly come to understand why Lord Grégoire of La Société in Paris had been so insistent we take him. After this last stunt of creating a cult for himself, I'd send him home to Larissa, Greece, assuming I could get him out of human custody, of course.

'Ah...' Agent Benet grunted, his eyes lowering nervously. 'The French *and* the Americans prefer he stay in our custody. He also killed one of our arresting officers, so... the Director is not eager to see him released.'

'Why did the human attempt to apprehend him?' I asked, and Benet's eyes widened at me. I realized it was probably one of those situations where logic was irrelevant. Humans were sensitive about offending the dead.

'When can I see him?' I asked instead.

'I could arrange something next week,' he suggested. I nodded and he scribbled it down in his mustard-stained planner.

There was a sudden crash behind me, which was painfully loud to my sensitive ears, and the diner went silent. Agent Benet looked up, but I didn't turn. I expected everyone to begin applauding some clumsy waitress; however, the silence stretched on. When I saw Agent Benet's eyes widen, I was obliged to investigate.

To my dissatisfaction, I saw James had yanked a redheaded waitress into his lap near the back of the diner.

'What do you want?' she growled angrily between her teeth, and I was impressed but confused by her aggression. Usually, humans possessed instincts that made them defer to vampires. This female seemed defective in this regard.

'Is it not obvious?' James purred to her, twirling his finger around several of the waitress's loose red curls.

'Stop it!' she snapped at him, and she slapped his fingers away. She tried to rise to her feet, but his arm around her was as immovable as steel.

'Fine,' she hissed, hesitating in her struggle to reach for the cup of water on the table in front of her. I watched, stunned, when she deliberately dumped the glass over James's head.

'I hope this will help you sober up,' she goaded him.

'I'm.... gonna go,' Agent Benet advised me worriedly. 'You should probably deal with that. I'll call you next week!'

I ignored the bumbling human as he collected his things and made a hasty exit. I was intent on the incredibly strange episode before me and, anticipating James's reaction, I rose from my seat to intervene before things escalated too far.

James sprang up furiously, dumping the waitress to the floor as his chair screeched over the diner tiles. He gave his wet hair a quick shake, and his lips lifted in a distinctive vampire snarl. Luckily for him, his eyeteeth had not lengthened, or I'd have been forced to kill him for his carelessness.

'Ye ungrateful *wench,*' he growled.

When the waitress tried to scramble to her feet, he stepped on her leg. I could tell he was using too much pressure when she immediately cried out in agony.

'James,' I said in warning, and he turned toward me in surprise. I watched the anger in his eyes become realization as he glanced around the establishment at all the staring humans.

Looking humble, he bowed his head and strode by me quickly. I heard the bell on the door ring as he exited the diner.

I might have simply returned to my seat at that point as the mundane existence of humans had never interested me. The way the female had dealt with her situation had been incredibly strange, however, and I was obliged to investigate.

I looked down and met clever green eyes speckled with gold. Her lips were parted in disbelief, and her cheeks were flushed from embarrassment. Some of her lovely red curls had fallen out of her messy bun and were caressing the fair skin of her neck and shoulders.

She was *beautiful*.

It had been a long time since I'd even glanced at a human woman. They were far too fragile to be taken as lovers, and five hundred years ago, they were liable to try and kill me. Yet, despite her unsightly beige uniform and apron stained in steak sauce, I couldn't help noticing all her ample curves. Her bare legs were long and lean from hours working on her feet.

At first I thought my reaction to her was bloodlust. I would've made a swift exit had that been the case, but it was something else. *Desire...*

'Are you all right?' I asked her.

X X X

Gwendolyn

Gwen sat gazing up at the gorgeous man, who had come to her rescue. When his brow rose in concern, she remembered he'd asked her a question, and she cleared her throat.

'I'm fine!' she lied as the leg James had stepped on throbbed painfully when she got to her feet. She was already feeling stiff, and she knew she'd be sore in the morning.

Brushing her uniform off, Gwen looked up to see everyone around them seemed intent on ignoring her. Even Sonia, behind the bar, was concentrating deeply on pouring someone's orange juice. Feeling incredibly hurt by the collective insensitivity, Gwen wondered how far they would've allowed the incident to go.

She looked up again at the only man who'd been willing to intervene for her, and to her surprise, he actually looked similar to James. They were both around six feet in height with lean, muscular builds. They both possessed magnetic sexuality, which had initially drawn the other waitresses toward James, but her rescuer's dark eyes lacked malice. His lips were too full for a cruel, thin smile, and while James was sometimes unkempt, this man was impeccable. His midnight black hair was nicely styled, and he was dressed in an absurdly expensive Armani suit and Italian leather shoes. The shadow of stubble on his stern jaw gave him just the right hint of rugged appeal. Even with his hands casually tucked into his pants pockets, he had immaculate posture, and he *exuded* confident authority. It was not difficult for her to recognize he occupied some position of power. She'd been familiar with men like him at Welford Accounting before she was fired.

'Thank you,' Gwen assured him, trying very hard to eliminate the edge of anger from her tone.

She reached for his hand, but he made no move to accept her shake. After an awkward moment, she lowered her arm.

'Why did you antagonize him?' he asked. His voice possessed the unexpected hint of a sexy, central European accent, but her appreciation for it was lost under a tide of indignity.

'*Excuse* me?' she growled.

Gwendolyn Rhys had been on her own since her mother was killed when she was seven years old. Her father had become a drunk who'd barely kept her out of foster homes, so she was used to looking out for herself. The beautiful stranger still managed to take her by surprise when he devolved suddenly from noble knight to another ignorant asshole.

He looked impressed by her renewed irritation. The amused lift at the corner of his full mouth might have even been devastatingly hot had Gwen not been so offended by him.

'You have quite the temper,' he remarked, and she swore steam blew out of her ears.

'I'm sorry,' she growled sarcastically. 'Have a nice day.'

She turned away from him and met Sonia's

scandalized expression from behind the bar when she reached the counter.

'Gwen,' her co-worker hissed. 'Don't you *know* who that is?'

'No,' Gwen retorted impatiently as she grabbed a tray to clean up the shattered plate.

'It's Mr. Santos,' said Sonia, and the revelation gave Gwen hesitation. She did in fact know that name although she'd never been able to put a face to it until then.

Mr. Miguel Santos was a world-renowned businessman, billionaire and philanthropist. He competed with princes and celebrities as the most eligible bachelor in the world, but that wasn't what Gwen knew him for. She'd always appreciated him for his work in languages and anthropology, which Gwen had studied in university. She'd even heard him speak before but only from the doorway of an auditorium. He was even rumoured to be connected to the old Austrian monarchy: the Habsburgs.

Gwen wondered whether she'd been too harsh on him. When she saw he was crouching to pick up the shattered pieces of the plate she'd dropped, she thought so.

Sighing reluctantly, she approached as he rose, and he placed the shards on the tray she was holding. In the napkin in his other hand, he'd collected the food.

'Thanks,' she muttered, blushing as he continued to be kind after her rebuff.

'My pleasure,' he assured her. 'Add his meal to my bill.'

He returned to his booth nearer the front, and Gwen watched as he attempted to melt seamlessly back in among The Diner patrons.

x x x

Miguel

I tried to ignore the gaze of the beautiful redheaded waitress who had, immediately after aggressively challenging a fellow vampire, turned her fearsome ire upon *me*. I wanted to depart, but I was reluctant to leave her unprotected since James had been as intrigued by her as I seemed to be. The difference was he wanted to hurt her, and he *would*.

My initial objection to his behaviour had only been in the interest of preventing a public incident that might have exposed our people. Now, I was far more concerned James's pride had been hurt and the infamous hothead would return whilst the pretty object of his intentions was far less exposed.

This bothered me so much that I began to debate options.

The easiest solution would be to kill James and file it as a necessary precaution with the Tribunal due to his negligence. I worried, however, that the girl's strange allure would bring another vampire upon her later. It was absolutely ridiculous to consider having a human shadowed for her protection, but it was a possibility.

I sensed her presence seconds before she took a seat across from me at the table. In the direct light coming through the window next to us, I could see just how stunning she was.

'Look, I need to just say thanks,' she said reluctantly.

More wisps of her red curls had escaped her bun, and the fine strands gleamed like fire in the sunlight. Her soft, bee-stung lips were pressed firmly together with her resolve. There was a faint frown line between her slender brows as she waited for me to respond. I sensed she was still angry with me for insinuating she'd encouraged her attack although that had not been my intention.

'You already expressed your gratitude,' I reminded her. Her face reddened further and a faint spattering of charming freckles appeared on her cheeks.

This had been the reason James couldn't resist her, I realized. It was no excuse for his actions, but I could better understand his behaviour when the sight of her was pure temptation.

'You know James?' she asked suspiciously.

'We are unhappy acquaintances at best,' I guaranteed her, and she made an unladylike snort of derision.

'Do you have many acquaintances like that?' she wondered cheekily.

'Unfortunately, more than I care for,' I admitted guardedly.

'Well,' she said dismissively, 'I'm Gwendolyn Rhys.'

She extended that warm hand toward me again over the table. 'You can call me Gwen,' she invited.

I was immensely fascinated by her challenging gaze as one of her brows lifted ever so slightly at my hesitance. She waited more patiently this time, and I tried to remain calm as I reached for her. I was thankful I'd fed the night before so my skin felt warmer than usual.

'Miguel Santos,' I said politely before her fingers wrapped around mine, and I was filled with unspeakable violence.

For five hundred years, I'd been overcoming my very nature so I could be the political instrument I'd become. Then she touched me, and all that carefully honed control melted away in a matter of seconds. It was a firm reminder that under the prudently layered civility, that creature of instinct endured. Usually, he only emerged when it came time to feed or to fuck, so I had not been faced with him, unexpectedly, in hundreds of years. In the midst of a perfectly innocent conversation, his presence was inexcusably dangerous.

'It's... a pleasure to meet you,' I assured her. I was thankful when my voice remained steady.

Chapter Two

'I know who you are,' she assured me casually before she took back her hand. I was amazed she couldn't know how unsafe her situation was. It was difficult to keep my expression unclouded as I struggled for composure.

'You do?' I asked.

'I didn't recognize you at first,' she admitted sheepishly. 'I read *An Instinctive Species,* and I heard you speak about human origins last year.'

I was impressed and immensely thankful for the distraction.

'That's an interesting way for a diner waitress to spend her time,' I hinted, and she glared outright at me. This time it was more playful and less genuinely hostile.

'In your speech, you said your family came from Austria, but you don't *sound* Austrian,' she informed me boldly. I was taken by surprise.

'Not many North Americans can tell the difference between Austrian and German,' I noted.

'It's faint,' she acknowledged, 'but I think you must have grown up closer to Berlin than Vienna.'

'Luxembourg, actually,' I corrected her.

'And yet your name is Spanish,' she pointed out evenly, and I felt a smile starting to work its way across my lips.

'I'm beginning to see why you were at my lecture,' I observed with interest.

26   A. A. G O R D O N

'I studied accounting at my father's insistence. My interests always lay in culture,' she clarified. 'You are one big contradiction,' she added. As if I didn't already know it. I was a five-hundred-year-old vampire who had lived all over the world in the past five centuries. Obviously, I wasn't about to explain that to her.

'My father was Spanish, and my mother was Austrian. I grew up near Gaichel.' I humoured her at last.

'How many languages *do* you speak?' she wanted to know. 'You never said in your lecture.'

'I don't want to brag,' I assured her a little cockily.

'How many?' she insisted as she shared my smile. It made her look incredibly breathtaking as she leaned across the table eagerly toward me.

'Do you want me to include the ancient ones?' I asked her and was pleased when her eyes widened.

'Yes!'

'Most of them,' I admitted, and her mouth opened.

'Be serious!' she chastised.

'I am! While not proficient in all, I know enough to at least recognize the roots of almost any language. With the obvious exception of some localized dialects,' I amended.

She gazed at me in uncertain wonder. 'Why didn't you say that in your speech?' she asked suspiciously.

'I didn't want the interest of the crowd shifting from the ancient roots of language to how many ways I knew how to curse,' I explained. To my surprise, she laughed and nodded in agreement.

'So, what are you doing in Toronto?' she wondered.

'I live here. In Yorkville,' I advised her. 'You?'

'Victoria Street,' she answered with some reservation. 'It's near Dundas Square.'

I knew the area. It could be rather unsavoury for most humans and especially at night.

'I see. I've humoured you, so now humour me. Why do you work *here*?' I asked, inclining my head to indicate the diner.

'What do you mean?' she demanded, seemingly

offended.

'Come on,' I chastised her gently. 'You are obviously very highly educated, Miss Rhys. You could be putting your attributes to much better use, I think.'

x x x

Gwendolyn

Gwen felt her anticipation rising as Miguel smiled knowingly when he stunned her with his compliment. The man was gorgeous and ridiculously charming when he wanted to be. She hadn't expected to feel such a strong attraction to him, but then knowing who he was had made her helplessly curious.

'I used to work at Welford Accounting,' she said, which seemed to surprise him. 'I got fired.'

Luckily, the weight of his attention was lost when Sonia arrived at the table to fill his coffee mug. Her co-worker's curious gaze flickered covertly to Gwen, who decided to take the opportunity to avoid an awkward conversation. She quickly rose from her seat.

'I should get back to work,' she admitted.

'I didn't mean to keep you,' he apologized as Sonia moved reluctantly away from them. Gwen quickly shook her head.

'No! This has been the most cultural conversation I've had since fourth-year anthropology,' she advised him sadly.

'Well, it was my pleasure,' Miguel reassured her, and he also rose from the table.

Gwen stepped back, impressed again by his height and presence, as he pulled his wallet from his jacket. He dropped some cash on the table while she tried not to let her gaze linger on the definition of his wide shoulders. She wasn't going to see him again, so there was no use getting attached.

'Maybe I'll see you next time you decide to honour us with another lecture,' Gwen suggested as she grudgingly backed away toward the bar.

'Or, maybe you will see me later tonight?' he proposed, and she came to an immediate stop.

'Oh?' she uttered. *Remain calm,* she thought.

'There is a gala at the NTM,' he explained. 'It's the—'

'The museum's Annual Patron Appreciation Gala,' Gwen blurted excitedly. 'I'm sorry,' she gasped, horrified she'd cut him off. Miguel simply laughed.

'Would you care to join me?' he wondered.

Gwen felt like she couldn't draw in enough air to answer him, so she simply nodded.

'I can pick you up at six,' he offered.

'Why don't we meet here?' she suggested after regaining her powers of speech. She did *not* want him seeing the atrocious building where she lived and changing his mind.

'Until six then,' he agreed and reached for her hand. Instead of shaking it, he lifted it to his lips and placed a chaste kiss on her knuckles.

After he'd gone, she realized she had absolutely nothing to wear to a gala.

x x x

Miguel

I wasn't sure what had possessed me to invite the human woman out on a date since it had easily been four hundred years since I'd been on any such thing. I tried to dismiss it as necessary if I wanted to learn Gwen's secrets, but the truth was she'd piqued my curiosity.

When she'd turned away, insinuating we would never meet again, the thought had been strangely unbearable.

Outside the diner, I met the watchful eyes of one of my agents. Darius of Gilan was a four-hundred-year-old Persian vampire. He was leaning casually against the brick wall with his corded arms crossed over his chest. Human females glanced at him appreciatively as they passed by.

'Ensure James does not follow her,' I advised him in Dari on my way by. He inclined his head and remained standing against the wall facing the diner.

Across the street were Natalia and Luka Menshikov. The five-hundred-year-old vampire twins from Saratov, Russia, had been at my side for hundreds of years. They also stayed put. With such fearsome guardians, Gwen couldn't have been safer had she been locked in a bomb shelter.

I returned home to the Royal Alton Hotel on Yorkville Avenue. The luxurious building occupied the ten breathtakingly beautiful acres of Alton Park and was completely private in the midst of downtown. During the Toronto International Film Festival, it was not uncommon to bump into celebrity guests there.

I passed through the enormous Greco-Roman designed lobby to my private elevator, which ascended directly to the presidential suite. I had been residing permanently in the ten million dollar residence for nearly five years.

I went quickly to the walk-in closet of the master bedroom to exchange my Armani jacket for my favourite Belstaff leather jacket. I heard my butler come into the room behind me.

'I was not expecting you home so early, Sir,' he said.

'The meeting was cut short, Ainsley,' I explained briskly as I glanced at myself in the closet's full-length mirror. 'We will not be seeing Rosie or Alexion until next week.'

'I see. Shall I get anything for you?' Ainsley replied. His deep voice hinted at a Cockney accent.

'Have Anthony bring the SV for five thirty,' I responded, and my butler made a sound of intrigue.

'My,' he murmured speculatively. 'I might wonder at the occasion.'

His curiosity was warranted even if it was impertinent. I was a vampire, and my fastest mode of transportation was usually my own two feet. If I didn't walk or run somewhere, it was only because I was required to arrive stylishly to an important event. For those occasions, I generally had Anthony drive me in the Mercedes-Benz or the Bentley Mulsanne limousine.

'I have a date,' I admitted with an amused smile.

There was a long silence behind me, and I looked up to meet Ainsley's uncertain grey eyes in the mirror. He said nothing, however, and simply turned to do as he'd been told.

Whether he believed me or not, I was unsure.

Ainsley Westin had come very highly recommended to me by my Ambassador predecessor. He'd been in my employment for the five years I'd been living at the Royal Alton and for ten years before that. While he'd gotten older, I had remained as utterly unchanged as I had in the last five hundred years. Some vampires might have found his unusual comfort insubordinate, but I liked him a great deal for it. In addition to his proficiency as a man-servant, there were other useful qualities of Ainsley's skill set that were much more unsavoury. I knew Gwen's mystery was probably a mission I should have passed on to him, but I couldn't. The thought of my butler going anywhere near the redheaded waitress with his fearsome expertise was unacceptable. I would learn her secrets, gently, myself.

I stood looking at my reflection in the mirror as I began to plan luring the fiery waitress into giving up her ambiguity. I was a man who was used to getting what he wanted, and that seemed to be Gwendolyn Rhys. If that desire lined up with my intentions to unravel her secrets, the only question was whether I'd be able to touch her human skin without bruising it. Vampiresses were as durable as I was, but Gwen would be warm and soft.

I began to imagine her seduction. I could almost feel her pressed beneath me with her legs wrapped firmly around my waist. I could almost hear how her breathless cries might sound.

I could almost taste her passion-spiked blood...

My pupils dilated almost instantly and blackened my

eyes in the reflection. Blood pooled beneath my eyes, making them appear bruised, as my vision instinctively switched to infrared.

I looked away from the face of the beast within.

x x x

Gwendolyn

'Hello—*dammit!*' shouted Charlotte Wells.

Gwen held the phone away from her ear when a loud bang echoed over the line. When she replaced it skeptically against her cheek, she could hear the sound of plastic spinning on tiles.

'Fucking great,' Charlotte growled, and her voice drifted nearer to the phone. 'Hey!'

'Hi. Did you drop the phone?' Gwen guessed.

'Yah, it cracked. What's up?'

'Just on my way home from work. I, um... I met a guy,' Gwen admitted hesitantly. She was always nervous to tell Charlotte these things. Her friend had a habit of overreacting, and the momentary silence was promising. Gwen pre-emptively held the phone away from her ear again just in time for Charlotte's shriek of glee.

'Tell me *everything*!' her friend demanded greedily.

'I don't have time! He's picking me up at six, and I don't have anything to wear,' Gwen reminded her. 'He's taking me to that gala I was telling you about. I need a nice blouse or something.'

'Say no more! I'll be there in twenty,' Charlotte promised.

'Tha... nk you,' Gwen said haltingly when Charlotte immediately hung up on her.

She quickly tucked her cell into her purse as she reached her building. There were no stairs, so she had to wait on the elevator just to get to the second floor. The man standing with her in the lobby followed her inside when the doors finally opened. His stench of cigarettes and cats nearly overwhelmed her in the confined space.

The doors opened on her floor, and she raced down the hall to her apartment. She fumbled impatiently with her key and pulled up on the handle so the door would open and close on uneven hinges.

Luckily, her roommate wasn't there as she began to leave a trail of clothing from the front door to the bathroom. She turned on the shower and was in and out almost before the water was warm. She cursed colourfully when she saw the bruise forming on her leg where James had stepped on her.

Gwen heard the familiar sound of an animal pawing at the sliding doors in the living room. She went to the kitchen for a tin of soft cat food and to the concrete balcony. The tabby stray she'd been feeding for the last two months was waiting and meowing persistently.

Gwen stood shivering in the chill of late summer while the cat finished, and then she picked up the bowl. Before she could close the door, she was distracted by the man leaning against the side of the neighbouring apartment building. She recognized him from outside The Diner. He was still catching a lot of feminine attention with his enormous arms folded over his chest.

She thought it was a strange coincidence but quickly forgot about him when the grey cat wandered between her legs and into her living room. Shrugging, Gwen closed the door behind her.

There was a stern knock, and Gwen went to let Charlotte in. Her friend's eyes immediately swept Gwen's bare legs, damp hair, and towel-clad body skeptically.

'Your hair's not even dry yet!' Charlotte chastised before she hauled a large overnight bag through the door with two hands.

'What did you bring?' Gwen demanded as she closed the door behind her friend.

'I brought everything!' Charlotte assured her before dumping the contents of her bag onto the couch. She fished through the cans of hairspray and mousse to present Gwen with a black cocktail dress.

'I asked for a blouse!' Gwen snapped. 'I don't have time to shave my legs, Charlotte.'

'This is all I brought for you,' Charlotte revealed with great satisfaction. 'You're *not* wearing pants!' she added seriously when Gwen frowned. 'Work with me here. I'm trying to get you laid tonight.'

'*Uh*!' groaned Gwen with bitter regret she'd had no choice but to ask for Charlotte's help.

After they broke up, and she was suddenly fired, her ex had cleaned out her closet. His reasoning had been that he'd bought her some nice things over the course of their short relationship. Apparently, that meant anything expensive she owned, and there had never been any use arguing with Jonathon Welford. He was the notoriously temperamental son of Mr. Welford, the CEO and founder of Welford Accounting and Gwen's old boss.

'I have a bruise—' Gwen began to protest.

'I have makeup,' Charlotte cut in.

'Fine,' Gwen growled in frustration, 'but you haven't even asked me what his name is yet.'

'You said he was a nerd,' Charlotte dismissed as she began to usher Gwen toward the bathroom.

'His name is Miguel Santos,' Gwen said expectantly, and Charlotte stopped in her tracks.

'Mr. Santos? As in that hot billionaire guy?' verified Charlotte in disbelief.

'The very one,' Gwen proclaimed as she sat down on the edge of the tub to run water over her legs. She enjoyed Charlotte's shocked silence while she lathered her skin with shaving cream. 'He's pretty incredible,' she admitted, blushing.

'He's pretty gorgeous,' Charlotte retorted 'and *loaded*. He invests with us,' she revealed, referring to the bank she worked for. 'I obviously have never seen him. He deals with the bigwigs upstairs.'

'Charlotte, you aren't supposed to tell me where people bank,' Gwen reminded her.

'Maybe if tonight goes well, I'll finally get the chance

to meet him,' Charlotte hedged hopefully, and Gwen felt suddenly giddy at the thought. It had been a long time since she'd been out on a date, and she'd never been this interested in a man. She wondered whether he'd want to kiss her at the end of the night.

'Derek is obsessed with his car collection,' Charlotte prattled seamlessly. 'Maybe he'll come with you for dinner tomorrow.'

'His car collection?' asked Gwen to distract herself from fantasizing about Miguel's lips.

'Lamborghinis, Aston Martins, Ferraris, Porches. You name it, apparently he has it,' Charlotte informed her.

'You wouldn't know the difference between any of those cars if they ran over you. You're just naming cars you've heard Derek mention,' Gwen berated her in amusement. Charlotte shrugged nonchalantly.

'At least I'd know I'd been smoked by something super-hot and hella expensive,' she pointed out, and Gwen rolled her eyes.

It didn't take them long to get her ready, and once she was, Gwen was thankful she'd asked for her friend's help. The black cocktail dress looked perfect.

'Drive me to The Diner? I can't walk that far in these shoes,' Gwen admitted, and Charlotte snorted.

'I'm not missing this!' she swore.

They climbed into Charlotte's yellow Ford Fiesta and drove to The Diner where they pulled up and sat waiting anxiously across the street.

'Nervous?' asked Charlotte, and Gwen nodded.

'I never thought I'd do this again,' she confessed. For the first time, she wondered if maybe it had been a mistake.

'Don't let Jonathon get in the way tonight,' Charlotte begged.

Gwen had been trying to banish the violent memories of her ex for almost a year. Sometimes she could still feel his bruising grip and taste blood in her mouth after he'd hit her.

It was the first time she'd been out since that vicious attack, and Miguel's gentlemanly behaviour had distracted her. After Charlotte's teasing, Gwen remembered men usually expected intimacy after a date, especially men with the power and money to have whatever they wanted.

What if he became impatient like Jonathon had?

'Oh... my... God...' Charlotte breathed dramatically, and Gwen looked up as the rumble of a vehicle neared them. A beautiful, dark grey car had parked across from them and was drawing the attention of passing pedestrians. 'I may not be a car girl, but even I know *that's* a Lamborghini,' Charlotte gushed excitedly as she turned toward Gwen. She saw Gwen's nervous expression, and her grin faded. 'You okay?'

Gwen nodded as the Lamborghini's driver door opened, and Miguel stepped out onto the street. He'd exchanged his Armani jacket for a classy leather coat that made him look so much edgier and sexier.

'It *is* him,' Charlotte hissed in disbelief. She leaned over her steering wheel to examine Miguel incredulously through the windshield.

Gwen watched her date glancing with disinterest toward the people lining up on the street. They shouted compliments and took pictures, but none of it seemed to faze Miguel who, Gwen realized, wasn't like Jon at all. Her completely self-absorbed ex would've been posing for the pictures. Miguel was looking toward The Diner and waiting only for her.

'Want me to walk over with you?' asked Charlotte sympathetically, and Gwen nodded. She closed her eyes to muster her courage and opened the car door before she could change her mind. Charlotte followed her across the street.

Miguel caught sight of Gwen, and his pleased smile made her stomach flip in a way she'd never felt before.

'Miss Rhys,' he greeted her politely. 'You look beautiful.'

Gwen was relieved when his appreciative gaze filled her anew with anticipation rather than the anxiety Jon often had.

'Thank you. This is my friend, Charlotte.'

'It's a pleasure,' Miguel responded, but Charlotte shook her head at him.

'The pleasure is *definitely* mine,' she assured him. 'This is a beautiful car,' she added and indicated the Lamborghini.

'It's new,' Miguel informed them. 'I thought tonight would be ideal for breaking it in.'

Gwen smiled privately when his accented voice seemed to have the same effect on her friend that it had on her. She saw Charlotte blink and step back from them.

'Right!' she exclaimed. 'Well, I won't keep you. Just make sure she's home by morning,' she instructed Miguel jokingly with a wink. Gwen lowered her eyes nervously.

Miguel inclined his head in agreement, and Charlotte left them.

'May I?' he asked, and Gwen turned to see he'd held out his arm chivalrously. She was glad when he continued to distance himself from her ex and happily hooked her arm with his. 'I hope you have not eaten yet. I should have warned you dinner was going to be served,' he admitted apologetically.

'I didn't eat,' Gwen told him as she stepped toward the passenger's side of his car. She was confused when Miguel gently tugged her aside, but then the Lamborghini's door opened upwards.

She slid into the passenger's seat, and Miguel closed her door while she gazed around the leather interior with amazement. The controls glowed orange and yellow and looked almost like something out of a science-fiction movie.

Miguel got into the driver's seat. Glancing over at him, Gwen's eyes helplessly travelled the length of his lean body with deep appreciation.

'My friend's husband is apparently a fan of your car

collection,' she advised him as nonchalantly as she could manage. 'I think I see why now.'

'He is welcome to test-drive whatever he likes,' Miguel promised as he flipped up an oddly shaped lever between them. He pressed the Start button, and the car growled throatily to life.

A grin spread across Gwen's face.

Miguel

Chapter Three

I tried to prepare for her touch, but it still shocked me when her body came so near to mine. Even through the leather jacket, I could feel the heat of her warming me as I walked her to my car.

I'm not sure what possessed me to offer up my prized car collection to her acquaintances. I wanted to think it was because I had to make a good impression on her, to get close enough to deduce her secrets, but I was afraid I'd only wanted to impress her. When she beamed in anticipation after the car started, I felt a telling spike of pride.

The car shot forward at the lightest touch on the gas, and Gwen made a sound of exhilaration as we darted out onto the quiet city street. The crowd on the sidewalk cheered us.

'So, what brought you to Canada?' Gwen asked, and I could tell she was nervous. Vampires are apt at sensing emotions of fear and anxiety. Usually, we savoured them, but it was different with her. I wanted to put her mind at ease.

'My father,' I responded truthfully. I kept my eyes on the road as I tried to find a safe way to navigate my long past with her. 'Some time ago, he and his business partners decided to solidify their... territories,' I explained.

I remembered that Summons, almost two hundred years ago, when the vampires had come together to hammer out the Accords. For the first time in our history, we'd all been bound under one law and one Tribunal. Not everyone had been pleased by the prospect, and some had even tried to resist, but the majority had understood the necessity. As humans evolved, so did our methods of discretion.

'They divided the world up between them?' Gwen verified incredulously.

'Yes,' I told her. 'My father wished to experience the New World. North America,' I amended quickly. I glanced at her to see if she'd caught my slip, but she merely laughed.

'Do Europeans still think of us that way?' she wondered teasingly.

'In all honesty, I don't know,' I evaded. 'My father is old-fashioned.'

'Hmm,' she grunted, and I could sense she'd relaxed with me again. 'What about your mother?' she wanted to know, and I was momentarily taken off guard. The loss of one's human mother is the first, but not the last, wound all vampires must inevitably endure.

'She died. Shortly after I was born,' I told her.

'Oh! I'm so sorry,' she whispered.

'I didn't know her,' I lied. 'I don't remember.'

Gwen was quiet a moment while we weaved in and out of traffic.

'My mother is dead too,' she finally revealed, and I glanced over at her. I was alarmed when I felt an alien swell of tenderness toward her.

'I'm sorry,' I said in uncertainty. Thankfully, she didn't notice my internal struggle with foreign emotions.

'It was a long time ago too,' she assured me. 'The police said it was likely a robbery gone wrong.'

I did not believe that for a second. There was something very strange about Gwendolyn Rhys, and I was willing to bet it had something to do with why her mother had been killed. The revelation reinforced my need to protect her.

'I'm sorry!' she exclaimed, embarrassed when the atmosphere in the car became melancholy. 'You must be a museum patron. Do you collect?'

'I have an extensive collection of which I'm rather proud,' I admitted freely, and she grinned in appreciation.

'Well, if Derek gets to see your car collection, I insist on seeing your art collection,' she bargained. I nodded readily.

'You're more than welcome, Miss Rhys,' I answered.

'You can... You can call me Gwen,' she invited softly. I could feel her anxiety spike as she wondered whether she'd been too bold in giving me this freedom.

'Gwen,' I corrected myself, and she smiled shyly.

We arrived at the National Toronto Museum, which was an enormous building resembling a Greek temple. The Ionic columns and ornate walls were illuminated beautifully by the solar lights in the surrounding gardens.

A small crowd jostled eagerly at the sight of the fancy cars pulling up in front. Cameras flashed vigorously as prestigious patrons and intellects ascended the stairs of the museum.

Gwen was enraptured as we got in line behind a Porsche. I was sure she'd been to the museum often, so her excitement was strangely endearing. I wondered how she'd feel if she knew she was sitting next to a man older than some of the artifacts inside.

'Is that Dr. Anita Johansson?' Gwen demanded. She leaned nearer her window as the Swedish anthropologist privileged the crowd with a few words.

'She and Dr. Michael Turner are giving a speech tonight,' I explained. I didn't tell her the research presentation was the reason I'd accepted the invitation.

Anita publicly focused on human mythology and its origins. Privately, however, she knew how real the lore was, and that made her dangerous, so we kept a close eye on her research endeavours. Tonight, I'd see for myself what she'd uncovered from the Middle East and what conclusions she'd drawn from it.

I handed the valet my keys and drew Gwen a little closer to my side in spite of the discomfort it caused me. Her safety was paramount until I determined her secrets, and some of the reporters could be rather aggressive.

'Mr. Santos, have you heard Dr. Johansson has uncovered another Sumerian cult? Any theories?' shouted one of them.

My face betrayed nothing, but my gut filled with dread. If she'd already published her findings, it would make our efforts to subdue her ideology more difficult. She knew we were watching her, and she was getting bolder and trickier.

We kept moving, avoiding all questions, as I guided Gwen up to the door. We entered a marble lobby.

'She's found a new cult?' Gwen asked with interest as we approached the coat check.

'She's been uncovering them all around the world, but this will be the oldest. Perhaps the origin,' I illuminated.

'What kind of cults?' Gwen wondered in fascination.

'Blood-worshipping ones,' I said. I hoped I'd infused my tone with the appropriate amount of disbelief.

'What's that?' Gwen asked as I handed the attendant our tickets and my jacket.

'It's an ancient cult of blood-drinking fanatics worshipping monsters, evidently,' I clarified sarcastically as if it were not possibly the truth.

'Vampires?' she guessed doubtfully.

She'd turned from me as she slid her coat down her shoulders. My eyes trailed from her slender shoulders to the swell of her hips and ass. The black cocktail dress she was wearing hugged every subtle curve and made my hands twitch with the need to touch.

I took her coat and turned my eyes away from her.

'I suppose,' I answered huskily.

She checked my expression curiously when my voice deepened, but I'd composed myself. I offered her my arm again, and we moved into the next room where there were music and mingling humans.

Almost every academic person on our watch list was in attendance, which meant something compelling had been uncovered. I began to wonder whether inviting Gwen had been prudent, but Luka Menshikov caught my eye with a conspiring wink. The Russian was still wearing his leather biker jacket, and blended poorly with the formally dressed crowd, but I was relieved to see him. Where Luka was, Natalia was never far.

Gwen was in such awe she didn't say anything until we reached the bar at the end of the room.

'This is incredible' she whispered to me excitedly as I handed her the martini she'd ordered. 'I really can't believe I'm here right now!'

'You will like what's next even better,' I promised as I gently took her arm.

In the adjoining room were the items on display for the silent auction. It was a relatively small event, and there was nothing I wished to purchase, but Gwen was fascinated. Whether it was an antique hairbrush from West Virginia or the Blue Dragon brooch of Empress Wu, she marvelled. I was surprised to feel so patient with her. I was even enjoying myself.

Then we came to the last display case, which had a tiny brass "Not for Sale" sign on the glass. I immediately stiffened in recognition of the glinting object within.

'This is a ceremonial cup from an underground temple uncovered by Dr. Anita Johansson near the City of Ur,' read Gwen unnecessarily. 'Dr. Johansson believes the temple was devoted to the worship of the *akaharu,* which is a Sumerian blood demon,' she continued with interest. 'Humans drank an opium tea called Hul Gil, the "joy plant," from the goblet. This allowed the *akaharu* to partake of their victims without violence.'

Gwen looked up at me innocently once she was finished reading aloud. 'This must be part of what Dr. Johansson brought back,' she guessed.

'Among other things,' Dr. Johansson answered her suddenly from behind me.

I turned, fighting hard to mask my irritation, as I faced the Swedish anthropologist who continued to create such difficulty for my people. 'Anita,' I greeted her.

'Miguel,' the tall, elegant woman responded with a tight smile. In a black gown, with her wrinkled features prettily powdered and her silvery hair elegantly styled, she looked very different. I'd felt confident discrediting the dusty, obsessive anthropologist while she'd been playing in the ruins of old things. Now, I wasn't so sure.

'Please allow me to introduce you to my guest, Gwendolyn Rhys,' I said. I saw Anita's eyes flicker over Gwen with immense interest.

'It's a pleasure to meet you, Dr. Johansson,' Gwen said eagerly, and Anita inclined her head.

'Tell me, what do *you* think of my research?' Anita asked. Gwen glanced back at the ceremonial cup in uncertainty.

'Humans have always had strong believes about blood. So, I think it's plausible they drank it. Even in the Bible—'

'We have evidence it was not *Homo sapiens* drinking the blood,' interrupted Anita. Gwen was hesitant.

'You mean another humanoid?' she deduced. 'Something like *Homo erectus*?'

'One *more* advanced, not less advanced,' Anita corrected Gwen. 'A predator with superior strength and senses,' she explained. She glanced at me, and I wondered, as I often did, whether she knew what I was. 'We call them *Homo occisor*. It means "man-killer"'.

Gwen maintained her composure admirably, but I could see her features tensing.

'You mean like vampires,' she finally conceded reluctantly.

'Why not?' challenged Anita, and Gwen laughed nervously.

'We would probably know if there was such a thing,' she reasoned with an edge of impatience.

'Unless steps had been taken to protect their

existence,' Anita pointed out logically.

'By whom?' demanded Gwen dubiously, and I felt reassured.

'Their leaders or our own government,' suggested Anita casually. 'The cultural evidence alone is compelling, Miss Rhys. The fact is that in a time when humans had no contact with one another, there were tales of these creatures in every civilization all over the world.'

'By that logic, dragons should be real too,' Gwen pointed out dismissively.

'Who is to say they were not?' Anita persisted, and Gwen looked flabbergasted.

'I think we would know if there were giant lizards living among us!' Gwen told Anita a little sharply. Her cheeks were beginning to flush with that temper I admired so much.

'Whether they still exist today, I don't know,' Anita granted. 'All I know is what our ancestors have indicated about the ways in which our world has changed.'

I was deeply amused by the idea of Anita attempting to uncover dragons. The Murhyaeli shapeshifters didn't fear humans the way the rest of the paranormal world did. Their wrath would've been utterly destructive if she went digging.

Gwen was fuming silently when Anita turned curtly to me. The anthropologist nodded her head respectfully.

'Thank you for being here, Mr. Santos. I'm sure you will enjoy my seminar tonight,' she assured me before returning to her colleagues.

'Wow,' Gwen breathed, 'I didn't realize how crazy she was. You could've warned me!'

'I didn't want to disappoint you in her,' I lied.

We began mingling among the other guests. Under the guise of introducing Gwen to some of the world's leading experts, I tested the reception of Anita's theories. Most were doubtful, but I took note of anyone who was undisturbed. Of course, not everyone was a scientist, historian, or anthropologist. The wealthy were only there for the artifacts, and they didn't care whether there was such thing as vampires.

Luka's sister, Natalia, arrived in a stunning white gown, which had every head in the room turning her way appreciatively. With long blonde hair and slanted dark eyes, Nat always made an impression. I was pleased to see she was getting close to Anita's American colleague. Dr. Michael Turner had been Anita's partner in the Ur excavation.

Despite these important developments, my attention was being more and more captivated by Gwen. Instead of analyzing the room for threats, I was becoming distracted by the way she pursed her lovely lips.

'Do you dance?' she asked hopefully, gazing toward the dance floor and a string quartet playing classical music. Their authentic sound reminded me of Carl Friedrich Abel playing the *viola da gamba* in Dresden, Germany, in 1756.

'Yes,' I confessed cautiously as I imagined holding her. The thought was strangely intimidating.

'Won't you be a gentleman and ask me then?' Gwen proposed, and I smiled in enjoyment of her playful impudence. When I obliged her with an ironic gesture toward the dance floor, she looked pleased with herself.

The other couples were performing an American style waltz, which didn't seem to intimidate Gwen. She eagerly took her position, and the heat of her thigh pressed against mine. I was familiar with the physical allure of a woman's body against mine, but the intimacy was unexpected and foreign. Sex had always felt primal to me. It had never been sentimental in the way humans often engaged.

'You do know how to waltz?' she verified when I hesitated in uncertainty.

'Of course,' I said immediately. 'I didn't expect you would,' I covered, and she laughed as we waited for the tune.

'Charlotte and I took a classical dance class for her

wedding. Her husband is a bit of a geek,' she explained as she began the first turn with admirable elegance. 'I was pretty good at it,' she added proudly when she came back to me.

'You think classical dance is the prerogative of geeks?' I confirmed. She smiled coyly.

'Maybe not in high society,' she acknowledged evenly, and I snorted at the underhanded slur.

'I don't know whether to be insulted,' I informed her, and she laughed. She was breathtaking when she was laughing.

'Don't be insulted!' she begged me as she completed the reverse turn.

'Miguel,' said a familiar voice firmly, and I turned in surprise. Hudson of the Wendat, one of my dearest friends, was standing behind Gwen.

The twenty-five-hundred-year-old Etruscan had been named Natula for an Etruscan demon. His mother had then abandoned him as a bad omen because he'd been born during a solar eclipse. He was one of the Lamia, who were the eldest and strongest of our kind, and who'd been our unofficial rulers before the Accords. There were four half-brothers of which Hudson was the youngest. Thanos and Anatolius of Demeter, five-thousand-year-old Minoan twins from Crete, were now called Tyler and Liam Demetrius. The final brother was Nirgal Enkara, and he was the eldest of *all* vampires. The formidable eight-thousand-year-old Sumerian from Mesopotamia was best known either as Quinn O'Connor or as the Destroyer. It was widely believed that the origins of our race were hidden in his dark past. Some even claimed he'd been endowed with great power, but there were few alive who'd known him, and Hudson would never say. He had a reputation for ending civilizations, but luckily, he'd been asleep for nearly a thousand years.

'May I have a moment with him?' Hudson asked Gwen politely. She nodded, and I gave her hand a gentle squeeze before she departed. Luka was still acting as her protective shadow, and he subtly followed her across the room.

Certain of her safety, I returned my attention to Hudson, who was watching me warily when he didn't glean my attention right away. He was the only vampire to have ever been born with blue eyes, and their intensity was deeply disconcerting.

'Your date is rather spectacular,' he commented.

'I know,' I assured him.

'I knew I'd find you here,' he informed me more seriously. I cocked my head suspiciously at his tone.

'Nervous about what they have uncovered in Ur?' I estimated in concern. As far as I knew, Hudson was nearly invincible because of his age. Anita's research should not have alarmed him.

'I have this sense,' Hudson disclosed delicately, and my apprehension deepened. It wasn't uncommon for older vampires to develop intuition. Hudson's premonitions had even saved my life before.

I looked anxiously toward where Gwen was standing before I could think better of it. I felt Hudson appraise me knowingly.

'An assignment?' he guessed.

'My own,' I admitted. 'She is unique.'

'She is one of the Dowrra seeking a mate, Miguel,' he revealed resentfully. 'I believe she has Chosen one' he added significantly.

I followed his gaze back toward Gwen, who was glancing back at us. She met my eyes and smiled before returning her attention to the humans near her.

'Dowrra,' I repeated, stunned I hadn't thought of it myself. I'd come across so many of them in my lifetime but never one who wanted me. She could give me children! Such a rare blessing when vampiresses are infertile.

'Just remember,' cautioned Hudson when he saw my growing intrigue, 'many vampires have loved a Dowrra mate. Very few have ever been loved in return by one.'

Gwendolyn

Chapter Four

Gwen thought Miguel and his dark-haired acquaintance with the strangely luminous eyes seemed to be having an intense discussion. She'd learned quickly that Miguel was a master of his facial control, but this time, she could see he was troubled. His glance at her made her even more nervous.

After several uneasy moments, Miguel and the stranger parted, and her date returned to her side.

'Who was that?' she asked as innocently as she could. Miguel offered her a quick smile.

'His name is Hudson,' Miguel answered. 'He's an old friend from home who wanted to give me my father's regards.'

'I see,' Gwen responded, perfectly aware he was not being fully honest. She also knew his private affairs were none of her business, however, so she put the incident out of mind.

A man's voice was suddenly amplified over a microphone. He requested they take their seats so Johansson and Turner could begin their presentation. Gwen joined her arm with Miguel's, and he led her into the dining room adjacent to the cocktail party.

She noticed Hudson leaning against one of the columns at the edge of the room. The majority of the guests were dressed formally, but he was wearing leather and jeans. He was very handsome, in that rare and breathtaking way, but there was something missing from his eyes. She thought he felt old and full of memory in the way old buildings do.

Gwen tore her gaze from him as she sat down at Miguel's table. She looked speculatively at her date as he began to read the presentation program, and she realized he and Hudson were eerily alike. Miguel was better at hiding whatever it was that made them different, so it had taken Hudson's extremity for her to see it, but they felt *alien*. They reminded her of wolves in sheep's clothing, and she was suddenly afraid.

Miguel looked up at her, caught her watching him, and he smiled so beautifully he couldn't be a wolf.

'Are you all right?' he asked her.

'Yes,' she assured him, shaking off the ridiculousness of her imagination.

'Thank you all for being here,' said the coordinator, drawing their attention and quieting the room again. 'It is with great pleasure that we invite Dr. Johansson and Dr. Turner here tonight to share with us their findings from a site near the ancient ruins of the City of Ur. Please,' he added, holding out a hand invitingly toward Dr. Johansson.

Anita stepped forward, and she smiled coolly for the room.

'For those of you who don't know me, I'm Dr. Anita Johansson of Uppsala University in Sweden, and this is my colleague, Dr. Michael Turner of Harvard University in the United States,' she said in her deep, Swedish accent.

'We would like to thank our team for all their hard work over the years and all of you for being here tonight,' continued Dr. Turner. 'You know for some time now, we have been digging in the Middle East in search of the origins of our darkest mythologies.'

'What initially drew us to this expedition was the evidence, in every civilization, of an unidentified underground movement. It was spanning not only the millennia but also every continent,' explained Johansson.

'For a long time, we supposed these cults arose from some innate fear or respect shared by all humanity,' said Turner. 'There was always the possibility, though, that something real was instigating them. It was this prospect that prompted us to try and find the origin. To see whether they were all somehow connected.'

Gwen was grudgingly awed by their stirring presentation but still skeptical. It was going to take a lot more than a pretty cup and some supernatural stories to make her believe in vampires.

The white screen at the front of the room flipped to a picture of a shaft in the ground.

'It took us a long time to find it. Then, just outside the City of Ur, we finally discovered an underground temple we think was the first devoted to the cult,' continued Johansson. She flipped the screen to a picture of an earthy wall carved in cuneiform. 'According to the scripts on the temple walls, these cults first arose from a feud between sisters. Ereshkigal was queen of the Underworld and Inanna, the goddess of love, fertility, and war. Their children were given thrones in both heaven and on earth to be worshipped by humans.

Lilith, Ereshkigal's youngest, was desired by her cousin Utu, who was Inanna's only son. When Lilith refused his advances, Inanna cursed Lilith with infertility. Enraged, Ereshkigal avenged her daughter by cursing Inanna's children never to enter the heavens where their mother ruled. Cut off from the goddess of love, they became deeply despised by humankind. Inanna fired back so Ereshkigal would never again see her children either. Cut off from their mother, Lilith and her brothers were forced to drink the blood of mortals to sustain bodies that had come from the cold depths of the underworld.

Anu, the Sumerian king of the gods, grew tired of the feud. In order to mitigate, he made it so the daughters of Inanna could bear the children of Ereshkigal's sons and the sons of Ereshkigal would find love with the daughters of Inanna. Thus, he connected them all forever,' Johansson finished.

Gwen glanced back at Miguel with a smile of appreciation for the semi-romantic story. He was already looking at her, and there was an expression of curiosity she didn't understand in his eyes; her heart started thumping from a sudden rush of adrenaline.

'This gloomy conclusion is just the beginning for the cults,' Johansson admitted. 'The sons of Ereshkigal still inspired fear, and they ruled over humans. Temples continued to be built and sacrifices given to appease their appetites for human blood.'

'These texts are clear in describing how the artifacts we found were used in these ceremonial offerings,' picked up Turner. 'They are also precise about the physical attributes of the sons of Ereshkigal,' he added seriously. 'We may not choose to equate these inhuman differences with those of demigods, as the Sumerians did, but it's apparent they were not a race of hominid with which we are familiar today.'

There was a moment of silence before a hand lifted determinedly from the audience. Gwen was impressed to see it was the blond man in a biker jacket. He was sitting next to the beautiful blonde in the white dress.

'Are you implying these early people were catering to a superhuman race?' he asked in a thick Russian accent.

'Yes,' was the simple answer.

'You have no proof of the actual creature these stories describe. Just the myth of how early people thought they came into existence,' the Russian pointed out.

Dr. Johansson was not deterred. She casually lifted her hand to flip the screen again.

Gwen saw a picture of shattered pottery on the earthen floor, but what caught her attention most were the countless teeth. They were long and sharp. The room buzzed with excitement.

'DNA confirmed they were hominoid but nothing like anything we'd ever seen before,' Johansson said proudly.

Gwen's brow lifted in disbelief. She grudgingly began to reconsider her stern position.

'They were filed,' dismissed one man.

'They were not. They were carefully studied for any tampering by our team,' promised Turner. 'These teeth are perfectly authentic and not from a *Homo sapiens*.'

Anita flipped the screen to an image of a closer look at one of the teeth on a white counter. 'The root, as you can see, is larger than average human teeth with a ridge that retracts. See here,' said Turner abstractedly. He used a pointer to outline the ridge of the tooth.

'We think this is because the teeth could extend longer above the gums, perhaps when it came time to feed, much like snakes can unhinge their jaws,' explained Johansson.

Gwen glanced to the side when Hudson suddenly turned toward the door. With an angry frown, he disappeared as silently and seamlessly as he'd appeared.

'If there was indeed another race of humanoid at the time, why has there been no other physical evidence until now?' asked a woman from the audience.

'Our testing has indicated the new species might be very old. What I mean,' Johansson said delicately, 'is that they lived a long time. Carbon dating on the teeth suggested they were removed around 5000BCE. However, our tests indicate the individual from which they were taken was already five-hundred-years-old.'

Immediately, the room was filled with hushed whispering. Harsh voices rejected this possibility.

'You have done something wrong,' insisted the woman who'd asked about the evidence.

'We completed the tests many times. The teeth came from three individuals over a long period,' claimed Johansson.

'Over five hundred years?' verified the woman doubtfully, and Dr. Johansson nodded.

'It is not impossible. There are other creatures on this planet that regularly outlive us,' Turner reminded them.

'Not by five hundred years!' dismissed someone.

'Coral can live for thousands of years and bowhead whales for centuries,' Turner asserted.

'If what you're saying is true,' cut in another man a little more reasonably, 'are you suggesting the reason we have no evidence of this race is they rarely die? Therefore, they have been living among us all this time?'

'That is one theory,' admitted Johansson. 'Tales of them have cropped up all through the centuries, and we have proof of their worship in every culture. It is only now, in the modern age, that we reject the possibility of such a creature. We don't see them, but it is perfectly reasonable to suspect they would be intelligent enough to hide themselves from us.'

'Why hide?' demanded another man mistrustfully.

'You have but to consider the policies of the Church for your answer,' Johansson pointed out drolly.

'As a species, we are much stronger than we have ever been,' Turner chimed in logically. 'It is possible that in the modern age, we would've found a way to drive a stronger predator to extinction. In this sense, *they* are now surviving *us*.'

Gwen heard Miguel make a sound of derision, but she was captivated by this idea. It all seemed much more plausible now with the addition of the physical evidence. DNA!

She glanced back to see Miguel's expression of dissatisfaction.

'You don't believe this?' she whispered in uncertainty.

'Not at all,' he assured her quickly.

'Are there any other questions?' asked the uncertain coordinator, but there was a long silence as the room processed what they'd been shown.

A woman wearing a purple hijab rose from a table near the back of the room. Her abrupt movement drew everyone's attention.

'What about the daughters of Inanna?' she asked sternly. 'What more have you found on *them*?'

Gwen marvelled at the woman's powerful stance. Her

features were firm, and she had a faint scar on her cheek.

'Nothing,' acknowledged Johansson. 'We have only this origin story and the promise they would forever become outcasts to society. In the earlier writings of the temple, it *does* suggest they too were worshipped for a time. It seems after the age of the Sumerians, the cults were forced underground by newer religions. It's quite possible the so called "Dowrra" also went underground.'

Johansson hesitated and smiled slightly as if deciding whether to impart something more.

'I'm once again tempted to draw similarities between this origin story and the manic crusade to eradicate women consorting with the devil.'

There was another long stretch of silence.

'Thank you for your time, this evening,' said Turner, and the screen behind him went blank.

No one quite seemed to know what to say. Obviously, everyone was skeptical, but it was difficult to argue with the facts that had been placed before them, and many people seemed agitated. Hudson had left, the Russian and his pretty companion were bent together whispering, and Miguel was withdrawn.

'What do you really think of all this?' Gwen asked him, and Miguel considered her thoughtfully.

'I think Anita is going to wish she hadn't made this presentation,' he admitted. Although the words seemed initially threatening, Gwen sensed they were not meant to be.

'What do you mean?' she asked apprehensively.

'If these cults *are* real, they will not appreciate being exposed,' he pointed out. Gwen considered what he was saying with interest.

'You think she is in danger?' she guessed as the food began to arrive in the room. Miguel nodded. 'You're saying there could be vampires in this room?' Gwen verified, and he laughed.

'I do not, for a moment, believe in such creatures,' he assured her. 'On the other hand, human enjoyment of the same sort of ritual has been common enough,' he reminded her.

'The teeth?' she pressed.

'Hardly evidence to believe in vampires,' he reasoned, and Gwen grinned at him, purposely mischievous, as she prepared to challenge him.

'I don't know. *You're* pretty twitchy. Are you sure you're not one of her vampires?' she teased.

She could have sworn, for just half a second, he betrayed real alarm at her suggestion. It was so quickly followed with a dismissive laugh it was impossible to know.

'I'm quite certain. But if I *were,*' he added, his tone dropping dramatically in a way that made Gwen smile, 'you can be sure I'd be immensely upset with *anyone* trying to drag me out into the light.'

Miguel

Chapter Five

G wen laughed, dispelling her suspicious expression, for which I was glad. I was still seething with anger.

What the *fuck* did Anita think she would accomplish by exposing us? Surely, if she'd seen the DNA, she knew we were among humans. She *had* to have suspected there would be some of us in the room with her and we'd come for her after this. Not only had she threatened my people and me, but she'd uncovered the Dowrra! Gwen was mine to protect, and I'd do it with my life if necessary. I would have to be careful, of course. If Anita disappeared after such a discovery, people would wonder if she'd been onto something.

Our food arrived, and I did my best to put aside my mounting rage to enjoy the remainder of the night with Gwen. I decided to steer us away from the topic of vampires.

'If you could go anywhere, anytime in history, where would it be?' I asked her curiously. She looked intrigued by this question as she took a sip of her drink.

'That's a hard one! There are so many things I wish I could have seen,' she complained.

'If you had to choose *one,*' I maintained unconditionally, and she was thoughtful.

'The Renaissance,' she answered finally, and I nodded in approval. I couldn't help wishing she could have seen Italy then. She would have charmed Da Vinci, Raphael, and Michelangelo.

'You'd have enjoyed it,' I agreed absentmindedly.

'What about you?' she wondered, and my answer was immediate and obvious to me.

'Here and now.'

'*Really*?' she asked in disbelief. 'Today is so boring!'

'That is not a bad thing,' I promised her.

'It's *not* the most interesting time,' she accused me in disappointment, and I laughed.

'My father used to say nothing is ever interesting until the agony has faded, and it is romanticized,' I told her. Although she appreciated my point, she was still not convinced of my perspective. I was prepared to persuade her. 'Modern medicine, higher standards of living, basic human rights, unlimited access to information,' I listed. Gwen sighed and grudgingly agreed.

'Not everywhere, but sure,' she granted.

'Then there's you,' I added, which surprised her. 'I mean *this,*' I clarified, and I motioned between us.

'I don't understand,' she admitted.

'You were free to choose to come with me tonight. You didn't defer this decision, we aren't accompanied by a chaperone, and no one mandated we spend time together. So, I know it is where *you* want to be. Women have never been more honest,' I finished as an appreciative smile crossed her lips.

'I hadn't ever thought of it like that,' she said coyly.

'So, you know I grew up in Luxembourg. What about you?' I asked her.

'Oh!' she gasped in surprise at the topic change. 'A boring little place called Silver Springs.'

Her admission took me off guard, and I immediately searched her expression suspiciously.

Silver Springs was not only the site of a Dowrra convent, but it was also close to Highberry Park, which was a Wayside Coven estate. I'd built a halfway house there for vampires transitioning from human custody to freedom. It seemed incredible I'd been so close to Gwen so many times and we'd never crossed paths before.

'Do you ever go home?' I inquired, and she immediately shook her head.

'I haven't spoken to my father in years,' she revealed, and I felt a sudden desire to comfort her. It was a strange sensation with which I had no experience.

'Hasn't he tried to get in touch with you?' I wondered.

'Nope,' Gwen assured me. 'I remind him of my mother.'

Almost of its own accord, my hand lifted and rested over hers on her lap. She stilled, her entire body thrumming with awareness, and I had to take my hand back after a reassuring squeeze.

'So, you moved to the city for school and never looked back,' I assumed.

'Something like that,' she acknowledged. 'I got a Bachelor of Commerce from U of T and spent three years working on my CPA at Welford Accounting.'

'Where you got fired,' I recalled. 'What happened? You didn't say,' I reminded her.

'Oh, yah,' she grunted, suddenly uncomfortable. 'I... started dating the boss's son,' she admitted nervously. 'We broke up about a year ago, and confidential material went "missing" from my desk. It was considered a breach of my contract.'

'They fired you because you broke up with Jonathon Welford,' I said, and she looked horrified.

'You *know* him?' she gasped sounding worried.

'Of course,' I assured her angrily. 'He's an arrogant ass.'

She burst out laughing, despite my being perfectly serious, and nodded in agreement. I watched her intently as she continued eating for a moment.

'What did he do to you?' I asked suspiciously. When she looked nervous, I knew my instincts were not wrong.

'What?' she breathed.

'He must have done something. Otherwise, there would've been no need to fire you,' I pointed out logically.

'Maybe he was just offended,' she suggested quietly. She avoided my eyes.

'I don't think so,' I persisted, and she became defensive.

'I don't know what you want me to say,' she advised me sadly. 'He was an asshole.'

'Did he hurt you?' I asked sternly, and she sighed impatiently.

'He tried. Let's leave it at that,' she recommended. I could suddenly taste venom on my tongue.

Dowrra didn't possess sexual appetite before Choosing a mate, so human partners had always been forced upon them. Jonathon Welford was an embodiment of that kind of entitlement. I knew he would've demanded what he thought he deserved whether Gwen wanted it or not.

'Have you told anyone?' I asked, trying to keep my tone light despite the rage boiling within me.

'Only Charlotte,' she said, still avoiding my eyes.

'Will you?' I asked, and she snorted derisively

'No. Even if they believed me, it's been too long,' she reasoned, and I knew she was probably right.

It was brutally hard wrestling down my temper, but I did so my touch was gentle when I lifted her hand to my lips. I could sense her relief, and I knew she'd given up the only secret she thought she possessed.

'You know more than you should about me now,' she mumbled in an attempt to lighten the mood. 'Tell me more about you.'

I was more than prepared to humour her after her exceptional honesty with me. 'Anything you wish,' I invited.

'How did you meet your friend, Hudson?' she wanted to know.

'He used to date my sister,' I told her. I left out the fact that this had been before I was born.

'I didn't know you had a sister!' she exclaimed.

'Mackayla is my older sister,' I advised her. 'She raised me after my mother died.'

'What about your father?' Gwen wondered.

'He didn't know about me,' I admitted. 'You see...' I added hesitantly, 'my mother was thrown out when her family learned she'd become pregnant out of wedlock. I was born on the street.'

I looked up and saw she was staring at me in stunned disbelief at what had been perfectly normal behaviour in 1501.

'Your mother died on the street,' she realized, and I nodded.

'My sister found me, but by then I had no wish to know my father,' I assured her. 'It took me a long time to forgive him.'

She was gazing at me with new appreciation.

'So, not related to the Hapsburgs,' she assumed, and I had to work hard to keep the bitterness out of my smile. It is an unspoken law among vampires that we do not kill our human family. However, prejudice and hateful circumstances often make them the first of many murders.

The topic of conversation lightened considerably after that. By the end of the night, the chemistry between us had reached a nearly unbearable friction.

'Shall I take you home?' I asked when we were almost the last people in the room.

'Charlotte will pick me up where she dropped me off,' she informed me, and I agreed. I was perfectly aware she was attempting to keep me at a distance, but I was respectful. I knew her reasons must have to do with her ex.

We went to the coat check, and I helped her on with her coat. My eyes lingered on her slender neck as she lifted her hair out of her collar. The way the strands of red glinted in the artificial light was breathtaking.

Outside, the valet got out of my Lamborghini and abruptly tossed me my keys. Moments like that, when humans are expected to be quick, often prove most difficult for my kind. Controlling how fast we are is always a conscious concern. Nevertheless, I managed to both catch the keys and not react too quickly.

She texted her friend as we drove back to the diner. I parked on the street and told her I was more than prepared to wait with her. There was no way I would leave her on the road. Not if she were one hundred percent sober and not even if Luka, Natalia, and Darius had all been there watching her. Not now that I knew how precious she was to me.

Gwen's phone dinged, and she checked it. 'She'll be here in a minute,' she promised me.

'I'm in no rush,' I assured her once more, and she nodded before glancing uncertainly down at her phone again. I thought there was something she wanted to say, so I waited patiently.

'So... tomorrow is Charlotte's anniversary,' Gwen began, and I assumed her friend had reminded her of this on purpose. 'My date bailed *again,*' she confessed with a sigh.

'Bailed again?' I asked while trying not to betray any of the hints of jealousy I felt budding.

'His name is Anthony Benet. He works with—'

'Benet?' I repeated, wondering how I knew that name. It took me some time, but I had to repress a laugh when I realized he was my human contact, Agent Benet.

'He works with Derek,' Gwen continued, looking suspicious. 'Charlotte's husband,' she clarified.

Charlotte's husband working for the Protective Services Agency could pose some serious issues for me. The PSA didn't just act as a liaison between me and the human government. They worked with me to police vampire behaviour.

I wondered if Benet had chosen the diner because of Gwen. Then I recalled his hasty retreat when James had attacked her, and I doubted they'd ever met. Next, I pondered the possibility I'd been set up to meet Gwen. It wasn't unheard of for PSA agents to do undercover work to investigate vampires.

I looked warily down at my companion, but I could tell she was concerned only with what she was trying to ask me. She didn't seem to realize what she'd unintentionally revealed about her friends. If she was as perfectly naive as most humans, she would think Derek was some kind of detective.

'Are you lining me up as a second choice?' I asked her teasingly.

'No! I mean, yes...?' she corrected herself in confusion. She nervously tucked her hair behind her ear. 'It won't be fancy like tonight. Probably just dinner with Derek and Charlotte,' she explained.

'I don't know if I could handle that,' I advised her jokingly, and she became agitated again. I couldn't help it when she riled so easily, and the scent of her embarrassment was delicious.

'Do you want to come or not?' she finally demanded, and I laughed, dispelling the act.

'I'd love to accompany you,' I assured her although privately I was a little apprehensive about her companions. Her friend could easily recognize what I was, and I doubted he'd appreciate my dating Gwen. There was no law against it, but he could tell her what I was. It would jeopardize both their lives, but I didn't know what sort of man this "Derek" was. In my experience, humans could become extremely irrational when faced with my kind.

Gwen was so pleased I'd accepted she was oblivious to my preoccupation.

'Can we meet you here again tomorrow at six?' she wondered, and I nodded.

'I'll be here,' I agreed, and she smiled.

There is a common expression which comes into the eyes of a woman when she decides to kiss you for the first time. I became utterly still in anticipation as Gwen leaned forward. The moment her lips touched mine, I deepened the kiss. She groaned softly, and both her hands slid up my shoulders. I wanted to be gentle with her, but it was all I could do to prevent myself from coming across the car. I was not used to controlling myself with women, and to make things more difficult, my eyeteeth abruptly lengthened.

Luckily, car lights flashed through the windshield, and Gwen shrank back from me with a nervous giggle. Charlotte had arrived not a second too soon.

I felt my nails biting into my palms as Gwen collected her shoes. I kept my head lowered and out of the light until I was certain my eyes no longer betrayed me.

'Thank you, for tonight,' Gwen told me, and she leaned forward again to sweetly kiss my jaw. 'I'll see you tomorrow.'

'Goodnight,' I whispered just before she closed the door.

Gwendolyn

Chapter Six

Overwhelmed with excitement, Gwen walked briskly to the yellow Ford Fiesta where Charlotte was waiting in anticipation.

'*Well*?' Charlotte demanded as soon as Gwen closed the door. Miguel's Lamborghini rumbled off into the night, and Gwen grinned. Charlotte shrieked knowingly. 'You totally just kissed him!' she accused happily.

'How could you know that?' Gwen laughed. She sank contentedly into her seat as Charlotte began to drive her toward her building.

'You're grinning like a girl who just got kissed,' Charlotte informed her, 'and *well,*' she added with a wink.

'I invited him to join us tomorrow night. He said he'll come,' Gwen said.

'Good! Derek is all anxious,' Charlotte groaned.

'Did you tell him dating one asshole doesn't make me susceptible to them all?' Gwen asked, and Charlotte rolled her eyes.

'For the thousandth time,' Charlotte insisted. 'He just knows Benet. He thinks he's a good guy.'

Benet's efforts to avoid meeting her had bothered Gwen initially, but now she felt a little relieved. She smiled at the memory of Miguel's kiss that had been filled with need and yet tenderly cautious. Charlotte was glancing at her thoughtfully.

'You know that thing we talked about years ago?' she

asked hesitantly. 'How you... never *wanted* a man,' she clarified.

'I remember,' Gwen assured her with a coy grin. 'He makes me want him.'

Charlotte seemed shocked by this. 'Would *not* have guessed that,' she muttered cryptically. 'Derek is going to have a *fit*.'

Gwen decided to ignore her eccentric friend as she wondered how things might play out with Miguel. She knew there were things he wasn't telling her, but it was useless to find reasons not to want him. No one had ever made her feel the way he did, and it felt *so good* to taste real desire for someone.

Charlotte was quiet all the way to Gwen's building, and Gwen was thoroughly impressed. She'd expected her friend to lose her mind over Gwen finally experiencing the passion most women were privileged to every day.

'See you tomorrow, horndog,' she saluted Gwen obnoxiously.

Gwen's roommate was already in her room with the TV blaring, so she went straight to bed.

She lay in silence for a short time, but it was impossible to ignore the new way in which she was thrumming with arousal. She kept remembering how incredible he'd smelled, the hardness of his body under her hands, and the command he'd taken of her mouth.

Losing her patience, Gwen turned over. From the bottom drawer of her nightstand, she retrieved a pink box Charlotte had bought as a gag gift years before. It was ridiculously bedazzled with the words, "*In case of emergency*" printed on the lid. Inside was a pink bullet and remote, which she'd never needed to use before.

Nervous, but determined for relief, she wiggled out of her sleeping shorts. She set the vibrator to the first setting and was thankful the little thing started to buzz between her fingers. After a momentary hesitation, Gwen slipped the quivering toy between her thighs. It touched her aching flesh, and she groaned before sinking against her pillow gratefully.

She'd expected pleasure to be difficult to achieve by the way everyone talked about women and their elusive orgasms. To her pleasant surprise, her body responded eagerly to the stimulation, so she turned up the vibration. It didn't take her long to discover her clit, and then it was only a matter of moments before her muscles all began to clench expectantly.

She heard herself groan, and at first, she was mortified. She listened carefully to make sure Sandra's TV was still on down the hall. Confident her roomie couldn't hear, she ignored the involuntary sounds. Her mind automatically returned to Miguel.

Her abdominal muscles twitched just before ecstasy began pulsing through her. Her mouth opened, and her back arched, but she was able to rein in her cry at the last second. Then she collapsed back into the mattress with a sense of release, unlike anything she'd ever felt before.

x x x

Miguel

'Hudson.'

My friend answered his phone sharply with irritation as if he'd been in the middle of something.

'It's me,' I growled back. 'We've got to talk.'

'Let me guess,' he said disapprovingly. 'This is about your redheaded girl. You're not listening to my advice.'

'Don't play games with me, Hudson,' I grumbled as my fist tightened on the steering wheel. 'This is important to me.'

'I know,' Hudson assured more soberly.

'Then tell me about her. How do I...? I have never been with a human this way,' I admitted. 'I'm afraid to hurt her.'

It is not the nature of a vampire to humble themselves. I hated expressing vulnerability, but I had nowhere else to turn, and I trusted Hudson above almost anyone.

He sighed, and I knew he was preparing to humour me even if he found my humility as irritating as I did.

'The combination of bloodlust and desire is normal. Eventually, if she is ever comfortable enough with you, the two need not be distinguishable,' he revealed.

'You mean bite her?' I demanded in shock. Part of me found the potential harm this would cause her inexcusable, and part of me was helplessly intrigued.

'Well, yes,' Hudson said as though this were the most obvious thing in the world. I felt my teeth lengthen, and venom numbed my tongue just at the thought of it.

'What if I envenom her?' I wondered.

'Immune. In fact, I always found they had an erotic reaction to it,' he added with some amusement.

'How am I supposed to hide the change?' I asked as I recalled the way my fangs had suddenly lengthened. If we hadn't been in a dark car, Gwen would have seen my eyes blacken. All hope for future intimacy had been momentarily suspended.

'As you become more intimate with her, you'll find it easier to control any bodily reactions,' he promised, and I was immediately relieved.

'Her friend works for the PSA,' I informed him, and he laughed.

'It was nice knowing you,' he responded and hung up.

I dropped the phone on the passenger seat and sat a while thoughtfully staring out into the darkness of the parking garage. Did I really mean to go through with committing myself to just one female who was a *human*?

My mind wandered back to that kiss in the car and the intensity she'd made me feel so swiftly. I'd have killed any vampiress that caused me that kind of weakness, but with Gwen, it was strangely liberating.

So, yes...

It wasn't only because she would one day provide me with offspring, which was something few other males could boast of. She also made me feel something I'd never known I could feel before. It was something I'd never realized I'd needed, or wanted, until the moment she'd unleashed it.

Hudson had said I'd share it with her one day if she were willing. I wondered whether she'd ever be willing.

x x x

Gwendolyn

'I really can't believe you forgot. *Again,*' Charlotte reiterated from the back of the taxi.

Gwen had been content with Derek's excuse that a high-profile murder had kept him from making the dinner reservation. Charlotte Wells wasn't letting it go that easily, however.

Mrs. Wells was usually harmless, but she had an uncanny ability to evolve quickly from devoted wife to fearsome monster. Gwen still wasn't satisfied the busty brunette wasn't harbouring a twelve-foot demon inside her.

Agent Derek Wells, Charlotte's dedicated husband, was *well* beyond making apologies by this point in their argument. Gwen knew from experience their fight had begun long before she'd gotten into the cab.

'Well, *I* can't believe you invited a total stranger out to dinner with your best friend,' Derek fired back with all the satisfaction of a man who has held his tongue long enough.

Oh, Gwen thought, *this is only going to get worse.*

Derek was no pushover, and he was a cop with a naturally suspicious nature. He didn't look particularly intimidating, with his average height and beer belly, but Gwen had seen him happily go toe-to-toe with six-foot ruffians. He dealt primarily in sensitive cases and had even been asked to consult in the States. Whatever it was he did exactly, he did it extremely well, which was just one of many reasons he didn't know about Jonathon Welford. Even Charlotte knew Derek would have gotten locked up for murder if he knew about that.

Charlotte growled ominously from the backseat, and Gwen anxiously resisted the urge to make sure she hadn't eaten her husband.

'It's not like she dated an asshole who ended her career, took everything she owned, and dumped her less than a year ago,' Charlotte ranted sarcastically.

The taxi driver was an older man with distinguished salt and pepper hair. He glanced skeptically at Gwen, who offered him a tentatively reassuring smile.

'This guy could be *anyone*!' Derek reprimanded.

'You're such a cop! Relax! She's already gone out with him once, and she lived to tell the tale,' Charlotte reminded him. 'Not everyone is a murdering psychopath.'

'We don't even *know* him!' Derek asserted with disbelief.

'Well then, tell your friend to stop cancelling on us!' Charlotte quipped dismissively. Derek was grudgingly silent again after the reminder it was his friend who continued to neglect meeting Gwen. Agent Benet was a really busy man, evidently.

They managed to ride in tense silence all the way to The Diner after that.

'Sorry,' whispered Gwen to the cabby, and his bushy brows lifted wordlessly at her. She climbed out of the car next to Charlotte, who was still silently fuming while Derek paid the fare. Once he'd joined them, the car quickly sped off.

'Where is he?' demanded Derek, glancing around as though expecting a monster to come tottering out of the shadows at them. 'Is he late?' he added with evident satisfaction.

'We're twenty minutes early,' Gwen informed him quietly. Derek looked disappointed and didn't respond.

Gwen fidgeted uncomfortably in the dress Charlotte had insisted on despite numerous objections. She had little choice but to submit when Charlotte treated her like a mannequin since she still couldn't afford to replace what Jon had taken. Minimum wage wasn't exactly livable.

Ignoring her discomfort, she focused on seeing Miguel again. She'd been thinking about kissing him all day. She'd even fantasized about what it might be like to let him wring some ecstasy from her instead of doing it on her own.

She was, nonetheless, admittedly nervous to see how he'd find her friends. He was the epitome of class and yet just informal enough she'd been able to relate to him. She wasn't sure how her odd friends would fair. Jonathon had never liked them.

'Whoa,' breathed Derek, 'now *there's* a nice car. Looks like an Aston Martin Rapide S,' he guessed to himself.

Gwen followed his gaze up the street toward the white vehicle coming toward them. It was gorgeous but not in the obvious way Miguel's Lamborghini the night before had been. Charlotte even grunted with disinterest at its misleading austerity, and Derek gaped at her in disbelief.

'It's a two hundred thousand dollar car!' he exclaimed. She shrugged nonchalantly, which only further agitated her husband.

'I looked up Miguel's Lamborghini,' she advised him smugly. 'The SV is a *five*-hundred-thousand-dollar car.'

'Well, the Aston Martin is the car *James Bond* drives,' Derek returned evenly, and Charlotte became a little more curious. She leaned forward to peer through the tinted windows for a glimpse of the driver as the car approached. Then it abruptly pulled over to the curb, and she laughed knowingly.

'*Nice!*' she exclaimed, glancing triumphantly up at Derek's tense expression.

Gwen's heart was suddenly in her throat when Miguel stepped out of the driver's door. She hadn't realized how nervous she felt he wouldn't come until he was finally there. She'd never seen anyone look so good in jeans and a leather jacket.

Derek twisted unexpectedly next to her so his back

was to her date. Gwen could see he looked wildly uncertain.

'Miguel… *Santos*?' he hissed in verification, and Charlotte smirked with a nod. Gwen realized her friend hadn't told her husband who they were meeting, which was why he'd been so anxious.

Derek didn't look apprehensive anymore, though. At first, he looked terrified, and he swayed a little as though he might stumble sideways. Then he looked angry and his cheeks mottled.

'Are you okay?' Gwen whispered, and Derek seemed to remember himself. He turned back toward Miguel, who was walking toward them.

'Of course,' he assured her. 'I just wasn't expecting you to go for *another* rich asshole,' he muttered. Gwen frowned at him as he began to eye the other man from head to toe as if he were searching for evidence of his suspicions. Gwen disregarded his behaviour when Miguel reached them.

She felt suddenly uncertain how to receive him after their kiss the night before, so she let him approach her first. She had no idea how people dated all the time! It was surprisingly stressful deciding how to behave with him when all she wanted was for him to kiss her again.

'Gwen,' he greeted her softly, and he stopped much nearer to her than she'd anticipated. He smelled as incredible as she remembered, and the memory caused her a newly familiar twinge of anticipation.

'I'm glad you came,' she told him sincerely. Her nerves were suddenly gone now that she was looking up into those dark eyes again.

'As am I,' he responded, and he smiled as he reached for her hand. His lips were soft on her knuckles before he turned toward Charlotte, who was watching him almost as closely as her husband. 'Charlotte, it's good to see you again,' he told her.

'Thank you for coming,' Charlotte responded politely in stark contrast to her earlier tone. 'This is my husband,

Derek Wells. Derek, this is Miguel,' Charlotte said rather proudly. Gwen thought her friend seemed exultant as though she'd accomplished something.

Gwen looked at Derek and was disappointed to see him frowning slightly at Miguel. He barely remembered to hold out his hand.

'Pleasure,' he mumbled insincerely, and he wore an arrogant smirk with his hand outstretched. There was expectation and challenge in his eyes as though he'd already guessed Miguel might be averse to shaking his hand.

Chapter Seven

Gwen wondered if she'd missed something when Miguel again seemed hesitant to shake. He did it more readily than before, however, and she forgot about it.

'I hear you have an impressive car collection,' Derek commented stiffly. He gave Miguel one solid shake and retracted his hand as though he'd touched something unpleasant.

Gwen was utterly indignant and mortified, but she was too proud to say anything in front of her date. Thankfully, Miguel seemed either oblivious or politely indifferent.

'I do,' he responded simply, and he turned toward the car he'd driven. 'I thought you might enjoy this one.'

'The only one you have with four doors,' Derek anticipated with brazen cheek, and Miguel looked back at him. Gwen knew he wasn't blind to Derek's impoliteness because his smile hinted just a little at ready cockiness.

'Aside from the Mercedes-Benz and the Bentley Mulsanne limousine, yes,' he responded evenly. Derek's smile was brittle and faded completely once Miguel returned his attention to Gwen.

'Is it all right if I drive?' he asked.

'Of course!' she assured him.

'You're forgetting that *someone* forgot about tonight. We'll be lucky to get into a Jack Astors,' Charlotte reminded Gwen angrily. Miguel looked thoughtful, and then he smiled playfully at Gwen.

'I could certainly get us a reservation, but I'm afraid it

would seem fancy,' he advised her teasingly. Gwen laughed at his reminder of her apology for an "ordinary" dinner.

'If you can get us in somewhere, please do! It's their anniversary,' she explained.

'I hope you don't mind?' Miguel inquired of Derek who looked as though he did mind very much. Charlotte looked at her husband sternly, and he forced a smile.

'Of course not,' he dismissed, and Miguel nodded. He retreated to the car to make his call, so Gwen rounded on Derek fiercely.

'What the *hell* is wrong with you?' she snarled.

'Did you not learn anything from your experience with the last wealthy son of a bitch?' Derek demanded stonily.

'It's none of your business who I date, Derek!' Gwen hissed forbiddingly. 'All I ask is that you're polite to them. Besides, Miguel is *nothing* like Jonathon. You'd know that if you gave him half a chance,' she claimed.

Derek looked like there was something he desperately wanted to say, but he couldn't seem to find the words.

'Gwen, he's dangerous,' he implored. 'Can't you just trust me on this one?'

'No!' Gwen snapped. 'I really like him.'

He was initially surprised by her declaration, but then he looked with sudden clarity at Charlotte. His wife was waiting for him to meet her eyes, and something passed between them.

'You *knew*?' he realized aloud.

'Knew *what*?' snapped Gwen in agitation, and Derek opened his mouth as he searched for an explanation. He didn't have the chance to enlighten her before Miguel returned to the sidewalk.

'I have reserved a place for us at The King's Court,' her date informed them. He hesitated as he took note of their agitation, and their unease skyrocketed with his revelation. Charlotte made a choking sound, and Miguel was suddenly uncertain. 'Was that a poor choice?' he guessed.

'No!' Charlotte and Gwen tried to assure him together.

'Yes!' Derek chimed with disbelief after them.

Miguel looked bewildered by their chorus, and Gwen stepped forward calmly. She tried to find a way to tell him there was no way Derek could afford such a place, but Miguel held up his hand.

'The owner owes me a favour,' he explained. 'Tonight's dinner is on him.'

'You don't have to waste your favour on us,' Charlotte objected quickly, but Miguel shook his head.

'I insist!' he told her adamantly.

Some men might have taken the opportunity for arrogance or entitlement, but Miguel was purely sincere in his offer. In the end, that was the only reason Charlotte conceded, and when Gwen saw Miguel's smile, she knew it was genuine.

'Please,' he said with a gesture of invitation toward the car.

Charlotte snatched Derek's hand to drag him toward the Rapide. He managed to salvage a portion of his dignity by sullenly opening the car door for his wife.

Gwen looked up at Miguel, who was watching her apprehensively with his hands tucked into his pockets. She thought that uneasy expression was endearing on the face of a man so competent. She knew it meant he was unsure of himself with her, which was testament to how much he cared.

'Too much?' he wondered, and she shook her head.

'No, it was perfect,' she promised, but her eyes slid guiltily down from his. 'I'm sorry about Derek.'

'Don't be,' he advised her immediately.

'He's acting terribly!' she lamented. 'I don't know why.'

'Gwen,' Miguel said firmly, and her breath caught when his fingers brushed under her chin. He tilted her head so their eyes could meet again. 'I didn't evolve from a homeless orphan to my current position easily. I had to overcome many people who were a good deal more ruthless than your friend. He cares about you, and that's more important to me than my pride,' he assured her with a gentle smile that immediately set her at ease. She wanted to kiss him and taste the rapture he'd left her struggling with the night before.

He lifted his arm cordially, and she took it so he could lead her to the passenger side of his car. Inside, Gwen admired the red leather interior. She could tell, from the uncomfortable silence in the backseat that she'd interrupted an intense discussion.

'Come on, guys,' Gwen groaned while Miguel crossed in front of the car. 'It's your anniversary, for Christ's sake!'

There was no reply as Miguel got into the car. It started with a throaty rumble, at which Charlotte hummed appreciatively.

'What other cars do you have?' Charlotte asked. Gwen knew her friend had no real interest in cars. She expected this diversion was for Derek's benefit.

Miguel looked doubtful as if he anticipated this topic might irritate Derek further.

'The Aventador Superveloce you saw last night is the newest,' Miguel began as he pulled away from the curb. 'In addition to this one are the Porsche 918 Spyder, a Ferrari F12 Berlinetta Coupe, a Lamborghini Veneno Roadster, and an Aston Martin Vulcan. I also have a couple of driver cars and a lot of antiques.'

'I have no idea what any of that means,' Charlotte exclaimed. Gwen could tell she was trying to bate her husband's obsession, and Miguel finally saw this too.

'All those cars are beautiful, but my most prized possession is the 1959 Ferrari 250 GT Interim. My father bought it for me for my birthday,' he told her as Derek finally broke his silence with a squeak of disbelief.

'*You're* the one who bought that car?' he blurted. He leaned forward a little.

'My father did,' Miguel repeated.

'What's so special about this car?' Charlotte prompted her husband helpfully.

'*Uh,*' Derek groaned in disbelief as if he didn't know where to start. 'It's an 8 million dollar antique, and it was previously owned by a Saudi Arabian Prince.'

Gwen looked at Miguel quickly, but he didn't indicate whether this was true. She realized that meant it probably was.

'Where do you keep it?' Derek wanted to know.

'At home,' Miguel answered. 'It's too aggressively sought after by collectors to keep here in Toronto.'

'I thought you lived here?' Charlotte pointed out just as Gwen was about to mention the same.

'I do, but "home" has always kind of been in Prague,' Miguel clarified. Gwen realized there was still a lot she didn't know about him despite his honesty regarding his upbringing.

'You're from the Czech Republic,' Charlotte assumed with interest. 'I would have thought you were Spanish,' she admitted.

'No,' said Miguel hesitantly. He glanced knowingly at Gwen, who returned his smile. 'I grew up in Luxembourg.'

'*Oh.* So, you're... German...?' Charlotte guessed. 'I guess that makes sense with the accent,' she babbled casually.

'Luxembourg is a country,' Derek informed his wife.

'I thought it was a German city!' Charlotte exclaimed.

'They speak German, but they also speak French and Luxembourgish,' Derek explained. 'In any case, he's Austrian.'

'Wait, *wait*!' Charlotte laughed. 'So, you're an Austrian, with a Spanish name and a German accent, who grew up in Luxembourg, who now lives in Toronto, who's from Prague?'

'I think it's safe to say Miguel is kind of from everywhere,' Gwen intervened when Miguel began to look uncomfortable. He seemed to appreciate it as they reached The King's Court Steakhouse.

Gwen had never been to the famous restaurant, but she recognized the elegant building the same as everyone else in Toronto. It was legendary, not only for its steak and lobster dishes but for its medieval embellishment. The stunningly beautiful grounds surrounding the castle included waterfalls and koi ponds.

They drove under a bright red canopy, and four men opened all their doors at the same time. Gwen accepted the offered hand as the attractive gentleman welcomed her to The King's Court.

Miguel met her on the sidewalk as she gazed up at the well-lit terraces on the side of the building. Music drifted out into the night air, and Gwen could see several people walking in the gardens.

The door was opened for them, and they entered into a reception area where a pretty hostess smiled.

'Mr. Santos.' She acknowledged Gwen's date. 'Mr. Boerio informed us you would be joining us tonight. We are very happy to have you and your guests! Your room is ready.'

Gwen cleared her throat and leaned into Miguel a little.

'Did she say *room*?' she whispered, and he nodded.

'I believe she did,' he confirmed tentatively. 'Boerio has outdone himself, as usual.'

'This favour Mr. Boerio owed you...?' Gwen hedged, and Miguel grunted in comprehension.

'Probably not worth what he will give,' he assured her evasively as they passed into the main dining room.

The first half of the ground floor was a traditional restaurant with quiet music playing. Then they passed into the second half, which was open with white and black marble flooring. There were three pairs of French double doors to the balcony and a live band playing classical instruments on the stage. The guests all wore evening gowns and tuxedos.

The hostess led them up the antique, cherry-wood

staircase and down a wood-panelled corridor carpeted in a red runner. The stern Gothic portraits, armoured suits, oil lamps, and sombre statues gave the passageway a medieval charm.

They passed by several doors until they'd reached the end of the dark hallway where there was a door left open. They passed into a truly elegant room with the same white and black marble floors as below and floor length windows with silk drapes. There was an enormous fireplace at one end, with couches arrayed around it, and a dining table at the other. A waitress and waiter were already waiting for them in front of the private bar.

'Welcome to The King's Court,' said the waitress politely. She and her companion pulled Gwen and Charlotte's seats out for them, but Charlotte was too distracted to sit. She stared around them in wonder and craned her neck backwards to take in the ornate ceiling inlaid with gold.

'This is beautiful, Miguel!' Charlotte exclaimed as Derek impatiently waved the waiter away from his wife's seat.

'I'm glad you like it,' Miguel responded as he took his place at the table next to Gwen. Charlotte finally joined them.

'Can I get you some drinks?' asked the waitress.

'I think I need a scotch,' Derek advised her sounding tired.

'We have twenty-one-year-old Balvenie PortWood,' she suggested.

'That will do, I'm sure,' Derek dismissed sharply, and Gwen glared at him. He had the decency to look guilty.

'Wine for me,' Charlotte cut in, 'whatever is good that you have in red.'

'Penfolds,' Miguel recommended. 'Block 42 Kalimna Cabernet Sauvignon is Niccolò's favourite. I'll have that as well.'

'Me too,' chimed in Gwen, and the staff departed with nods.

Derek sighed worriedly as he lifted the menu they'd been left to examine the options. 'No prices,' he muttered to himself.

'So, Miguel,' said Charlotte pointedly, 'tell us what's good to order,' she proposed.

'Everything,' Miguel promised readily, 'but the salmon and the porterhouse are particularly excellent.'

'How do you know the owner?' Gwen asked as the waiter returned with a bottle of wine and Derek's scotch. Miguel seemed momentarily hesitant.

'We met at Sapienza, the University of Rome,' Miguel revealed to Gwen's amazement. 'Niccolò was studying political science, and I was studying law.'

'You studied law?' asked Gwen at the same time Charlotte said, 'You lived in Rome?'

Miguel laughed. 'Yes, to both.'

'Don't bother asking him where else he has been or what else he has studied,' interrupted a deep voice with an Italian accent. Gwen turned toward a man with black eyes and shoulder-length hair who was approaching them in an impeccable suit. He moved effortlessly over the floor like he was floating. 'I think you may find the list of *have nots* is far shorter, *buona donna,*' he explained.

'Boerio,' Miguel greeted him. 'Thank you for the accommodation tonight.'

'My pleasure, *mio amico,*' assured the gorgeous Italian with a pleased smile. 'It has been *far* too long.'

As he reached the table, Gwen saw he had a strange scar across his throat. It seemed to her as though he'd nearly been decapitated at some point. She tried not to stare.

'This is my date, Gwendolyn Rhys, and her friends Charlotte and Derek,' Miguel introduced them. 'Gwen, this is Niccolò Boerio.'

'Thank you so much for letting us come here,' Gwen said sincerely. 'It's beautiful!'

'It is no trouble. Anything for Miguel,' Niccolò added with a wink toward her date. 'We go way back, as he told you. Back to Rome,' he said enigmatically. 'Have you spoken to the Macedonian, of late?' he asked Miguel with sudden interest.

'Angjelko?' verified Miguel with evident confusion. 'Not in years,' he admitted.

'Well,' dismissed Niccolò drolly, 'he *was* exceedingly upset after we burned down his castle in Thessaloniki,' he recalled.

'I'm sorry, you did *what*?' Gwen demanded, and she looked to Miguel for an explanation. Niccolò laughed although Miguel looked ashamed.

'Greeks are notoriously temperamental,' the Italian pointed out. 'He will get over it in time.'

Miguel cleared his throat, and the methodical way he rose from the table made Gwen think he was upset. 'I will have the porterhouse,' he said to the waiter, who nodded, and Miguel turned to Gwen. 'We'll just be a moment' he promised her, and she nodded skeptically.

'It was an absolute pleasure, *bellezza rosso,*' Niccolò declared with a dramatic bow before following after Miguel.

Gwen tried to decide whether the Italian was pulling Miguel's chains or if her date had been disguising a rebellious youth. He'd said he grew up on the street. She hadn't thought that meant he'd done much partying in castles.

'Wow,' Charlotte giggled once they were alone. 'The more I get to know about this guy, the more I *like* him, Gwen.'

Miguel

Chapter Eight

Once we were far enough down the hall that Gwen could not hear, I turned on Niccolò angrily. My hand seized his throat, and I pushed the four-hundred-year-old Italian effortlessly against the wooden wall.

'What are you doing?' I snarled as he choked. He gripped my wrist to lift himself up so he could get enough air to speak.

'I said nothing!' he objected, and I dropped him. He slumped to the floor, rubbing his neck as he glared up at me.

'It was unnecessary bringing up Angjelko or the castle at Thessaloniki,' I reprimanded him.

'What do you care? I assume they will be dead by the morning,' dismissed Niccolò.

'I'm not Mickaël of Burgundy anymore,' I growled, resenting him for the reminder. 'Gwen is Dowrra, Niccolò. She is *mine*.'

Realization filled his eyes, and he got slowly to his feet.

'Dowrra,' he said softly in awe. 'She does not yet know?'

'No,' I confirmed. I was relieved he seemed to understand how reckless his behaviour had been.

Niccolò Boerio had always been the most thoughtless creature I'd ever known. Not malicious precisely but wilfully careless at times. Once we'd been close, and we'd ravaged Europe together, living in excess and wild abandon, for centuries. Now, he was in exile, and I had garnered too much respect and responsibility to abide his childish mind games. He'd always resented that a little.

'I am sorry, my lord,' he said humbly, and he bowed his head. 'I did not intend insult.'

'You're forgiven,' I acknowledged. 'Now go, before I finish what I started a hundred years ago,' I recommended. I indicated his scarred throat, and he quickly melted into the shadows of the corridor. I returned to the table where the humans were bent together whispering fiercely.

'So, you were a party animal,' Charlotte hinted eagerly, and I sighed regretfully.

'Haven't we all been, at one point?' I redirected.

'Sure, but most of us haven't burned down a castle,' pointed out Gwen expectantly.

'Then again, most of us didn't party in castles,' Charlotte added thoughtfully.

'I did a lot of partying, in a lot of places, but I still managed not to burn anything down!' chastised Derek impatiently.

'It was an accident and rather tragic,' I cut in. 'It was five-hundred-years old,' I admitted sadly.

'Oh, my God,' Charlotte murmured in horror, but there was a hint of laughter in her voice. 'Did you get in trouble?'

'No,' I assured her.

I glanced at Gwen, who was gazing at me, and I wondered what she thought of me now. I supposed, based on Charlotte's apparent enjoyment, it could not have been too detrimental.

'Why do I feel as if it wasn't the first, or last, castle you burned down?' Derek asked rhetorically with his eyes on the fireplace.

The man knew I was a vampire, which was evidenced by his abominable behaviour toward me. What he didn't know was that I was the Ambassador of Human Affairs and the Prince of the Wayside Coven. It was highly privileged information which was classified for my privacy. Had he known these things, he would have been far more careful about the way he spoke to me. I trusted that once he investigated me, he might be very afraid for his life but for now, I let him continue digging a grave.

'It was the first one I burned down *accidentally,*' I dismissed.

The women thought I was kidding, and they laughed, but Derek met my gaze knowingly as the food arrived at our table.

'So, when you're not burning down castles and eating at fancy restaurants with crazy friends, what do you like to do?' Charlotte wanted to know.

I thought better of telling them I mediated between human and vampire agencies, passed judgment, and enacted justice against unruly vampires. I went with my hobbies of the sixteenth century instead.

'Art and music,' I told her.

'Can you play?' asked Gwen in surprise.

'Piano and... I play the Spanish lute,' I admitted.

'What's a lute?' asked Charlotte.

'It's an old guitar,' Derek substituted dourly.

'I want to see that art collection you keep talking about,' Gwen advised me sincerely. I could hear the longing in her voice.

'It's early,' I pointed out. 'When we are done here, you could all accompany me back to the Royal Alton.'

Gwen's eyes widened lustfully. She was about to accept this offer, but Derek nearly choked on his food in his haste to intervene.

'No!' he cried and quickly regained control of himself when both women glared at him. 'What I mean is... perhaps another time?' he suggested more civilly.

'I want to see it tonight,' Gwen growled at him.

'Very well,' I agreed, and I clinked my wine glass first against hers and then against Charlotte's. Derek glowered at me from across the table, but his ire only encouraged me. Perhaps there was a bit of mischievous youth left in me yet.

Derek remained composed for the rest of the meal, but I could see his ire was provoked whenever the ladies laughed at anything I said. By the end of the meal, both women had become dismissive of his attitude.

While we waited outside for the car to be brought around, Derek asked if he could speak to me. I obliged him, despite objections from the women, and we walked around the corner of The King's Court. He rounded on me viciously.

'What the hell are you doing?' he snarled at me. I had not been verbally abused in centuries, and my patience with him was done.

'I'm trying to enjoy the night, in spite of your continued efforts to ruin it for everyone,' I commented snidely.

'Don't give me that shit! I work for the PSA, and I know what you are! I will haul your ass in for questioning so fucking fast,' he promised explosively.

I was impressed by his stupidity, but I wanted to respect him for Gwen's sake. It was just impossible to prevent a smile of amusement from touching my lips.

'You're mistaken—' I assured him.

'I'm not,' he cut in. 'I've been with the Agency for ten years, and I can spot your kind in a crowd,' he promised.

'That is not what I meant,' I said, my voice deepening when he interrupted me. 'You're making a mistake, Derek. You have no idea to whom you are speaking.'

He snorted scornfully at me.

'You're the one messing with the wrong guy,' he assured me. 'Gwen and Charlotte are not going to your place tonight, *leech*. I suggest you come up with an excuse to take us home.'

I don't need to explain why being likened to a blood-sucking worm is insulting, but above all other derogatory names, it's the one I hate *most*.

I grabbed him, more roughly than I'd intended to, and I shoved him against the brick wall with enough force to knock the air out of him.

'I've... texted superior... your name,' he grunted as if this would protect him.

'Have you checked your phone since then?' I asked, and he shook his head. I dropped him, and he went to his knees as he gasped for air.

'Check it,' I commanded, and he scrambled to pull his cell out of his pocket. He probably meant to call for help, but with trembling fingers, he decided to open the message from his supervisor first. I saw his eyes go wide, and I turned away from him. I was thoroughly annoyed he'd incited me to violence.

'You're... the Ambassador,' he gasped, his voice going a little high, and he looked up at me. 'You're a coven prince! I'm... sorry,' he said awkwardly, as though apologies were a foreign thing to him. 'What is it you want with Gwen?'

'Is it impossible to imagine I might genuinely care about your friend, Mr. Wells?' I asked him.

'You still kill,' he defended his concerns logically. My position as the Ambassador may have been as good as sainthood to the PSA, but they still mistrusted me.

'Get up,' I commanded, and he did so quickly as though I'd reminded him he was still kneeling on the ground. 'I'm on a date with a woman whom I care very much about impressing,' I told him frankly, and he looked amazed by my candour. 'I have been exceedingly patient with you, and I've even tried to make your anniversary memorable. You're more than welcome to accompany us to see my collection, but I'm not done with my evening, and neither is Gwen.'

With a great deal of reluctance, he nodded in understanding. I held out my hand for him to make his way back toward the car.

'Miguel, do you like theatre?' Charlotte asked doubtfully, and I got the sense the women had been debating this fact.

'Immensely,' I answered, and Charlotte rolled her eyes

when Gwen smiled triumphantly. 'Probably my favourite venue is Teatro La Fenice, in Venice.'

'Opera,' noted Gwen with admiration as I opened her door. 'Which one is your favourite?' she wanted to know. She remained standing close to me, looking expectant, and I could sense her pulse quickening in excitement.

'Oh, Gwen,' I chastised her teasingly, and she grinned. 'There can be no such thing.'

She got a stubborn look in her eyes even as colour flooded her lovely cheeks.

'If you had to choose one,' she insisted, repeating my words from before regarding what period in history she liked best. I met her challenging gaze well aware Derek and Charlotte were watching us.

'I suppose *Dido and Aeneas,*' I decided softly, 'even if only for Dido's lament.'

'That's a very romantic one,' Gwen pointed out. 'I thought you might choose *L'Orfeo* or *Giulio Cesare.*'

I was impressed she was familiar with opera, and my hand rose to touch her flushing cheek. I could sense the blood rushing excitedly beneath my fingertips.

'Most operas are,' I reminded her, and I saw her pupils widened a little as her eyes shifted to my lips. Charlotte cleared her throat, which spoiled the moment.

'I prefer rom-coms,' she informed us as Gwen startled away from me. 'So, are we going to see some art?'

Gwen offered me a coy smile before she sank into her seat. I reluctantly closed her door, and I noticed Derek staring at me over the roof of the car. There was a peculiar expression of amazement on his face I didn't understand. No sooner had I spied it, it was gone.

Charlotte plied me with questions about my hobbies and where I'd come from on the way to the Royal Alton. Like many before, she was continuously frustrated by a lingering sense of not having all the facts.

We finally reached the hotel where Anthony had come down to wait for me and take the car down to the parking garage. Carlton, the doorman, opened the door, and I took my gaping guests to the private elevator, which opened directly into the presidential suite.

'Do you have a room where you keep everything?' wondered Charlotte naively as she wandered into my apartment.

'No,' said Gwen before I could answer. 'It's everywhere.'

I hung back to appreciate her amazement as she moved from the foyer into the reception area. Her hand ran absently over the white Lexington sofa as she took in the Grecian statuary and paintings on the wall. Eventually, I gently took hold of her arm to lead her through the kitchen and into the dining area. Her eyes latched onto the rusty red Egyptian pillars, but then she saw the famous painting, *Ladies of Troy,* by Fernando. I was suddenly afraid she might faint.

'Is that a wine cellar?' Charlotte demanded, peering into my private study.

'Help yourself,' I encouraged her distractedly.

I followed Gwen into the games room where I kept the majority of my modern art. Her eyes feasted off the abstract sculpture, *In Pieces,* by Ariel Thomas. Next, she was drawn in by the bookshelves filled with volumes I'd collected and restored hundreds of years ago. Her fingers traced with gentle reverence over their spines as she read the familiar names and authors.

'Air tight, I presume,' said Derek as he motioned toward the glass room where all the oldest of my things were kept. He'd helped himself to the Fernando de Castilla sherry in my office.

'Yes,' I admitted as Gwen pressed herself against the glass to gaze at the scrolls, books, and artifacts.

'Can I stay here forever?' she breathed wistfully, and my laugh seemed to sober her. She turned quickly toward me, and her eyes flitted over me appreciatively.

'A lot of wealthy men have a taste for art, but you *know* art,' she said. 'I don't think I've ever seen a collection like this.'

'I'm happy you approve. Would you care for a drink?' I asked her, and she nodded.

I went to my study where Charlotte was fondling a bottle of 1971 Château Léoville-Las Cases. I got them each a glass and opened the chosen bottle for her.

'Let it... breathe,' I said as Charlotte immediately lifted the bottle and started pouring once it was open.

'You have quite the place here,' she said.

'Thank you,' I responded, assuming she meant to compliment me.

'You seem to like my friend,' she added causally, and I smiled at her brazen inquiry.

'Yes, I do,' I confirmed readily.

'Good,' Charlotte nodded. 'She seems to really like you too. Which is different for her, you know?'

'I do,' I said without thinking, and she looked up at me with sudden inquiry from the corner of my eye.

'You *do*, don't you?' she asked hopefully, and I looked up at her as I realized something intriguing.

'As do you, I see,' I pointed out knowingly, and Charlotte hid a cocky grin in her glass as she took a sip. I waited impatiently for her to elaborate on how she knew about the Dowrra. Once she'd lowered her glass, Charlotte shrugged.

'You must be royalty,' she guessed. 'Gwen has come unknowingly across many *akaharu,* but she has never Chosen.'

Akaharu was Ancient Sumerian for *vampire...*

I glanced back toward the games rooms where I could hear Derek and Gwen talking. I only returned my full attention to Charlotte once I was sure they were distracted.

'Who are you?' I demanded, and my lips lifted defensively. Charlotte waved her hand at me in dismissal of my uneasiness.

'Derek and I are Nasaru,' she explained. 'You need not be concerned about us. Gwen is our responsibility.'

There were two classes of Dowrra inside their cult.

Foremost were the Tatamora whose ancestors could trace their lineage back to Inanna. These women could form the bond with a vampire of their innate Choosing, and they were like royalty. The cult was very stringent about keeping those bloodlines pure and uncontaminated. The second class, the Nasaru, were bloodlines which had lost the ability to form the bond after millennia of breeding with humans. They became cult guardians.

'If the cult knows about Gwen, why are you allowing her to live outside your walls?' I needed to know.

'It was the wish of her mother,' Charlotte illuminated, and I snorted with understanding.

'Her mother didn't die, did she?' I guessed, and Charlotte averted her eyes shamefully.

'She Chose,' she admitted.

'Abandoning her daughter,' I added accusingly.

'She left her well protected,' Charlotte defended. 'Besides, you know a coven is no place for an unmated Dowrra. Certainly, no place for a human child,' she added.

I couldn't disagree, but it still tore me apart. Gwen's mother had allowed her daughter to think she was dead when the truth was she'd just moved on to another family. There was no way to tell my mate this without exposing myself to her.

'Why are you telling me this now?' I asked suspiciously.

'Clearly, she has formed the bond with you. I know you will protect her, and I fear she will need it,' Charlotte admitted. 'The temple Johansson found contained stone tablets listing the bloodlines. Soon, the humans will begin their witch hunts anew, and they will know who we are, even if we don't yet know it ourselves,' she pointed out as my gut turned at her revelation.

I considered what Hudson had said the night before about how he felt something terrible was about to happen.

Humankind had always hated vampires, but they'd conceded to cohabitation with us because they had no other choice. Once the humans learned of the Dowrra, there would be no reconciliation with them. They would recognize them as the key to our undoing.

'Where is Quinn O'Connor?' I asked the Nasaru directly and was rewarded for my perception when she smiled.

'He wouldn't be helpful to us now,' she promised. 'He'd only end the world. Again,' she clarified.

'Perhaps that's what we need,' I suggested gravely.

'You cannot be serious,' she hissed in disbelief.

'You said it yourself,' I reminded her. 'I will do anything to protect Gwen.'

She stared into my eyes nervously for a moment as she recognized how sincere I was. Finally, she nodded.

'I will see if the Matrons will awaken him, but *Miguel,*' she stressed my name seriously, 'you weren't there when he went to sleep. You might not wish to be here when he awakens, either...'

Gwendolyn

Chapter Nine

Miguel and Charlotte entered the library as Gwen experimentally pressed the keys of the grand piano. Several hauntingly beautiful notes flowed into the air. She could almost feel Miguel's proximity as he came near to hand her the glass of wine he'd gone to get for her.

'Do you play?' he asked, and she shook her head sadly.

'No, but I always wished I'd learned,' she admitted. 'My mother knew how to play. I remember that,' she told him.

'There is still time for you to learn,' he reasoned.

'They say it's harder after adulthood,' she dismissed and looked up at him. '*You* play.'

'Would you like to hear?' he guessed, and he set his wine aside in anticipation of her nod. She'd been prepared to convince him but instead was impressed by his confidence as he took a seat at the piano.

Gwen gazed down at his long-fingered hands longingly. A beautiful melody filled the room, and she closed her eyes listening to the emotional tones. She didn't notice Derek and Charlotte drifting nearer until the song ended, and their clapping shattered the spell.

Derek suggested they play pool; Gwen objected, but Charlotte overruled her. She was even more nervous for Miguel to know how badly she played after realizing he was frighteningly good. Initially, his help was restricted to verbal suggestions and directions while she was shooting, but it wasn't helping much.

Gwen grew even more anxious when he decisively set down his pool stick to come around to her side of the table. Standing so close to him was difficult, but it also felt wonderful. He was gentle as he adjusted her shoulders, the way her arm was stretched across the table, and how she was holding the cue. He reminded her strangely of marble that had warmed in the sun but remained cold underneath.

'Which pocket?' he asked.

'Right corner pocket,' she indicated, and he nodded.

'We're crowded down there, so we should try and mix it up a bit. Any targets in the current tangent line?' he tested her.

'No, so I should move,' Gwen suggested.

'If you want,' he agreed, and she edged around the table. She was careful to remember the pose he'd shown her.

She lined up and made her shot. Charlotte cried out prematurely just before the target ball darted into the pocket, and the cue ball broke up the congestion.

'Good job!' Derek congratulated her. Once she started playing better, they even managed to win the round.

They migrated to the balcony to smoke some of the cigars Derek had found in Miguel's office. The grounds of the hotel were exquisite, and at night they were lit up with solar lights. The hotel was far enough from the road that only the occasional honk reached them, so there was an illusion of privacy.

It was almost two in the morning before any of them thought to check, and Derek was scandalized. Gwen was reluctant, but it would've been foolish to argue, so she relented.

'Are you sure you don't want Anthony to take you home?' Miguel verified.

'No need to wake him up!' Derek dismissed before Gwen could decline. 'The taxi is already on the way.'

Gwen wanted to be alone with Miguel so she could

have the chance to say goodbye, but Derek was rushed. He shooed her and Charlotte toward the door.

'When will I see you again?' she finally worked up the courage to ask. Derek sighed impatiently, but he held the closing elevator for her. Miguel looked pleased she'd asked.

'I've thought about it,' he admitted, and he glanced behind at her friends. 'I wondered if you would like to accompany me to Stoney Creek. There's a track there I have access to and—'

'Are you inviting us to drive cars?' Derek demanded, and suddenly he was more interested in the conversation.

'I thought we could take a few of mine,' Miguel explained. 'Whichever ones you preferred,' he assured them.

Derek looked unbearably eager as he waited impatiently for Gwen to accept this offer. She might have enjoyed toying with him a little, but the truth was she was just as enthusiastic.

'When can we go?' she asked Miguel.

'Sometime this week,' he suggested. 'I have some things that require my attention, and I'm not sure how long they will take. Can I call you?'

Gwen nodded, and she watched him pull out his phone so she could give him her number. She wanted to kiss him, and suddenly, she didn't care if her friends saw it. It was like she'd been possessed by someone bolder. He was not going to be forward after what she'd revealed about Jon, so she knew she had to initiate.

Luckily, he anticipated her, and he bent his head down so she could reach his mouth. She was not as indecisive as she'd been in the car. This time, she kissed him more deeply so she could taste the scotch on his tongue, and she stood against him with her hands on his chest. Despite the recklessness of the hunger between them, his hand was gentle as his fingers combed her hair back from her temple.

Their first tentative kiss had elicited a strong reaction

from her, but now he showed her a little of what he was capable of. She could count the men she'd kissed on one hand, but she could still tell Miguel would be an experienced lover. She'd never felt someone promise her that in a kiss before, and it was intriguing and intimidating at the same time. White hot desire erupted from the pit of her stomach and radiated down.

The kiss ended when he bent his forehead against hers, and she felt his pleased smile against her lips.

'We're still here,' Charlotte hinted sarcastically, and Gwen jumped. She bit her lip as she backed away from Miguel without meeting his eyes.

'Sorry,' she stuttered once she'd stepped into the elevator. When she turned back, she saw he was watching her hungrily with eyes that almost seemed darker than usual.

'Until the track, then,' he said a little roughly, and she nodded.

'Good night,' chimed in Charlotte as the elevator closed. Gwen kept her eyes on his until their view of one another was blocked, and she released the breath she'd been holding.

'Looked like a good one,' Charlotte teased her, and Gwen cleared her throat in discomfort.

'It was,' she promised as the biggest smile enveloped her face.

x x x

Miguel

The sensation of her breath lingered on my skin, and the taste of her lips teased me long after the elevator doors had closed. I could still smell her perfume clinging to my shirt where she'd pressed against me. It lingered in the games room where we'd spent most of the night. With my heightened senses, I'd never sleep, so I decided to take a shower. Even under the stream of the water, she was still with me.

Desperate for relief, my hand trailed down to my hardened cock. It only took a few moments, imagining her mouth on me, before I was groaning in release. I wrung every last tremor of pleasure from my body as the hot water pounded my back. I'd never known such helpless desire for a woman.

My phone woke me a few hours later.

'Agent Benet,' I growled. 'It's six AM.'

'I'm sorry!' the young man promised. 'There's a serious situation you'll want to deal with yourself,' he advised me. I sat up quickly, and the silk sheets slid from my bare shoulders.

'What is it?' I demanded.

'Offence 666,' the agent explained to me nervously. 'Someone's dead,' he added unnecessarily, and I closed my eyes in dread. I was pretty sure I knew who.

'Tell me,' I prompted him.

'Dr. Anita Johansson from Sweden,' confirmed Benet. 'She'd just given a presentation—'

'I know,' I assured him. 'I was there.'

'You were?' he asked nervously. 'That... makes you a suspect.'

'I have an alibi,' I dismissed. 'Who else do you have?'

'The list is long,' admitted Benet.

'I'll come in,' I said shortly, and I hung up.

I remained sitting quite still for some time as I pondered the implications of her murder just after Anita had outed vampires. It was going to convince a lot of people she'd been on to something.

Agitated, I got out of bed and got dressed. Ainsley was having his breakfast in the kitchen.

'Call the others. Anita is dead,' I informed him, and he reacted with amiable speed for a human.

'Where do you want them to meet us?' he asked.

'PSA Headquarters,' I answered reluctantly.

If there was anything I hated more than public restaurants, it was the PSA Headquarters. I despised it so much I hadn't been there in fifteen years. On the outside, the building looked like an average police department, and the first floor was devoted to that appearance.

Darius, Luka, and Natalia were waiting for me in front of the building. While Darius seemed adequately prepared, the Russians were still dressed for the party from the night before. The buttons on Luka's shirt had been ripped off, so he wore it open despite the chill of the October morning. Natalia's long hair was mussed, and I had to use my thumb to smear away the blood at the corner of her mouth.

They fell into step behind me as I strode up the enormous steps and into the open lobby. It had been cleared of all civilians, so a small task force of suits were free to meet us. They sprung to attention when I arrived, and Agent Benet came forward to mediate. I was too irritated to deal with his stuttering welcome.

'Where is Director Donaldson?' I demanded.

'Here,' said a deep voice, and I looked up as the man stepped forward in his navy suit. His black hair had gone white, and his dark skin sagged around his jowls and under his eyes. His strong frame stooped with age, but he still squared his shoulders smartly. He eyed me with evident amazement.

'You haven't changed,' he commented offhandedly.

'You'll excuse my impatience,' I advised him.

'Of course,' he agreed, and he indicated the elevator doors, which were all standing open.

I stepped forward to follow him, but I caught a familiar scent. I glanced aside and met Derek's wide eyes amidst the crowd. I chose not to acknowledge him.

We joined Director Donaldson and Agent Benet and, using a key, Donaldson assumed control of the elevator. The doors closed, and we moved upward.

'You told me she'd be watched,' I reminded Donaldson. 'We knew she would be a target.'

'My men were not equipped to deal with a vampire,' he pointed out seriously.

'It was not one of mine. They wouldn't dare,' I

assured him firmly. 'Our existence will be questioned after this.'

'As will ours,' insisted Donaldson calmly in response to my defensive tone. 'We are not prepared to publicly accept responsibly for fostering a political relationship with our own predator. We'll be held accountable for every human life we have allowed your people to take.'

'Perhaps someone has an agenda to expose us both,' I suggested, seeing his point. 'What about her colleague, Dr. Michael Turner?' I asked.

'He's alive, and we're keeping an eye on him,' said Donaldson.

'I will handle it,' I advised him, and he nodded as we arrived at the thirteenth floor.

A glass hallway stretched out before us with patient rooms covered by curtains and separated from labs by solid metal walls. We entered a room at the end which was full of humans in white lab coats and masks. I immediately scented cold blood, death, and Anita, but I didn't smell vampire.

The lab coats stepped back, and I saw a long lump lying on a cold aluminum table under a white sheet.

Dr. Anita Johansson would no longer be a problem for me.

Chapter Ten

'Time of death was approximately eleven o'clock last night,' said the lead examiner. 'Method was strangulation, but she was also drained of blood,' she informed us. 'We are still trying to determine whether the attack was made to look like vampire molestation or whether it really was.'

I stepped by all of them, and they made room for me automatically. I peeled down the sheet to expose the bruising on Anita's throat and the little holes in her neck. I carefully extracted her arm to observe the haphazard bruising on her wrists and forearms. Relief consumed me.

'Not a vampire,' I concluded.

'How do you—'

'This murder was filled with the desperation of a human attack. Someone not much stronger than Anita killed her,' I interrupted Agent Benet. My finger brushed lightly over the raised edges of what had looked initially like a vampire bite. 'These were made after she was already dead.'

'These were my thoughts,' admitted the lead examiner reluctantly.

'Then someone wanted to make this look like a vampire attack,' Benet verified.

'Which suggests their target is you, and they don't care if we get caught in the crossfire,' Director Donaldson pointed out.

'Or someone irrational,' suggested the lead. 'Someone

desperate enough to protect vampires but not smart enough to think through their actions,' she clarified.

'That list is probably pretty short,' commented Benet jokingly. He looked down in embarrassment when Donaldson frowned at him, and Natalia glared outright.

'I will need a copy of the file,' I said, turning toward the door.

'It is waiting for you downstairs,' Donaldson told me. He had to scramble to keep up with us.

'While I'm here, I will see Alexion and Rosie,' I informed him. I could hear them whispering frantically as Benet told Donaldson about our conversation at the diner.

'Of course,' Donaldson agreed as we got into the elevator. We rode in silence past the ground level and all the parking levels to a dank corridor far below.

On either side of us were cells with ten solid feet of cement between each of them. The loud buzzing was from electricity pulsing through the bars at the front of each cubicle. They were comfortable by human standards, luxurious to the needs of a vampire, but we still considered them barely tolerable. They might not have held vampires over the age of a thousand, but they would have held me and my companions. That was the real reason I always brought backup. I never trusted the humans wouldn't somehow try to keep me.

We came to the first cell, and I saw Alexion rise elegantly from a plush chair. He stayed back from the bars.

'My noble coven prince comes to rescue me,' he said sarcastically in Greek.

'Not this time, Alexion,' I responded in the same language. 'This time they're keeping you a little longer.'

'That is what I thought,' he admitted. His eyes flickered resentfully over the humans, and Benet stepped back with an audible gulp.

'What's a hundred years?' asked Darius in amusement and purposefully with his native Persian language.

Vampires rarely tended to get involved in human

affairs, yet Darius and Alexion had never liked one another. It was testament to the depth of animosity between the Persians and the Greeks which had even affected vampires of the time.

'Hopefully, it will not be that long,' I assured the Greek and moved toward another cell.

Rosalina was waiting for me, and she smiled tensely. She was from another coven, so our interaction would be as short as possible.

I jerked my head in her direction, and the electrical buzzing of the bars was muted. Once the door was opened, she stepped out in relief.

'There is paperwork—'

'I will fill it out and send it to you,' I told Benet as I guided my vampires out of the dungeon without glancing Alexion's way.

Back at the main floor, the humans were still waiting. I never understood why they all but ceased to work when I came, but I assumed it was to keep everyone out of my way.

A young female handed Director Donaldson a file, which he presented to me.

'Thank you for coming,' he told me, and I nodded briskly before turning for the door. I could almost hear a sigh of relief from inside once we'd gone.

'Take Rosie home,' I told Darius, who nodded.

'Do you want us to go to the scene of the crime?' asked Natalia, and she motioned toward her brother.

'Call me when you've finished,' I advised her, and I handed her the file I'd just been given.

Before they could depart to do as I'd asked, there was a shout from the top of the stairs behind us. We all turned, and I saw Derek scrambling to catch up. Natalia stepped in front of me, but I pushed her aside as Derek reached us.

'Go,' I commanded, and they reluctantly left me with Ainsley at my back. Derek waited for them to go before he looked at me.

'What's happened?' he asked.

'You don't have clearance,' I reminded him, and I turned toward the Mercedes-Benz.

'Is it to do with the alley murder?' he pressed, and I shook my head. I would've smelled it if Anita had been killed in an alleyway. 'There was a boy killed last night,' Derek continued before I could get into my car. 'He was badly mutilated.'

'Why are you telling me this?' I demanded impatiently. 'I have bigger concerns than a human child right now.'

'He was homeless,' Derek began.

'Then the vampire may have done the kid a favour,' I observed callously, and Derek glowered at me.

'This is different, Miguel,' he promised, reacting in frustration to my indifference. 'There was—'

'I know you think when a child is involved, it's different, but it's not. Not to us,' I assured him, and he looked disgusted.

'There was blood all over the alleyway,' he revealed angrily, and suddenly, I was more intrigued by what he was saying. I cocked my head thoughtfully.

'What is your evidence it was a vampire attack and not a human one?' I wondered.

'The car he was displayed on was smashed in,' said Derek.

'Displayed?' I prompted him petulantly.

'His head was severed and left sitting on his chest,' he said, and I knew immediately what we were dealing with. I didn't say anything, however, because my people had an agreement with them not to tell humans about them. It did mean one of them was in my city, and they would need to be dealt with before they inevitably started killing vampires.

I pulled out my cell to call Hudson. 'I need a favour,' I said when he answered, and he scoffed.

'I'm listening,' he growled grudgingly.

'Keep an eye on Dr. Michael Turner,' I bid him,

glancing at Derek who was listening. 'Anita is dead.'

Hudson cursed. 'I'm on it,' he promised.

'You were right. I think we're facing an unknown enemy,' I advised him in Latin, and I hung up before turning toward Derek.

'Get in,' I told him, and he appeared far too excited by the prospect as he climbed into the back of the Mercedes.

It was nearly a half an hour drive to the crime scene, and I insisted on silence. I also wanted to walk the last five minutes. I didn't want to show up in the Mercedes with Ainsley in case the agents figured out who I was. Field work wasn't a habit I intended to make.

'He's with me,' Derek assured the man standing guard at the crime scene tape. The human nodded and stepped back so we could duck under the border. I guessed Derek commanded quite a bit of respect.

We hadn't even reached the alleyway before I suddenly caught the scent of my people's most feared enemy. I came to a horrified stop as I recognized the stupid mistake I'd made in coming alone.

'What—?'

'He's still here,' I interrupted Derek. 'Now he knows I'm here too. You need to get all these people out of here.' Derek looked like he'd argue. 'Before they all die,' I emphasized.

Derek was unnerved. I could see him striving for composure as he made his way toward the forensic team meandering around the bloody car. I heard the captain begin to argue about abandoning the scene, but I ignored them.

I could still feel the vibrations of brutality and the emotions of fear and pain hanging on the air. The unrelenting hatred of my enemy was hot and vicious. Their auras were so much stronger than those of vampires, and I could tell he'd sensed me.

I looked down at my favourite shoes with a sigh of regret as Derek came back toward me.

'Miguel, the captain wants to know—'

'Derek,' I said calmly through my teeth as my frustration with the situation that was about to unfold skyrocketed. 'Just get them out of here.'

'Miguel, what's—?'

A thunderous roar cut him off and seemed to shake the buildings around us with its fury. Derek ducked instinctively, and I frowned at him before indicating the terrified bystanders. Looking more convinced, he ran back toward the alleyway to help the forensics team collect their things.

My muscles twitched readily when the scent of my enemy intensified just before he appeared at the end of the alleyway. He was shirtless and bloody as usual with his eyes recently cut out. I was not foolish enough to think this would make him any less of a foe to me. The humans cried out in horror when they saw him.

'*Leech*!' he snarled hatefully and loudly enough his voice echoed off the buildings. 'I can smell your filthy stench from miles away! You cannot sneak up on me.'

I could have attempted to be civil with him, but in my experience, it rarely worked. Instead, I shrugged off my expensive jacket and let it fall to the dirty ground.

He stumbled out of the heaps of garbage, and he began to contort his body. The snapping and ripping of a werewolf transformation is the most horrifying sound, and what follows can be almost just as ugly.

I loosened my tie and dropped it on top of the jacket.

The PSA, including Derek, was still between us. Normally, human casualties were inconsequential when I was about to fight for my life, but this time was different. The Dowrra bond I'd formed with Gwen was powerful, and it made me more sympathetic to the things she valued. Unfortunately, Derek seemed to be one of those things, so I was disinclined to allow him to be hurt.

I unbuttoned the cuffs of my shirt so I could roll my sleeves up my arms.

The werewolf's roar echoed again, and this time the humans were smart enough to drop their medical kits and run. Derek brought up the rear with his captain, but they were not fast enough.

It is rare to encounter a wolf with absolute control over their transformation, but this one was strong. Instead of completing his change into a two-hundred-pound ulfur wolf, he adapted a two-legged version between man and beast. He shot forward at a speed unperceivable to human eyes and in a heartbeat was right behind Derek.

I leaped over the screaming humans, and my hands fastened in his thick fur. Using my momentum as I landed, I spun him around once and launched him back into the alleyway from which he'd emerged. He crashed down among the dumpsters. It felt good to exert myself. I hadn't been in a real fight in several years.

I heard the feet on the pavement stop, and I turned to see the humans were looking at me. Their ability to harbour opposing sentiments toward something is the singularly most confusing thing about their race. They can abide both hatred and love and sustain both cruelty and purpose.

'Keep fucking running!' I shouted at them angrily, and everyone except for Derek scattered. He pulled the gun at his side and held it readily in both hands before him.

My attention was diverted when a dumpster abruptly slammed against the building near to me and landed heavily. My enemy sped out of the alleyway, and this time he wasn't distracted by fleeing humans.

I had counted on being faster, but I was unprepared for it when he bounded off the wall and landed behind me. I spun and looked up into his wolfish face that was twisted with a scowling snarl. The expression was made even more hideous by the emptiness of his eyes sockets.

'You should have run,' he growled deeply.

Chapter Eleven

I underestimated him when I reached out both hands to catch the clawed fist he swung my way. The force of the blow sent me careening into the brick wall, and I was showered in brick dust. I crumpled to the alleyway ground.

'Ouch,' I winced in surprise. It had been a long time since someone had been able to hurt me. To add insult to injury, I smelled blood a second before I tasted it when it rolled down from my nose.

I launched myself over him and landed gracefully behind while he bumped clumsily into the wall. Before I could manage a cocky smile, he spun and slammed me against the bricks again. I was heaved onto the pavement with enough might to crack it under my back, and he pummelled me with heavy fists. My ribs and leg snapped under his relentless assault, but I had to ignore that agony. His fangs were fatally venomous to me, and he was trying to force his open jaws toward my face.

It took me a moment to notice there were gunshots ringing out, and Derek was screaming. Not all the blood on me was mine anymore.

The constant stream of bullets to the wolf's skull finally stopped his assault, and he began ripping at himself viciously. The smoking bullets fell out of his skin and bounced around him on the asphalt.

I had underestimated him, and it had nearly cost me my immortal life. I would never make that mistake again.

I focused through the agony to trip him. I wrestled him as quickly as I could to the ground with my entire body protesting. My fangs had already lengthened, so I sank them into his arm to envenom him. Then I let him go as he shrieked immediately in unbearable pain. I watched him contort next to me until he was dead.

I took a moment to compose myself and glanced up at Derek, who was still holding his gun loosely in one hand. He was shaking.

'You're bleeding,' he muttered like an idiot.

'I noticed,' I growled as I struggled to get into a more comfortable position. With all my broken bones, it was impossible.

Derek looked at the twisted body of the monster that had almost killed us and back at me. 'What was it?' he asked.

'Usually, they live far away from people, and they don't prey on you,' I said evasively. 'Vampires probably cut out his eyes, and he came into the city when he was unable to hunt.'

Derek examined me incredulously.

'Are you all right?' he asked hesitantly.

'Indestructible, remember?' I demanded moodily, but Derek wasn't fooled.

'It didn't look that way from here,' he said sombrely.

'You were supposed to run,' I defended myself. 'Had you just done that, I would not be in this mess.'

I wiped the blood away from my nose and scowled at its stain on my shirt. Derek stared at it uneasily.

'I thought... I didn't think vampires could bleed,' he admitted, and I laughed humorlessly.

'It is just what they want you to think,' I assured him as I reached for my phone. Miraculously, it was undamaged.

I called Ainsley to pick us up, and I began limping out of the alleyway. Derek hung back in uncertainty of whether to try and help. I was immensely glad he wasn't stupid enough to try and touch me.

'Thank you,' said Derek softly, once I'd settled painfully against the wall outside the alley. I glanced up in surprise when he seemed so sincere, and then I snorted dismissively.

'I did *not* do this for you,' I insisted. 'Believe me, I'd have preferred to walk away and come back with backup after you'd all been slaughtered.'

'You knew he might kill you, but you stayed anyway?' he verified, and I groaned in aggravation at his persistence.

'I didn't think Gwen would enjoy the news you'd been ripped apart by an animal,' I explained reluctantly. He nodded as though this were what he'd expected.

'Charlotte told me she spoke to you. She's always been more understanding of your kind than I was,' he confessed. 'I was afraid bonding to you would put Gwen in danger, but... maybe it'll keep her safe.'

I endeavoured to ignore him as Ainsley pulled into the dirty alleyway in the Mercedes-Benz. My butler got out of the car, and he looked disturbed.

'Have you *any* idea what kind of wrath we'd be facing if he got killed?' he demanded of Derek as I limped to the car.

'Enough, Ainsley,' I chastised him as Derek walked guiltily around to the passenger side. My butler moodily retrieved my discarded clothing, and none of us said a word until we were back at the PSA building.

'I'll deal with our friend back in the alleyway and any questions that arise,' Derek informed me. I nodded mutely as he climbed out of the car and closed the door. Ainsley met my eyes with disappointment in the rear-view mirror.

'Not a word to anyone,' I commanded him, and although he appeared reluctant, he nodded.

It took me the rest of the day to heal properly, and even then it was painful to bend over on broken ribs. Rosie got home safely, and Darius returned to me the following day. Anita's crime scene was analyzed, and

Luka assured me Anita's killers had been human. Dr. Michael Turner was safe and finally in the custody of the PSA, who confiscated all his research material. I was not pleased by this, so they were in the process of getting me copies so I could monitor how much information they acquired about us.

Come midweek, I was feeling less overwhelmed by the crisis and ready to call Gwen. I'd been thinking about her, and I'd wanted to call her sooner, but it wouldn't have been wise while human relations were uncertain.

Her voice brought me relief almost immediately.

x x x

Gwendolyn

'It's been three days,' Gwen reminded Charlotte. 'Don't you think he would have at least texted me?'

'Gwen, even I know he's not a texter,' Charlotte laughed, and Gwen took a long sip of her wine as she considered this possibility.

'I hate this,' she finally declared. 'How do women just sit and wait all the time? Why didn't I get his number?' she demanded.

'Drink your wine, and keep your panties on,' chastised Charlotte. 'The guy's busy.'

There was something hinting in Charlotte's tone. It was almost as if she knew how busy Miguel really was, but Gwen knew that was a ridiculous thought.

Her phone had been left sitting conveniently on the table where she'd see it if someone texted her. It finally started to vibrate, and she darted forward eagerly. Charlotte paused the TV when "Unknown" came up on the screen.

'Told you!' squeaked Charlotte. She settled into the couch, clutching a pillow to her chest, and waited for Gwen to answer.

Gwen took in a deep breath for composure and answered the phone.

'Gwen, it's Miguel,' he said, and she smiled.

'I've been wondering when you'd call,' she chastised him playfully, and Charlotte rolled her eyes.

'I'm sorry,' he said sincerely. 'It's been a little hectic the last few days.'

'Is everything okay now?' she asked hopefully.

'Not entirely but much better,' he informed her. 'I still want to take you to Stoney Creek.'

'I still want to go,' she responded.

'Are you available tomorrow evening around five thirty?' he wondered. She was heartened by the sound of relief in his voice.

'I'll double-check with Derek and Charlotte, but I'm sure tomorrow is fine,' Gwen said. She looked curiously at Charlotte, who nodded vigorously.

'Would you like me to pick you up?' he asked.

'I can come with Derek and Charlotte,' Gwen declined hesitantly, and Charlotte cocked her head. She opened her mouth to protest, but Gwen waved her hand for her to be silent.

'Meet me at 385 Dublin Street in Midtown,' said Miguel, and Gwen agreed.

'Why wouldn't you let him pick you up?' Charlotte asked once Gwen had set the phone back on the table.

'I don't want him to know where I live,' Gwen admitted with her eyes lowered.

'I don't think he's dangerous,' Charlotte assured her in confusion.

'I know that!' Gwen swore. 'It's just… this isn't exactly the Royal Alton,' she pointed out, and Charlotte frowned at her.

'I don't think he cares about that.'

'Well, I do! You saw his place!' Gwen maintained. She motioned around them suggestively.

'Gwen, you're going to have to let him get close to you sooner or later if you want this to work,' Charlotte reminded her, and Gwen nodded knowingly.

The next day, Gwen met the Wells at their house on

Roselawn Avenue, and she walked in to find the house was in chaos. It turned out Derek might have been even more excited than she was to meet up with Miguel. He was torn regarding what to wear to the track, and Charlotte was doing her best to assist him with help from a glass of wine.

'You *do* know I'm the one dating him, right?' Gwen asked teasingly, and Charlotte discreetly high-fived her.

'I couldn't give *two shits* about what Miguel thinks,' Derek promised her in offence.

'The cars don't care what you wear either, sweetheart,' promised Charlotte with mock sweetness.

'For Christ's sake!' cried Derek in frustration at them. 'You're allowed to make a big ordeal out of what you wear on *every* other day,' he pointed out. 'I get just this once, *just this once,* to drive a Ferrari F12 Berlinetta Coupe!'

Both women did remarkable jobs of masking their hysterics, and they nodded.

It was less than a ten minute drive down Chaplin Crescent to the Midtown area. Initially, the warehouses made the area seem like a bad neighbourhood, but there were a lot of nice cars being put away for the winter.

They reached the address Miguel had given Gwen, which was a plain building with enormous garage doors. They pulled up in Derek's silver Audi Q7 as Miguel stepped out of the man-door. He was dressed in dark jeans and a light coloured sweater with the collar and cuffs of a white dress shirt folded neatly overtop. Gwen didn't think she'd ever seen him in anything other than black before, and he looked really good.

Derek seemed anxious, and he jerked the car abruptly into park. They got out and walked toward Miguel.

'Welcome,' he greeted them, and Gwen smiled when his eyes met hers. When she reached him, he took her hand to draw her nearer, and she was pleasantly surprised by a sweet kiss. Such a simple presumption might have irritated her with another man, but instead, she was left aching immediately for more of him.

'So,' Derek cut in excitedly, 'cars are in there?'

Miguel's mouth turned with an emotion somewhere between amusement and irritation as he nodded.

'Please,' he insisted, and he held out his hand. 'Lead the way.'

Seemingly oblivious to Miguel's sarcasm, Derek eagerly pressed through the door with Charlotte tagging along behind.

'Thank you for inviting them,' Gwen said pointedly, and Miguel laughed as they followed her friends inside.

'Whoa,' Charlotte breathed even before Miguel had turned on the lights. They flickered to life overhead, one section at a time, revealing several rows of cars. 'Wait, you made it sound like you maybe had like ten cars,' Charlotte accused.

'I listed the newest ones,' Miguel explained. 'I have quite a few classic cars, which are to the back. I've... been collecting a long time,' he described significantly.

Derek looked like he'd stepped into heaven as he approached the grey Aventador Superveloce Miguel had picked Gwen up in on the first night. His hands hovered in the air over the hood.

'Which one would you like to take?' Miguel asked Gwen, who looked around in bewilderment.

She saw the red Ferrari Derek so badly wanted to drive, so she passed by it for his benefit. Next was the orange Veneno Roadster, but it was far too aggressive in appearance for her taste. After it was the silver Vulcan, which she considered choosing, but then her eye caught the yellow Porsche Spyder beside it.

'This one,' she said decisively, and Miguel seemed to appreciate her choice.

'Ferrari,' Derek said firmly.

'Whatever that one is called,' Charlotte chimed in as she motioned to the Vulcan.

'What are you driving?' Gwen asked Miguel.

'The Superveloce,' he told her as he made his way

over to a board filled with keys hanging on hooks. 'I haven't broken it in yet, remember?'

Gwen watched him selecting the appropriate keys as she recalled what an incredible kisser he'd been. She couldn't help wondering whether a man who collected such beautiful cars did so because he lost interest in them quickly.

'I'd like to say,' said Charlotte nervously, 'I don't intend to hurt your car, Miguel. I just can't promise anything.'

'Don't worry,' Miguel laughed as he handed her the keys. Derek was more eager, and he went quickly toward the Ferrari for a closer look.

Miguel returned to Gwen, and she could hear the Porsche locks sliding in the car. She accepted the fob and sank onto the brown leather seat with orange stitching once he opened the door. She noticed a gold Porsche symbol on the steering wheel as she searched for the keyhole on the right side of the wheel. Miguel casually directed her to the left, and her hands trembled slightly as she inserted the key. The floating, touchscreen console lit up as Miguel knelt next to her open door.

'Wow,' Gwen breathed, looking around as the car came to life with a low rumble.

'The 918 is a hybrid,' Miguel told her, 'one of the first supercars to have an electric boost.'

'Does that mean it can go faster?' she verified, and he nodded laughingly. He spent a moment showing her the controls, before making sure her friends were both comfortable, and then he got into the Aventador. With all the cars running, the shed was filled with incredible sound.

Miguel pulled out first, and they followed behind. At a single touch on the accelerator, the car eagerly jumped forward, and Gwen felt her adrenaline spike. She'd never experienced anything so thrilling.

They spent several hours at the track, and all the supercars had to be refuelled *twice*! They even swapped a few times, so Gwen got to drive each of the other vehicles, but she was sure she preferred the Porsche.

She also became very sure of Miguel.

Each of the times she'd been out with him had been to formal or semi-formal events at which he'd been a perfect gentleman. At the track, he proved he could also be spontaneous and even a little wild. Knowing under all that sophistication was something a little more reckless was about as thrilling as driving a car that could reach 100km/h in 2.2 seconds.

The days were getting shorter, so it was dark by the time they were ready to head back to Midtown.

'Most incredible experience of my life!' exclaimed Derek enthusiastically once they'd parked the cars back in the shed. Gwen laughed when he suddenly kissed his wife before Charlotte could object to his declaration. The couple wasn't usually so affectionate, but Charlotte happily returned his kiss. Gwen knew how they felt. The supercars were like aphrodisiacs.

'Thank you,' Charlotte said breathlessly to Miguel, who was not remotely discomforted by their display.

'It was a good excuse to get these cars out on the track,' he said.

'Anytime,' Derek swore with his arms still around his wife.

Miguel nodded in agreement and turned to look at Gwen. Her heart hammered harder at his expression.

'I'd like to speak with Gwen,' he admitted.

'Of course,' Charlotte exclaimed, and she grabbed her husband's arm to tug him from the shed. He admired the Ferrari all the way out.

'There is something I wanted—' Miguel began.

Gwen had become impatient with desire for him, and she couldn't even let him finish. She went to her toes so she could reach his lips and cut him off. She might have been embarrassed by his surprise, but Miguel's reaction was fierce and automatic as he pulled her against him. It felt incredibly good when he seized her as though he couldn't wait to have her either.

Before she'd realized it, she'd tugged his shirt up, and her fingers had found the greatly anticipated contours of his abs. She knew she should have withdrawn in humiliation again, but his groan of encouragement was undeniable. Soon, her only regret was she couldn't see the beautiful body she was touching.

Wanting a man was exhilarating.

Despite the inexperience of her touch, Gwen was pleased to find Miguel seemed to love every moment of it. The incitement quickly became too much for him, and he groaned softly with impatience. He abruptly yanked her long-sleeved blouse open over her tank and stripped it from her shoulders. His hands brushed down both arms to grip her slender wrists, and he used his larger body to press her up against the Porsche.

She was trapped.

Jonathon had shoved her against a wall the night of the attack, and the terror had been absolute, but it wasn't the case with Miguel. There were no echoes of panic or fear as she'd dreaded there might be. His grip was superficial so she could pull loose, and she reached up to touch his shoulders curving around her protectively. His palms lowered to her hips as he pushed against her more fully, and she suddenly felt his erection through his jeans.

Gwen gasped involuntarily, and he instantly retreated.

'No, don't stop,' she begged him regretfully.

'No, you're right. Not like this, Gwen,' he whispered breathlessly against her neck. 'I don't want you like this.'

'Why not?' demanded Gwen in confusion. Jon wouldn't have cared if they'd been in a bathroom stall.

'There are many reasons, but come the time, I intend to make you scream. I don't want your friends to hear that,' he explained.

She shivered helplessly as the implications of his promise teased her imagination. Her longing for him sharpened painfully.

'You're not making it any easier to wait,' she advised

him, and he was quiet a moment.

'I want to erase whatever has been done to you,' he finally admitted. His words finally succeeded in alleviating her desire as he reminded her of the violence in her past.

'You do?' she asked, wondering if that were even possible.

'If I can,' he confirmed.

She felt almost completely sobered as he stepped back from her, and she looked up into his eyes. They seemed darker than usual, and his hair was dishevelled from where she'd run her fingers through it. His full lips were even more swollen from the roughness of their kiss.

'I was trying to ask you something,' he backtracked, fighting an amused smile, and Gwen smirked. 'I wanted to invite you to the Annual Toledo Charity Ball. It will be like the party at the museum only bigger and with more people. You'll enjoy—'

'The art auction,' Gwen interrupted knowingly. Her eyes widened as she recognized the event he was talking about.

'It is tomorrow night,' he laughed softly in enjoyment of her eagerness. 'I know that's short notice but—'

'It's fine!' she promised, feeling her face stretch under the strain of an impossibly ridiculous smile.

'Good,' he laughed again, and she watched as his eyes darkened ever so slightly anew with desire. 'If you feel the same tomorrow night as you do right now, then... perhaps we can explore that more,' he proposed softly.

Gwen swallowed in anticipation as all the heat in her body seemed to pool between her thighs. She nodded wordlessly, and Miguel turned to pick up the shirt he'd stripped from her. He handed it back to her, and she considered it as they began to walk toward the door.

'There's just one problem,' she admitted haltingly. 'What am I supposed to wear?'

Gwen worried Miguel would merely shrug the way Jon would have, but he seemed to genuinely consider her dilemma.

'Madame Rosetta makes my suits. She may have a gown for you to model for her,' he suggested. 'She's always looking for new faces, and she'd appreciate the publicity.'

'You want me to model a gown?' Gwen asked incredulously.

'My sister has before,' he assured her, and Gwen couldn't think of an excuse except it seemed too extraordinary. 'I can have Ainsley drive you to the boutique tomorrow,' Miguel offered once she'd nodded.

Gwen was about to decline politely, but she remembered Charlotte's insistence she let Miguel get close to her. She agreed and gave him her address.

Charlotte grinned when she saw their dishevelled appearances, and she was ecstatic when Gwen told her about Miguel's invite. She immediately predicted they'd end up sleeping together, and Derek grimaced at the windshield wordlessly. His enthusiasm had run out the moment they'd driven away from the cars.

Miguel

Chapter Twelve

I hesitated on Roselawn Avenue, which was a quiet and classy residential area to which I'd tracked them. I was standing in front of a row of dark red, brick buildings shadowed by elm and maple trees. Across the street was a baseball diamond and soccer field. Despite the nip of winter in the air, there were children and their parents playing in the park. It was all perfectly mundane and rather unforeseen.

I walked by the Audi Q7 parked in the driveway and stepped onto the porch. Next to the wooden planters blooming with Helenium autumnale were pumpkins reminding me Halloween was in a few weeks. There was an empty mug with "*BIG SEXY*" printed on it, which had been left on the arm of one of the Muskoka chairs. I smiled as I picked it up and knocked at the door.

'Just a minute!' called a voice before the door opened, and Derek leaned out. His eyes went wide at the sight of me. 'How the hell did you find me?' he snapped immediately.

'Hello, Derek,' I muttered and pushed passed him into the house. I handed him the cup on my way by.

'I did not invite you in,' he scolded me angrily as he followed me into his home.

'I'm not Dracula. I don't need an invite,' I pointed out drolly as I found the kitchen. I was immediately intrigued by the bottle of wine on the counter.

'What the hell are you doing in my house?' Derek demanded as I started to open all the cupboards in search of wine glasses.

'I have a date with Gwen tonight,' I advised him. 'Where do you keep—?'

He handed me a glass wordlessly from the drying rack on the counter, and I grunted in thanks.

'I heard. What about it?' he prompted impatiently. He crossed his arms defensively while I opened the bottle and began to pour the cheap alcohol.

'I'm not here for you,' I assured him. 'I'm here for your wife.'

'You're what?' he snapped, looking dumbfounded.

'It's fine, Derek,' interrupted Charlotte from the doorframe to the living room where I'd sensed her. 'I have a pretty good idea about what he wants to know.'

'What's that?' Derek demanded as he looked back to me.

I considered how best to word my question but ultimately decided it was best to be blunt with her.

'I don't want to hurt her,' I explained, and Derek groaned before quickly pouring himself an enormous glass of the wine.

'You won't,' Charlotte promised me soberly.

'Doesn't always feel that way,' I advised her distractedly as I doubtfully watched Derek take a swig of his wine. He was not a wine drinker, and he winced at the bitter taste.

'Bloodlust is part of it,' Charlotte reassured me as she moved to sit at her kitchen table.

'That's not my primary concern,' I admitted delicately. She looked confused, so I picked up an empty soup tin out of the drying rack. With the smallest of squeezes, the can was crushed in my hand. 'It takes a great deal of effort to consciously control the magnitude of my strength,' I clarified. 'I will hardly have that capacity if we become intimate.'

Charlotte was unnerved by the demonstration, but she

understood my concerns.

'Dowrra are built to be the lovers of vampires,' she reminded me. 'Derek, tell him what it is like,' she added, and I looked up at her husband, who was immediately antipathetic.

'I don't—'

'Do it,' Charlotte insisted, this time impatiently, and he sighed with great reluctance.

'Sometimes it feels like Charlotte could throw me through a wall,' he mumbled and took another huge swig of his wine. He winced again at the taste as I looked to Charlotte in suspicion.

'You mean you physically strengthen?' I verified in surprise and was immensely relieved when she nodded.

Intimacy with Gwen had terrified me because the last thing I wanted was to hurt her. If what Charlotte was saying was true, however, then Gwen's human body would rise to the occasion.

I was free to claim her that night if she still wanted me.

x x x

Gwendolyn

The black Mercedes-Benz was already parked in front of Gwen's building when she came downstairs. She hesitated as a man in a suit got out of the driver's seat and came around to the rear passenger's side.

'Good afternoon, Miss Rhys,' he said before opening the back door for her. He wasn't like any butler Gwen had ever imagined. She could tell he was strong and possessed the grace of someone who could move with great speed. His dark hair was streaked in grey, and his eyes were sharp, but they managed to be as warm as his smile. 'My name is Ainsley Westin, and I will be your chauffeur today. Are you ready to go?' he asked.

Gwen nodded quickly, and she walked toward the car.

'Thank you, Ainsley. I'm Gwen,' she said as he

stepped back to allow her access to the car.

'It is lovely to meet you, Gwen,' he responded as she slid into the spacious backseat of the car. He closed the door while she admired the warm tones of wood and leather around her.

'You weren't waiting long?' she asked when Ainsley returned to the front seat ahead of her.

'I waited just as long as I intended to,' the gentleman assured her with a quick smile in the mirror.

They drove to Yorkville in comfortable silence until Ainsley pulled up in front of a black and burgundy storefront. The sign deemed it *Madame Rosetta's Boutique.*

'Here we are,' proclaimed Ainsley before getting out of the car. He was nearly around to Gwen's side when she opened her door, and she could tell he was surprised. She obligingly accepted his hand as she stepped onto the sidewalk.

'I expect Madame Rosetta will be excited to meet you,' Ainsley advised her as they walked toward the store.

'She's expecting me?' Gwen verified, shyly avoiding the looks cast her way as she got out of the expensive car.

'Mr. Santos is a favoured customer of la Madame,' Ainsley explained as he opened the boutique door for her.

Gwen noticed the sign in the window clearly said the shop was "*Closed.*" She opened her mouth to ask Ainsley about it, but she was immediately enraptured by the incredible world into which she'd entered beyond the street.

The walls were white with black accents along all the corners, and there were mirrors on the ceiling. One side was designed for men while the other was obviously for women.

Gwen closed her mouth when a striking, middle-aged woman came toward them. Her white-blonde hair was collected at the side of her neck. Her green eyes were stern, but there were laugh lines around her red lips. She was dressed in a chic white suit, and her heels clicked with firm resolve against the tiles.

'*Bonjour*, Gwendolyn Rhys! Very pleased to meet you' she said briskly with a French accent. 'Mr. Westin, it is always a pleasure, *mon amour,*' she added with a wink for Ainsley that made Gwen flush.

'Madame Rosetta,' Ainsley acknowledged her. His hands folded behind him as he offered her a polite bow.

'Well, Mr. Santos surely did not exaggerate,' Madame Rosetta commented happily as she examined Gwen. She liberally began to comb her fingers through Gwen's long ringlets of red hair. 'You will be a stunning model for the Vaera Marietta.'

'Oh... thank you,' Gwen acknowledged with uncertainty.

'We will take some measurements, *mon petit chaton,*' the lady explained affectionately before taking hold of Gwen's elbow. She began to steer Gwen through the racks of clothing. 'What other gowns have you modelled?' the designer wanted to know.

'Um, this will be the first,' Gwen admitted.

'*C'est merveilleux*! That is wonderful,' the woman promised. 'Fresh faces always get more attention, *chére.*'

They entered a small waiting area furnished with white and gold Estilo styled lounger sofas and fainting couches. The archway in the wall was framed with heavy black drapes, which swept over the entry once they'd gone inside.

In the fitting room, Madame Rosetta released Gwen and floated over to the wall of white cabinets. Every door she opened displayed countless drawers of fabrics, buttons, needles, threads, and material.

Gwen saw a large alcove of mirrors with a pedestal at the centre. On the black and white mannequin standing next to the recess was the dress she assumed she was supposed to wear. Her heart sank into her stomach at the sight of it.

It had a compelling simplicity. The single chiffon shoulder sloped smoothly into the sweetheart neckline.

There was a sash around the waist with two tails trailing behind to the floor. She could tell the dress would hug her hips and hang from her thighs.

The problem was it was *red*. Gwen tried to avoid the sensual colour because her hair was already red, and it tended to attract notice. She was afraid to look obnoxious and for people to think she was vying for attention.

'Get undressed!' Madame Rosetta encouraged her.

Gwen reluctantly stepped out of her shoes and began to peel out of her clothing. Madame Rosetta approached with the red gown once Gwen was in her new bra and underwear. It was the first matching set she'd ever owned, which she'd gotten in anticipation of the night to come.

Gwen slid into the cool silk, and Madame Rosetta zipped her up. Gwen was glad she'd followed Charlotte's suggestion to buy a backless bra when the zipper stopped on the small of her back.

'*C'est formidable! Parfait*!' la Madame gushed. 'We will tighten the bust a little here, *mon chaton*.'

When the designer pinched the fabric, Gwen could feel her breasts popping out of the sweetheart neckline a little more. She felt a renewed spike of anxiety and kept her eyes down.

Madame Rosetta suddenly took hold of Gwen's chin and forced her gaze up to the stranger in the mirror.

The silken material clung to her in all the right places, which accented her hourglass figure perfectly. Gwen expected to feel naked when she turned, but the sight of her bare back was strangely gratifying. She lifted the folds of the dress and saw there was a slit all the way up to mid-thigh. Miguel wouldn't be able to resist her, and the thought was exciting.

'It will not take me long to make the adjustments,' la Madame assured her. 'I have diamond-studded red stilettos for you to wear.'

A man with flamboyantly spiked blue hair joined them with his assistant to apply Gwen's makeup and redo her hair. They were subtle with the dark brown eye shadow so the red lipstick became the focus. They trimmed the ends of her hair and enhanced the curls so they spilled silkily from her shoulders.

When Gwen walked through the curtains into the waiting room, Ainsley was waiting with a burgundy coat. He smiled with true pleasure when he saw her.

'Miss Rhys, you look beautiful!' he complimented her. Gwen walked toward him cautiously on the diamond-studded heels so he could help her into the coat. She buttoned it and admired the way the princess seams enhanced her figure in the mirror on the wall.

Madame Rosetta handed Gwen a diamond-studded clutch that matched the shoes. Inside, Gwen could feel the outline of the lipstick she had on.

'Don't forget to tell everyone you are wearing Vaera Marietta by Madame Rosetta!' cautioned the designer sternly.

Ainsley guided Gwen back to the car where he opened her door. She'd thought people were staring before, but it was nothing compared to the second time. When they pulled into the hotel drive, her stomach turned with nerves. She had to consciously remind herself not to twist the clutch or bite her lips. The last thing she wanted was to disrupt the perfection of her lipstick.

'Don't worry, Miss Rhys,' said Ainsley kindly, and his blue eyes caught hers in the rear-view mirror. 'You look perfect.'

'Thank you, Ainsley,' Gwen said with deep appreciation.

The car rounded a corner, and the hotel came into sight beyond the well-manicured trees. Gwen saw three men standing next to a stunning, black Bentley Mulsanne limousine. One man was the doorman, Carlton, and one she assumed to be Miguel's valet, Anthony.

The last one, of course, was Miguel.

Chapter Thirteen

Miguel was wearing a black tux with a red vest and tie, which Gwen knew meant Madame Rosetta had dressed them to match. He looked at once sharp and classy in his suit but also still a little rugged with a dark shadow on his stern jaw.

He opened her door, and she could tell immediately he was taken back by her appearance. She watched with pleasure as he seemed to recover himself and held out his hand.

'Gwen… You look beautiful,' he said with sincerity. His touch seemed electric as if he were still vivacious from their passion the day before.

Gwen stepped out of the car, and when he drew her near, she heard him groan softly. The sound filled her with anticipation.

'You smell good,' he explained in amusement with his helpless reaction.

'You look pretty good yourself,' she informed him.

'Have a lovely evening, Miss Rhys,' said Ainsley. 'Mr. Santos,' he added in acknowledgement of Miguel.

'Thank you, Ainsley! You too,' Gwen called over her shoulder. She regretted not letting him pick her up before when Miguel had offered. He was exceptionally sweet.

Miguel led her to where Anthony waited next to the limo with the door open. She was careful not to step on her dress as she climbed inside to sit on the white leather seat facing a purple bar. Miguel sat next to her, and he plucked a single rose from the counter of the bar. He handed it to her.

'I *really* like this colour on you,' he told her huskily as she accepted the flower. She suddenly found herself wishing she wasn't wearing lipstick so she could kiss him.

'Champagne?' he inquired, and Gwen nodded eagerly. He poured them both a glass as Anthony joined them in the front of the limo.

'So, what kind of art is going to be at the auction?' Gwen wanted to know as she took the champagne glass.

'Every kind,' Miguel promised her. 'I can't wait to see the Ferrari they'll be displaying. Most expensive car in the world,' he explained significantly.

'How much will it be?' asked Gwen in awe.

'I don't even want to say,' Miguel confessed, laughing, and Gwen gawked at him.

'That's disgusting,' she berated.

'Perhaps,' he admitted, smiling at her bold dismissal. Then he looked challenging. 'I wonder if you feel the same about rare art.'

'What do you mean?' Gwen demanded.

'I have heard that *La Dame en Rouge* by Philip de Marc will be there. Along with The Handmaiden of Aphrodite sculpture,' Miguel disclosed, and Gwen was speechless.

'*La Dame en Rouge*…' she said wistfully. 'What will it go for?' she asked, and Miguel was thoughtful.

'Last time it was sold was in 1984. It went for a hundred million,' he disclosed, and Gwen's jaw dropped. She suddenly began to agonize a little over where he was taking her.

'Just *who* is going to be at this thing?' she asked him suspiciously.

'The rich, the royal, the famous,' Miguel confided, and Gwen glanced down at her lap feeling nervous. She wondered whether she'd been wrong to accept his offer to take her with him.

They reached the location of the gala, and Gwen was amazed to realize it was at the Ian Dietrich Private Gallery building. The beautiful structure was only rivalled, she understood, by the extensive courtyards and ballrooms within. Cars were pulling up to the gated walkway where a crowd was held in check by security. She cringed when she saw the flashing of cameras as they got into line behind a stunning red car she couldn't identify.

'Maserati Alfieri,' she heard Anthony's voice saying over the intercom.

'I see it,' Miguel responded to him, equally impressed, as he touched the button on the top of the seat behind Gwen.

'What's that?' Gwen asked Miguel.

'It was a concept car originally. It's not due for production for another year,' he informed her.

'You're kidding!' Gwen groaned in disbelief as an elderly man in a white tuxedo got out of the driver's seat of the car. On the other side, a woman in a diamond-studded silver dress was helped out by the valet.

'It's the Duke and Duchess of Mavloh,' Miguel said her as if it all made sense. 'I didn't think they were coming.'

'I don't know if I can do this,' Gwen advised him anxiously, and Miguel's attention was diverted from the stunning car. He laughed as he gently rubbed her arm in consolation.

'Says the woman who nearly took my head off the first time I met her,' he teased her. 'You will be fine. This is the worst part.'

'Will it always be like this with you? Every time we go somewhere public, there are cameras,' she complained. Miguel smiled before he gently took the rose from her clammy fingers and placed it on the bar.

'Yes,' he admitted, and he lifted her arm so he could kiss the inside of her wrist. The sensation immediately warmed her, and she suppressed a sigh.

The door was opened and Miguel got out first. Gwen took a deep breath and unbuttoned her coat so she could show off the dress for la Madame. Then she took Miguel's offered hand and slid out of the car into the chaos on the street.

'Mr. Santos, who's your date?' called someone. Microphones were thrust toward them, but security held the crowd back.

'Who dressed you tonight?' asked someone else. Gwen felt ridiculous, but she owed la Madame.

'I'm wearing Vaera Marietta by Madame Rosetta,' she informed the reporters, and she saw several people scribbling it down eagerly.

'What's your name?' cried someone from the back.

'Mr. Santos, have you anything to say about Dr. Johansson's research or her sudden disappearance?'

'I was deeply sorry to hear about Dr. Johansson,' said Miguel.

'Do you think the murder was related to her work?' asked someone else.

'That is not what I was told,' Miguel answered, despite what Gwen knew he believed. He'd already told her he thought Anita's death was a direct result of her research. Apparently, he still didn't believe in vampires, though.

He put his arm around her, and they began to walk toward the building. Gwen made sure to keep her expression unclouded.

'Mr. Santos, are you dating? What's your name, sweetheart?'

The shouts followed them all the way to the door. Once they were inside, the crowd was tuned out by classical music.

'Whoa,' Gwen sighed, feeling a little overwhelmed.

'They have that effect,' Miguel admitted. They made their way toward the mahogany desk where men were taking coats in exchange for charitable donations.

'This is a very interesting world you live in,' Gwen said.

'Usually, it's rather boring. You spice things up,' he promised as he slid her coat down from her shoulders.

Gwen felt him hesitate. She could almost *feel* the intensity of his eyes on the expanse of her naked back, and it felt like her skin rippled in anticipation. She turned and was consumed by the heat of hunger in his gaze as it rose from her generous curves to her eyes.

'La Madame has outdone herself,' he said breathlessly, and Gwen watched as he looked for something else to say. She was fascinated when he seemed speechless, and her heart began to hammer when he stepped nearer to her. His head lowered, so his lips teased the corner of her jaw. 'You look stunning,' he said finally.

He was always so composed that it made the public demonstration of his affection all the more exciting. The simple brush of his fingers on her bare back was electrifying as they walked. His touch wasn't controlling, the way Jonathon's grabbing had always felt, and it was wonderful.

They passed several people chatting in the hallway, and Gwen was relieved to see her gown wasn't obnoxious. Other women were wearing fur, feathers, and diamonds, yet it was her everyone was taking an interest in. She couldn't be sure if it was because of the man on her arm, the dress on her body, or her anonymity.

They paused at the top of a wide set of marble stairs, which descended into a large white and gold room. The walls were lined in pillars, and between each set of columns was a piece of art. At the centre of the floor was the absurdly expensive car Miguel had been talking about.

'Wow,' she breathed, and her chest constricted as she immediately began to recognize some of the art pieces.

'We will start on the right and move around,' Miguel assured her with amusement before they began their descent.

Wine and finger food was brought to them on silver platters while Gwen drooled over the art. They chatted with duchesses, diplomats, princes, and pashas. People seemed to recognize Miguel, so they went out of their way to salute him and introduce themselves to Gwen. After several awkward encounters with some of the more intimidating ones, she began to relax.

She noticed Miguel was taking less interest in their surroundings and much more interest in her over the course of the night. He seemed particularly intrigued by her bare skin, and he couldn't seem to help finding excuses to put his hands on her.

'Charming,' the Duke of York complimented her enthusiastically before moving on to the next person of interest.

'You're doing well,' Miguel said softly into her ear, and once more his fingers found the curve in the small of her back. She allowed him to draw her nearer as she giggled nervously.

'I still feel sick,' she admitted.

'I have just the thing to make you feel better,' he promised.

He took her hand and led her to where the pinnacle of all the art in the room was hung. Gwen gazed up in awe at the famous *La Dame en Rouge*. Its elaborate, Victorian gold frame alone would have been outrageously expensive. The canvas was flawlessly textured, the deftness of the talent so evident, and the blending of colour effortless.

Gwen stood in such amazement before The Red Woman that she barely noticed someone request Miguel's attention. He touched her arm gently to tell her he'd be right back.

x x x

Miguel

I glanced back at Gwen, who was transfixed before the painting that seemed to have been made in her image that night. La Madame had dressed her with a simple modernism that put the expensive gaudiness of archaic diamonds, feathers, and fringes to shame. That wasn't what made her the singularly most stunning person in the room, though. The dress, the makeup, and the shoes were just material enhancements of what she possessed so naturally.

And she would be mine.

'Your father has been trying to reach you. I've come on his behalf to tell you there has been a breach of the Accords,' said Hudson, which effectively snapped my attention to him.

'What breach?' I demanded.

'My brother has evidence humans have been experimenting with *sanguinem furoris,*' he revealed quietly. 'There has been a Summons, and all coven lords will be in attendance.'

Sanguinem furoris, blood madness, was a fatal condition for humans who had consumed vampire blood.

'Why would they do such a thing?' I asked rhetorically.

'There's more,' my friend admitted. 'A Dowrra mated to Judas was killed, and he wants blood. The werewolves are restless after hearing about Anita's assassination. The Dowrra have reached out to us for protection for the first time in centuries.'

I looked immediately to where Gwen was still examining the painting, and the illusion of my night was shattered.

'She is not safe,' Hudson insisted. 'If things go badly at the Summons, it may lead to outbreaks of violence among the covens. You will be among the first targets, Miguel. You represent the peace we currently have with the humans.'

I'd already anticipated that. I also knew the ones I cared about would be in direct danger as well.

'When is the Summons?' I asked.

'The next full moon is in a few weeks,' Hudson answered. 'Contact me if you need anything else.'

'What of this evidence Liam has? Where can I get some for myself?' I wanted to know before he could go.

'Don't,' he cautioned seriously. 'Getting directly involved is an excellent way to make you their priority. I shouldn't have to remind you that you don't need anyone looking to hurt you or your father,' he added. He flicked his chin in Gwen's direction, and I grudgingly conceded his point. My primary concern needed to be Gwen's safety.

'Miguel,' said Hudson more lowly, 'someone is touching your mate.'

Gwendolyn

Chapter Fourteen

Gwen tried to imagine what it would be like to have enough money to buy the painting. The thought of a hundred million dollars was *absurd*. How could people have so much when she could barely pay her rent on time?

'You're standing in front of the most expensive piece of art in the room. Still, you manage to capture the attention of all,' whispered a startlingly familiar voice, and Gwen spun to face him. He hadn't recognized her until she looked at him.

'*Gwen*?' he gasped in disbelief.

'Jonathon,' she responded, and she edged away from him slightly. She was sure he'd never hurt her in public, but she hadn't forgotten the feeling of his hands bruising her skin.

'What the hell are you doing here?' he insisted and looked around in confusion. 'Who the hell are you with?'

'Hardly your concern,' Gwen reminded him, and he smirked as his eyes glanced over her thoughtfully. He turned to look around the room again in speculation.

'What old man have you conned into thinking he'll get laid tonight?' he mused to himself. 'We both know you don't put out.'

Gwen was sure her face gave away nothing of her offence, which seemed to irritate him more.

'Red is the colour of passion, you know. You shouldn't pretend to be something you're not,' he asserted, and he moved much closer. She recognized it as his attempt at intimidating her, so she held her ground.

'I think you should go before my date comes back,' she advised him calmly. She resisted the urge to glance around for Miguel.

'Why?' he laughed. 'Is he going to slap me with his cane?'

Frustrated, Gwen reluctantly decided to retreat and come back when he'd gone. She felt confident he wouldn't be brave enough to approach her while Miguel was with her.

Preoccupied with these thoughts, Gwen had forgotten how much Jonathon hated it when people dismissed him. She gasped when his hand fastened on her wrist before she could turn away.

'Don't turn your back on me, bitch. I could have you out on the street!' he swore. Gwen tried to yank her arm away as people began to look at them curiously.

'Stop it! You're making a scene,' she hissed as her tone grew sharp.

'I'm making a scene? *You're* the one who doesn't belong here,' he snarled, and he began to drag her away from the painting. 'I'll escort you out.'

Gwen wanted to put up a better fight, but her footing was already precarious in her heels on the tiles. She didn't want to slip in her efforts to wrench herself free, so she could do little but stumble after Jonathon.

'Leave the young lady alone, Jon,' recommended one of the elderly gentlemen Gwen had met earlier. 'I don't believe you know whom you're insulting.'

'Shut it, old man,' Jon muttered angrily.

Gwen tried to resist him again and, as feared, her heels suddenly skid dangerously beneath her. She was about to fall when Miguel's familiar hands pulled her upright and into his chest. His hand skimmed down her arm to Jon's, and she felt a surge of relief when he pried the clawing fingers off her

'What do you think you're doing?' Miguel snapped

angrily, and Jon looked shocked. 'I asked you a question!' Miguel reminded him impatiently, and Gwen was surprised by his temper. He'd always seemed so tranquil with her before.

'Do you know who she is?' Jonathon demanded sounding distrustful. 'She's an ex-girlfriend of mine. She stole stuff from Welford Accounting.'

Gwen could almost feel the ripple of rage go through her date, but he was gentle as he took her hands. He pivoted, so he was between her and Jon with his back turned to the other man. This only infuriated Jonathon further as he was shut out of their conversation.

'Did he hurt you?' Miguel asked softly, and Gwen shook her head with her eyes lowered. People were still watching, and she felt deeply ashamed. She wondered whether they believed Jon.

'This bitch is a complete fucking nun,' Jonathon interrupted, and Gwen's mortification doubled. Miguel was stiff as a board, and she couldn't muster the nerve to check whether he was as embarrassed as she was, or if he was angry. 'You won't get anything from her later—' Jon began to elaborate.

Gwen gasped when Miguel abruptly turned, and a single jab cracked loudly. Jon went sprawling to the floor as blood erupted from his nose, and he howled in a pain-filled rage.

'You're lucky I don't want blood on this tux,' Miguel assured him as he straightened his jacket with a deadly calm. Gwen's pulse quickened, and for the first time, she wondered how deep his darker side actually went.

There was some applauding in the room, and her unease vanished as security arrived. They scooped Jon up off the floor.

'Would you like us to take him outside, Mr. Santos?' asked one of the burly men, and Miguel nodded.

'That would be appreciated, Nikko. Thank you,' said Miguel as Mr. Welford, Jonathon's father, pressed through the crowd.

'What is going on here?' he demanded with that tone that had always intimidated Gwen.

'The situation has been handled, Mr. Welford,' Miguel told him coolly, and Jon's father looked horrified but deferential. Then he spotted Gwen, and the dismay became astonishment.

'Dad, *do* something!' Jon shouted as security began to yank him toward the door.

Mr. Welford looked at his son and back at Miguel. Evidently, he understood where the power resided because he made no move to protest.

'My most sincere apologies, Mr. Santos,' he said in earnest, and he walked away.

Once Jon was gone, the guests were quickly invited into another room with mauve drapes and dark wooden walls. Everyone took a seat on purple cushioned chairs in front of the podium where the items would be presented for the auction.

'So, what just happened back there?' Gwen whispered to Miguel next to her, and she felt the tension in his shoulder melting.

'I may have forgotten to mention I am one of the two benefactors for the Annual Toledo Charity Ball. My father is the other. Toledo, Spain is where my parents met,' he explained.

'*Oh,*' Gwen gasped. 'So *that's* why people have been trying to talk to us all night! Why didn't you tell me? Why were *they* here?'

'I thought if you knew, it might prevent you from accompanying me,' he answered her with reluctant candour. 'I'm only the benefactor, though. The committee apprises me of whether certain guests are coming, but I don't organize the event,' he admitted apologetically.

Gwen decided to forgive him for not telling her, and she began to think about his unexpected temper. His aggression should have made her nervous, but she'd been strangely thrilled by it. She wanted to know more. She wanted to know what had happened to him that had made him that way.

'Will you tell me about what happened to your mother sometime?' she asked him softly. He was quiet for a moment before he nodded. Then he turned his head toward her, and she felt his mouth brush her ear.

'I will if you tell me more about Jonathon Welford,' he bargained, and Gwen hesitated. She felt her face becoming warm again.

'He just thought I didn't belong here,' she hedged.

'I don't mean tonight,' he insisted, and Gwen leaned her head against his shoulder, so she didn't have to see his eyes.

'He wanted to sleep with me, but I didn't feel like that for him. I don't know why he even wanted to date me,' she muttered.

'He knew he couldn't have you, and that made him want you all the more,' Miguel advised her confidently. 'You said before he only tried to hurt you. Was that true?'

Gwen had been unable to find the words to describe the exact scenario even to Charlotte, but she wanted Miguel to know.

'He got angry when I tried to leave, and he started hitting me,' she began softly, and revulsion rippled through her at the memory. 'The butler heard all the screaming. He walked into the room just as I saw Jon look at me with this... realization. Like he remembered he could take what he wanted,' she recalled resentfully. The words offered her some relief. 'The butler got fired too,' she finished.

Gwen doubted Miguel had wanted so much detail, but it had felt incredibly good to finally tell someone. When he lifted her hand to his mouth to kiss her softly, she knew she'd made the right decision in trusting him.

'No one will ever hurt you like that again,' he promised her firmly, and Gwen snorted.

'I still won't ever wear anything so obnoxious again,' she confided in him and felt him hesitate in confusion.

'You think the dress...?'

'That's why he came up to me in the first place,' Gwen defended her logic. 'He said—'

'Gwen, what were you wearing when Jon attacked you the first time?' he interrupted, and Gwen thought about it.

'Jeans and a sweater,' she answered.

'Do you think what you were wearing had anything to do with his decision to hurt you?' he challenged her. Gwen grudgingly shook her head.

'No, but even you can't keep your hands off me tonight. The dress is—'

'I'm *perfectly* capable of keeping my hands off you if that is what you want, but I don't think it is,' Miguel interrupted, and he squeezed her fingers. Gwen smiled slightly when his voice deepened with confidence, and she shook her head.

'It's not,' she assured him as the auctioneer drew their attention to the front of the room. 'Are you going to bid on anything?' she whispered in an attempt to lighten the mood again.

'Was there something you wished for me to bid on?' he asked teasingly, but she said nothing. She was not about to ask him to spend a hundred million dollars.

They sat watching and listening as people paid millions and millions. Gwen was happy enough seeing the pieces going across the stage, and there was a thrill in seeing who bought what.

The final piece of art was *La Dame en Rouge.* The painting was too large to move from the wall, so a picture of it was displayed on the screen behind the podium. They commenced the bidding at one hundred million, and Gwen's jaw dropped when several hands shot into the air. The price continued to rise until Gwen was feeling anxious. The number of hands gradually decreased until the battle was raging between a man at the front and someone on the phone. Gwen was on the edge of her seat as the man at the front hesitated indecisively before he gave up. The auctioneer banged his gavel.

'*Sold* to the anonymous bidder on the phone!' he cried.

'Wait,' Gwen whispered in disappointment. 'We don't get to know who it was?' she asked.

'That's normal,' Miguel explained. 'Considering how sought after the painting is, I'm not surprised someone wanted to remain anonymous.'

Gwen tried not to show her disappointment at not having at least been able to see who'd acquired the piece.

They returned to the ballroom where a classical band began playing. The floor filled with couples, and Gwen was secretly thrilled with the excuse to put her hands on her date again. She was as subtle as she could be, but she could tell Miguel was aware of her sneaky exploration. He was more behaved after their conversation, and she regretted mentioning that he couldn't keep his hands off her.

They took a break to get a drink, and Miguel grunted in relief. 'Ms. Trolley,' he said, and Gwen detected a note of pleasure in his voice.

'*Where*?' she demanded as she glanced around excitedly. She followed him when he crossed the room.

Olivia Trolley, the American CEO of Trolley Accounting, had managed to age exactly the way every woman hopes she will. The sixty-year-old was still as gorgeous as she'd been when she was thirty. She was wearing a black, Gucci ruffle gown and white Christian Louboutin stilettos with the iconic red outsole. Her shoulder-length, white-blonde hair was pinned back on one side with a diamond clip, and her lips were red. When she saw Miguel approaching, she smiled.

'Ms. Trolley, I'm delighted you could join us,' he said upon reaching her.

'Well, I wasn't going to pass up an invitation from Miguel Santos himself,' Ms. Trolley assured him. Her wine glass clinked against his.

As Miguel turned back toward her, Gwen realized why he'd dropped her arm before they reached Trolley. She sucked in a deep breath for calm when he smiled for her.

'Please allow me to introduce you to Gwendolyn

Rhys. She's the one I was telling you about,' he explained
to Trolley.

'Yes,' said Olivia with great pleasure as she eyed
Gwen with deep consideration, 'the one who worked for
Robert Welford.'

Chapter Fifteen

Feeling blindsided, Gwen felt her mouth open in surprise, and Olivia laughed at her expression.

'Don't worry; it's a compliment! Not a chance I hire someone that *prat* could have working for him,' she assured Gwen with a roll of her eyes. 'I'm looking for an executive assistant for my CFO here in Toronto. I've always considered a woman with insider knowledge and a healthy distaste for the competition to be an asset.'

Gwen regained her senses, and she cleared her throat.

'I'd *very* much like to be that woman,' she responded, and Olivia tapped her glass against Gwen's.

'Then I shall see you at eight on Monday morning, my dear. We'll see what you're made of,' she proposed.

'Thank you, Ms. Trolley,' Gwen said in disbelief, and Olivia returned to her companions. Miguel guided Gwen back toward the dance floor, and she looked up at him suspiciously.

'You *told* her about me?' she asked in confusion.

'I did,' Miguel admitted. 'I didn't tell her about our relationship. I knew you wouldn't want to feel the job depended on me after Welford,' he pointed out. She could tell he was nervous she was upset, and she couldn't decide whether she was.

'So, the job doesn't depend on you?' she verified skeptically.

'Olivia doesn't let men define her opinions. That's why I told her about Welford. Not in full,' he added quickly when Gwen frowned at him. 'She was unfairly fired from her husband's company, and now she's the CEO of her own. I knew she'd appreciate you.'

'I'm not qualified to be an executive assistant, Miguel!' Gwen objected. 'What am I supposed to tell her?'

'You have your accounting degree and CPA,' he reasoned.

'I have next to *no* experience!' Gwen reminded him.

'This is an opportunity, Gwen. You don't have to take it, but don't ignore it. Please?' he insisted. He held her eyes until she nodded, and he smiled. 'Good. Now, can I have one more dance before we go?'

Gwen wasn't used to letting people help her, but the more she thought about it, the more she began to appreciate it. The tension gradually melted between them, and she leaned her head against his shoulder in contentment.

Near to the end of their last dance, she caught Mr. Welford watching them, and she knew he was confused. Jonathon had always complained about her lack of affection in order to pressure her.

By the time they were leaving, most of the reporters had gone, so the street outside was relatively quiet.

Gwen watched Miguel's lips moving as he arranged for his driver to pick them up on the phone. He looked gorgeous under the streetlights, and she was renewed with desire for him. She wiped her lipstick away, and when he hung up the phone, she pressed against him before he could say anything. He reacted instantly, pulling her against him, and he groaned hungrily against her lips.

She wasn't nearly finished savouring the taste of him when the car arrived, and Anthony got out. Gwen heard their door open, and she knew he was waiting, but it was almost impossible to pull away.

Miguel finally broke the kiss by leaning his head against hers as he caught his breath.

'You're welcome,' he whispered in amusement, and

she cocked her head at him questioningly. 'I can only assume a kiss like *that* was meant to be a thank you,' he explained, and she giggled.

'That was a "just-because" kiss,' she assured him. 'I am thankful, though,' she added sincerely. 'I was just overwhelmed.'

'I know I can be imperious. I'm used to being in charge, and I don't date a lot,' he admitted. 'If it's too much—'

'It's not!' she insisted, and she kissed him lightly again before the building doors opened behind them. Gwen stepped back from him shyly as several people walked by, but Miguel didn't let go of her hand.

'Home then,' he said, and he turned toward the car.

'Where are you taking me?' Gwen asked hesitantly, and Miguel turned back toward her in surprise.

'Wherever you wish,' he promised, and his voice had deepened. She knew he wanted her, but after everything that had happened, she'd have to be crystal clear with him that she wanted him back.

'I want to stay with you,' she told him, and his dark eyes searched her seriously.

'I'm not like Jonathon,' he promised her. 'I hope you don't think I expect—'

'I don't think that,' she interrupted quickly.

'Just because we talked about it yesterday—'

'Miguel!' she protested laughingly and she glanced down shyly. 'I *want* you.'

He stepped back toward her, and his fingers glided under her jaw to lift her chin so he could kiss her tenderly. With a smile, he turned back toward the car, but Gwen's eye was caught by something terrifying.

Jonathon was standing across the street. His jacket was open over his bloody undershirt, his face terribly bruised, but it was the murder in his eyes that scared her more than anything.

x x x

Miguel

Gwen wanted to be with me that night, and I wasn't going to deny her wish. The scent of her attraction had been toying with me all evening, and I was desperate for her. In the privacy of the limo, with the driver's divide up, I might have laid her down on the leather seat, but I knew better than to do that.

She hadn't indicated it explicitly, but I knew Gwen was a virgin. I didn't want her first time to be in the backseat of a car.

The car pulled away from the curb, and she toed off her shoes. Her thighs escaped from the slits in her dress as she abruptly straddled me with her knees clenching my hips. Immediately, the arch between her legs cradled my swollen cock, and I moaned.

She kissed me as her fingers ran up through my hair with her nails scraping my scalp. I tried to stay calm, but it was difficult when her innocent tugging finally succeeded in opening my shirt. She sat away from my mouth to see what she'd revealed, and she bit her bottom lip in appreciation.

I couldn't help it anymore, and I twisted so she was on her back beneath me. I worried briefly the assertion might have scared her, but she was giggling. She pulled my face down so she could kiss me again.

I bent her knee up through the slit in her dress so I could come between her legs more fully. Her skin was smooth and soft as I ran my hand from her thigh to her hip under the dress. She released her breath in relief against my lips, and I immediately felt my eyeteeth lengthening in response.

I inched back so she wouldn't see my face and bent my head down so I could kiss her inner thigh. I felt her become very still when my hand traced up toward the apex of her legs. The softness of her silk panties was the perfect material over which to stroke my thumb against her virgin flesh. She sighed deeply and dropped her head back to the seat. I had never seen a woman respond so helplessly and I realized it was further testament to the strength of the bond between us.

Vampire saliva contains a paralyzer which we often used during sex to make bites less painful. Humans were allergic, but Gwen was Dowrra, so her skin had numbed where I'd sucked on her. It was what another vampire's flesh would have done. She didn't feel it when I accidently scratched her with my tooth. I could have bitten her, and she might not have noticed until she inevitably discovered the teeth marks. I wasn't about to do that, of course, but I *was* curious whether she'd also have an erotic reaction to my venom. My tongue was tingling with it, so I deliberately tasted the tiny droplet of blood that had welled where I'd scratched her.

Her reaction was more powerful than any vampiress I'd ever seen, and a hoarse cry burst from her open mouth. I could feel her sex spasm in climax against my hand.

I smiled at this discovery as her stunned eyes met mine from between her thighs. I returned to her lips, and her kiss was fuelled with ecstasy as she grabbed my face. I wanted to test her again, but I heard us turning into the hotel driveway.

'We're here,' I informed her, and I sat up.

We were nearly put back together by the time Anthony opened the door for us. I could see his face was tense with the desire to smile, and I knew he'd heard Gwen. She saw it too, and her face was flooded with colour as she looked down.

'Thank you, Anthony. That will be all,' I advised the young man, who nodded and got back into the car.

Gwen took a step forward, and she hissed softly in pain. I knew it was her shoes, so I wordlessly scooped her up to carry her to the open door where Carlton bid us goodnight. I didn't put her down until we'd reached the couch in my living room.

I knelt in front of her and slid her heels off one by one. I lifted her feet and kissed each ankle while she gazed down at me in amazement.

'Would you like something?' I asked, and she was coy.

'I want you to do that thing again,' she advised me with a shy smile on her swollen lips. There was a gleam of sensuality in her green eyes I'd never seen there before, and I was almost immediately hard for her again.

I slowly pressed myself between her knees and kissed the swell of one breast. She ran her hands through my hair, and I closed my eyes. It was easily the best thing I'd ever felt when she used her nails against my scalp.

She suddenly leaned away, and she looked startled.

'Just so you know, I'm on birth control,' she told me impulsively, and then she flushed in embarrassment.

'Oh,' I said, realizing with her there was, in fact, a chance of pregnancy. It was the first time in my life that it had ever been a concern. 'That's good,' I assured her.

'I'm talking too much, right?' she whispered nervously.

'Not at all,' I dismissed, and I lifted her hands to my lips to kiss. 'The more you say, the more pleasure I can give you,' I explained with a wink.

I was eager for the unique opportunity of helping to shape her sexual experience. I could ensure she was never self-conscious or afraid to try something new.

'Are you sure there's nothing you want?' I verified, and she offered me that innocently devious smile.

'Just you,' she insisted, and I obligingly stood to scoop her up. 'What are you doing?' she shrieked in excitement when I tossed her playfully over my shoulder. My hand rested against that bountiful ass.

'Giving you what you want,' I warned her, and I carried her to the master bedroom.

I knelt on the king sized bed so she fell to the mattress beneath me. She was laughing, but her expression sobered quickly once I stood and began to unbutton my shirt. She watched with great anticipation, and I was pleased again with her smile when I stripped myself bare to the waist.

I pulled her to her feet so I could remove her coat and turned her back to me. I gently nipped my way along the nape of her neck and shoulder as I unzipped her dress. With a careful tug, it crumpled to the floor at her feet.

I ran my hands down to her wide hips, and her black panties dropped to the floor with the dress. Her breathing deepened when I reached around her to peel down the matching backless bra. I was finally able to cup each of her full breasts, and she moaned deeply as I rubbed my thumbs over each taut nipple.

I stepped back to admire her bare ass and slowly circled her so I could appreciate the full splendour of her nudity. Gwen was nervous, and her arms lingered over her body, but she still took my breath away.

Her skin was ivory except her seemingly perpetually reddened cheeks. There were green sparks of passion in her eyes, and her red curls cascaded around her shoulders. She looked like The Birth of Venus innocently covering her nakedness. I could still see her nipples were pink, and the hair between her thighs was dark red.

She saw the raw desire in my expression and slowly dropped her hands as I unbuttoned my dress pants and pushed them down. Gwen bit her bottom lip as I stepped forward, and she laughed when I suddenly lifted her up against me. I crawled onto the bed with her.

With the room lighting turned down low, she looked incredibly erotic stretched across the black sheets. I wanted to taste her, every inch of her, so I began with her puckering nipples. I had to be extremely careful with my teeth so I didn't cut her, but she seemed to like it when I tugged with my lips. Her skin rippled under my breath. My hand slipped up the inside of her leg until I touched the damp warmth between her thighs. Her legs jerked, and she sighed as I began again with the edge of my thumb against her. She wasn't concerned this time with how much noise she made, and I loved it.

'Remember what I said,' I told her. 'Talk to me, Gwen.'

'Harder,' she whispered longingly, and I was happy to oblige. She groaned gratefully, and her legs lurched again in response.

I was eager to taste her, so after a moment, I re-positioned myself so I could replace my finger with my mouth. Gwen gasped, and when her hand drove through my hair hard, I wasn't sure if she'd appreciated the change.

'Don't stop,' she hissed in assurance when I hesitated, and I returned my tongue to her clit. She arched back with her fists both clenching.

Her low groans became higher until she was panting, and she rocked helplessly against my mouth. After some time listening carefully to her cues, I pushed her over the edge of ecstasy again, and she cried out in relief. I kissed my way up so I was between her legs again.

'Is it your turn yet?' she breathed with her head still thrown back into the blankets. I froze when her eager little fingers skimmed down my stomach and found my straining erection.

'No,' I said breathlessly as she stroked the length of me experimentally. 'We haven't even gotten started.'

She lifted her head and kissed me with both her hands rising to either side of my head. She used her tongue in much the same way I'd just shown her to delve in search of mine.

'This might be uncomfortable at first,' I admitted against her lips once she'd finished kissing me. 'Just the first couple of times, and then I promise it will never feel anything but good.'

She nodded trustingly, and I manoeuvred my hips more directly between her legs. I'd never been with a virgin before, so I was admittedly curious to see what the fuss was about.

She was as eager as I was when I first guided myself to the entrance of her sex. As I began to press my way inside her, however, I could feel her tensing in unease.

'Easy,' I breathed for both of us. I had to fight for my composure as I revelled in the tightness of her.

'Have you been with a virgin before?' she asked me, sounding uncomfortable. She looked up at me hopefully, but I shook my head.

It was another awkward moment before she'd finally taken the entire length of me inside. I stopped moving, despite how hard I wanted to fuck her, to make sure she was all right.

'You okay?' I asked, and she nodded quickly, but her discomfort was still apparent. I knew she was becoming uncertain, and I felt guilty. I hadn't expected her to be so tight.

I resumed kissing her, and once she'd relaxed, I began to move again. It had to be slow until her sex adjusted, and then her legs opened more invitingly, and her nails stopped biting into my back. When she started to sigh in response to me, I knew it had finally started to feel good, so I quickened my strokes. Soon, her hips were rocking to meet mine, and I knew she was ready.

I changed the angle of my penetration for a bit more friction, and my cock began to graze along her clit with every thrust. She groaned more deeply and began to grip me again, but it wasn't in pain this time. I could feel her sex quivering, on the verge of release, so I gradually increased my rhythm until her head arched back. Her eyes closed, and her mouth opened as her cries grew hoarser. I was getting close, just from watching her, but I wanted her to come for me one last time.

'Come on, Gwen,' I hissed breathlessly into her ear. 'One more time for me, baby.'

'Faster,' she begged, and I was pleased she continued to take my advice. I obliged her direction, and she came hard.

I waited for every last shudder of ecstasy before I joined her and was surprised by the intensity. I even cried out unintentionally.

For a few moments, I couldn't move as she continued to spasm helplessly. I could barely breathe as I tried not to crush her under my weight. Her hand reached over my shoulder, and she brushed her damp hair out of her face with a contented sigh.

'Wow…' she breathed, and she began to run her fingers through my hair again. 'I didn't believe Charlotte when she said I was missing out.'

My laugh was muffled in her shoulder.

'It's not always that good,' I admitted, and I nearly bit off my tongue when those words slipped out. I immediately began thinking of an excuse.

'What made it so good?' she asked, as anticipated. I could hear the satisfaction in her voice.

'Compatibility, I guess,' I said hopefully. I couldn't say it was because of a connection between us, which was the reason she'd never had a normal love life before. I wouldn't tell her my eyeteeth had lengthened and were aching for her. I certainly wasn't about to disclose that she wasn't just the first virgin I'd ever been with. She was also the first *human*.

She sighed contentedly and turned her head to nuzzle my shoulder. I would have been happy to have stayed like that for the rest of the night, but she'd become uncomfortable beneath me. So I gently separated us to get off her.

'Uh,' she groaned, and she grimaced. 'Does it have to be so messy?' she demanded, and I laughed.

'You will learn to love it. It means you're mine now,' I growled, and *nothing* had ever made me feel so proud.

'You don't think it's gross?' she verified, and I groaned as I shook my head.

'Not in the least,' I promised, leaning over to suckle at her nipple again. I couldn't help it when it puckered for me so willingly. She moaned and melted underneath me.

'You're... ready again,' she pointed out with intrigue. I'd been trying to ignore that myself.

'I don't want to hurt you. You're going to be sore, and you're going to bleed a little,' I advised her.

'Doesn't feel like it,' she responded insistently.

I realized she was trying to convince me to make love to her again. I hadn't wanted to cause any more trauma than necessary in taking her virginity, but I wouldn't deny her either.

PART TWO:

*Only be sure that you do not eat the blood,
for the blood is the life,
and you shall not eat the life with the flesh.*

-Deuteronomy 12:23

Gwendolyn

Chapter Sixteen

Gwen opened her eyes, and silk sheets slid sensually against her when she stretched. Sunlight was teasing the drapes and flitting across the bed. There was a nice breeze kissing her skin from an open window, but the room still smelled like sex, which made her smile.

She turned over to see the bed was empty, and she sat up in surprise with the sheet clenched around her. Feeling a little anxious, she slid off the mattress, and noticed Miguel had been right. There was a bit of blood on the inside of her thigh and on the towel he'd put down for her to sleep on. Gwen used it to wipe her skin clean and folded it on one of the chairs. She found her panties and the shirt Miguel had discarded the night before, which hung to mid-thigh. His scent still clung to it, and she groaned appreciatively.

Gwen wandered cautiously out of the room and down the hall. She smelled food in the kitchen.

'Bloody hell!' she heard Ainsley curse suddenly, and she froze when he came angrily around the corner. The butler stopped, and she saw his gaze rise quickly from her bare thighs to her eyes. He looked as embarrassed as she felt.

'My apologies, Miss Rhys,' he said stiffly.

'What's wrong?' she asked nervously. She wrapped her arms around her breasts so he wouldn't see her nipples puckering from the chill of the hallway.

'Mr. Santos insists he can make coffee, but he

obviously can't,' Ainsley explained shortly. 'So, I am removing myself from the situation.'

Gwen laughed, and she nodded. 'I will help him, Ainsley.'

'Thank you, Miss Rhys,' the butler acknowledged her before he moved by her on his way to the guestrooms.

Gwen crept through the living room into the kitchen where Miguel was standing in front of the coffee maker. He was staring at it like it was some kind of demon with his hands braced against the counter.

'You okay?' she asked, and he turned toward her. He was shirtless in a pair of jeans, and all those rippling abs were just begging to be caressed. The man had the body of a god, and his morning-after look was the best she'd seen on him yet.

'Gwen,' he greeted her, his smile enough to make her day as he came toward her. She let him kiss her, but she didn't deepen it for fear of her morning breath.

'Did you make breakfast?' she asked and glanced around eagerly for the source of the food smell.

'No,' he admitted, and he indicated the trolley which had obviously been brought up by room service.

'Smells like pancakes,' she remarked with curiosity, and she moved nearer to investigate.

'I wanted to be there when you woke up, but this coffee machine is...' he grumbled. He trailed off as he glared at the offensive object.

'I will help,' she assured him, fighting an amused grin.

He was one of the most competent men she'd ever met, so it seemed rather ironic he'd never used a coffee machine before. Luckily, the night before had been more than incredible, enough to make up for his lack of domestic skills.

He had said sex wasn't always that good, which she might have been tempted to think was a lie, but she believed him. Charlotte had shared enough stories about awkward sexual encounters from before she'd been with her husband. Gwen didn't think it was simply because of their attraction to one another, though. There was no doubt the patience and guidance Miguel had shown her was unique and he was a highly experienced lover. That had caused her discomfort since she didn't want to become one of the many things he liked to collect, but there *were* benefits.

As they made coffee and ate breakfast, her concerns about his promiscuous past continued to fade. They had an incredibly comfortable dynamic, and soon her stomach muscles were aching from all the laughter. It felt very different from anything Charlotte had ever talked about, so Gwen felt reassured of Miguel's sincerity. They were having so much fun she nearly forgot she wasn't wearing any pants when a delivery man came to the door.

'Mr. Santos?' he asked, glancing with helpless interest at Gwen's bare legs.

'Yes?' Miguel prompted a little sharply, and Gwen fought a smile as she stepped around the kitchen corner out of sight.

'You've... got a large delivery, Sir.'

'That's all right. Bring it in,' Miguel assured him, and Gwen peeked curiously around the wall. She saw a large rectangular shape being carried into the living room.

'Just set it there,' said Miguel whose shirtless confidence was making the delivery guys uncomfortable. Gwen didn't blame them. He was intimidating.

Having recognized the shape of the frame, however, Gwen was no longer aware of their presence. She wandered toward the enormous covered frame, and her hands brushed over it while Miguel signed the delivery papers. He sent the intrigued young men on their way as Gwen abruptly pulled the cloth down from the canvas. Her suspicions were confirmed.

La Dame en Rouge.

She looked up at him with her eyes wide, and she could tell he was thrilled by her reaction.

'How?' she demanded.

'I told my appraiser to bid on whatever caught your

attention the most,' he explained casually.

'The person on the phone,' Gwen realized, and Miguel nodded. She wasn't sure whether to laugh or cry.

'Do you like it?' he asked, suddenly a little nervous when she became emotional.

'Oh, yes!' she exclaimed quickly before looking at him sternly. 'How much did you—?'

'It doesn't matter. It's for charity, remember?' he reminded her, and he moved closer to wrap his arms around her. She snorted at his assurance.

'How much of the proceeds actually go to charity?' she teased him. His eyes widened, and she remembered too late that the ball had been *his* event.

'I will pretend not to be insulted,' he informed her as she winced. 'Last night, we probably raised nearly a billion dollars for women all over the world. Ten percent barely covers what it costs to host the event, and I tend to be generous with my personal contributions.'

His hand rested pointedly on the frame of the painting, and Gwen was surprised by his sensitivity. It didn't take her long to make the connection, though, and she felt immediately guilty.

'For women,' she repeated. 'Is that because of your mother?' she guessed, and she saw his lips tense as he recognized his slip.

'Yes,' he admitted guardedly.

Gwen was dying to know what had happened to her, but she could see it was still not something he was prepared to discuss. There was some distant memory echoing in his dark eyes that pierced her with pain for him. So, she dropped it and took his hands in hers to squeeze them. She thought they felt cold.

'Where shall we hang it?' she asked to change the topic, and she saw his face soften.

'The bedroom,' he proposed with a wink, and she smiled before he kissed her. This time she didn't seem to care anymore about how she tasted in the morning. He seemed to relish her, and she giggled when he lifted her against his chest.

'Ainsley is here!' she reminded him when he began to carry her toward his room.

'Ainsley will leave the penthouse if he knows what's good for him,' Miguel promised her.

He closed the door with the heel of his foot and tossed her on the bed. He crawled over her and pinned her arms over her head. At first, she expected the sensation of him restraining her to frighten her, but she simply wasn't afraid of him.

His playful kisses began to tickle her neck and chest, and suddenly, she was laughing so hard she could barely breathe. Gwen was pretty sure he let her finally throw him over and straddle him, but once she had him subdued, she became unsure. He laid his arms down over his head in a gesture of surrender.

'All yours,' he promised her.

Grinning, Gwen slid down his body, so she had access to the belt around his hips. She heard his sharp gasp as she unbuckled him and began to pull the jeans down his thighs.

'You need sweatpants,' she mumbled as she discarded the jeans on the floor. She got the sense he was holding his breath and waiting for her next move. Only his hands clenching gave any indication of his anticipation.

He looked so inviting stretched out on the bed. Gwen lifted her hand curiously and trailed her fingers shyly over the muscles in his stomach to the part of him that was already hard. As she wrapped her fingers firmly around him, he groaned deeply, and she felt his cock jerk in her hand. Thusly encouraged, she tightened her grip and stroked him.

She'd expected him to be hairless, like the men on TV, but he wasn't. He had a light dusting of dark hair on his lower tummy, which thickened a bit in a line under and above his navel. He also had strange scars which she hadn't asked about the night before but now she had him at her mercy.

'What are these from?' she asked, and she leaned over to kiss the marks on his ribs while stroking him.

'Fighting,' he admitted breathlessly as he continued to tense at her touch. 'I lived on the street for quite a while,' he reminded her.

Gwen felt a potent desire to show him the same thorough care he'd given her the night before. She wanted to worship every inch of him. So, she sat forward and took the head of his penis into her mouth.

Miguel's entire body tightened, and a helplessly loud groan escaped him. She felt his hand sweeping through her hair as she twirled her tongue around him.

'Deeper,' he breathed huskily, and she obligingly moved her mouth farther down his length. She was afraid to scrape him with her teeth, so she tensed her lips protectively over them. Then she began to mimic the way he'd thrust in and out of her the night before. This seemed to be what he'd wanted, and he breathed in sharply as his stomach muscles clenched. After a few moments, he touched her shoulder.

'You have to stop,' he panted.

'Why?' she laughed. She rather enjoyed the sense of power she'd gained over him, but there was no teasing in his eyes. He sat up to kiss her lips.

'I want inside you,' he explained roughly.

He pressed her backwards onto the bed, and she happily opened her legs for him to come down on top of her. He began quickly unbuttoning the shirt Gwen had borrowed. He stopped impatiently once he'd revealed enough of her to tease her nipples with his tongue. Gwen lifted her hips for him when he tugged her panties off, and he used his fingers to begin circling her clit. Her soreness was long forgotten as two of his digits pressed inside her.

'Is that okay?' he whispered, and she nodded eagerly.

Miguel hooked his fingers a bit so they glazed repetitively over the bundle of nerves he'd discovered the night before with his cock. It wasn't long, and she was on the verge of release, but he stopped just before she could succumb. She whimpered in protest, but thankfully, he replaced his fingers with her new favourite part of him. She groaned deeply in satisfaction as he pressed inside.

He was still initially careful with her, for which she was grateful, but her sex adjusted more readily this time. She was able to meet each of his powerful thrusts, which gradually increased the pressure straining within her. The sound of skin slapping against skin filled the room along with their heavy breathing, and his groans became deeper and louder. His mounting pleasure was intensely provocative, and it didn't take her long to plunge into ecstasy.

Her body spasmed hard while he continued to piston into her until he finally came apart in her arms. His cry was the sweetest thing she'd ever heard as he sank against her in utter capitulation. Seeing such a powerful man become so passionate was thrilling, and she felt a great swell of emotion toward him. She couldn't help wondering whether he'd become like that for all his lovers.

He laid his head against her shoulder contentedly, and she ran her fingers through his hair the way she knew he loved. He moaned in appreciation. After a moment, he gingerly lifted himself off her to lie next to her on the bed. She was still not perfectly comfortable with the messy aftermath of sex, but he seemed to love it, so she was trying.

Miguel leaned over her again to kiss his way down her chest. She was still wearing his shirt open to the navel, so he slowly finished unbuttoning it.

By the time he was finished with her, it was almost noon, and she was going to be late to work. It didn't help that he kept grabbing her for kisses as she was trying to get out the door.

Luckily, Ainsley had had the foresight to retrieve the clothing she'd been wearing before Madame Rosetta's from the car. He'd left it neatly folded for her on the kitchen table alongside a coffee thermos. With the cup in hand, she kissed Miguel one last time before she got into the elevator with Ainsley.

She was reluctant to check her phone as they descended to the lobby, but she did. As expected, Charlotte and her roommate had called about a dozen times, and there were fifty unread texts. In the car, Gwen texted Sandra she was alive and to see if she'd bring her a change of clothes and her toothbrush to work; she decided to call Charlotte back before the woman had an aneurysm.

'*Gwen*!' Charlotte cried into the phone, causing Gwen to hold it away from her head. 'Why didn't you call last night?'

'I was busy,' Gwen said significantly, glancing guiltily at the rear-view mirror to make sure Ainsley was focused on the road.

There was a moment of silence on the other end before Charlotte gave a strangled cry of excitement.

'I knew it! I *knew* it!' she screamed, presumably at Derek.

'You're a genius,' Gwen sighed.

'How was it?' Charlotte demanded excitedly.

'I, *uh*.... I can't really talk about it right now,' Gwen whispered. Ainsley's eyes flickered up to hers, and she saw him smile when he looked back at the road. Her cheeks warmed.

'I bet his driver is taking her to work,' Charlotte estimated to Derek. 'Just answer yes or no,' Charlotte proposed to Gwen.

'Sure,' Gwen groaned.

'Was it good?' Charlotte asked suggestively.

'Oh, yah,' Gwen burst, and Ainsley's smiled again.

'Are you seeing him again?' Charlotte wanted to know, and Gwen could hear the squeak of excitement in her voice.

'I think so,' Gwen acknowledged in uncertainty.

'Derek wants to know if you guys talked about it,'

Charlotte persisted.

'Not really,' Gwen admitted. She began to wonder whether she should feel nervous about that.

'Well, *my* question is how hot he is naked—?' Charlotte paused. 'Oh, shut it, Derek! Like you watch the Victoria's Secret Fashion Show for my benefit!' she shouted, and Gwen smirked. 'Sorry. Seriously though, I need to know!' Charlotte insisted.

'Very,' was all Gwen could say conspicuously, and Charlotte seemed happy with that. 'Look, I'm almost at work, so can I call you later?' Gwen asked.

'Sure,' Charlotte agreed reluctantly. 'Talk soon!'

Gwen hung up and sat back in the seat thoughtfully.

Charlotte's question about whether she was going to see Miguel again had bothered her. She'd thought it was obvious they would see each other again, but now she worried whether it'd been obvious to Miguel.

Gwen asked Ainsley to drop her at The Diner, so she wasn't late. She grabbed the plastic bag Sandra had left for her from behind the counter. She ignored Sonia's skeptical glances and went into the bathroom to quickly brush her teeth and change her clothes. Once she was ready, she slung her hair into a ponytail and got to work.

Miguel

Chapter Seventeen

After Gwen had gone, I returned to the bedroom where her smell, and the scent of sex, lingered tauntingly on the sheets. It was nearly enough to make me chase her down and beg her to call in sick so we could spend the day together. The idea of rolling around with her for hours in broad daylight was strangely intriguing considering I was more of a nighttime kind of person.

I resisted the urge to climb back into the bed and turned my attention to the wall directly across from my bed. This was where I wished to hang *La Dame en Rouge*.

I hadn't told Gwen the exact truth regarding my charity. The money did go toward protecting women, but I cared very little about the circumstances of average human females. The only women I cared about were the ones like my mother and Gwen. I cared about the Dowrra.

My cellphone started ringing on the bedside table and distracted me from this contemplation. I retrieved it and saw the number was blocked. Usually, a blocked call was from my father or Agent Benet, but I almost always expected those.

After a couple of rings, I decided to answer.

'Hey, it's Derek,' said the familiar voice on the other end, and I sighed immediately with regret.

'How'd you get this number?' I demanded.

'I pulled some major strings,' Derek dismissed impatiently. 'Look, I wanted to see if you're free today.

There's been another strange murder.'

I took in a deep breath to regain control of my exasperation with him.

'I'm not a field agent, and I almost died the last time I went somewhere with you,' I reminded him.

'I know, but you might want to see this one,' he insisted, and my teeth set together in irritation. With everything that had been happening as of late, he was right. I had to take an interest in all things strange and abnormal. I could no longer rely on the humans to keep me informed.

'Where is it?' I relented.

'Just north of Lawrence West Station,' Derek answered. 'There are some old abandoned buildings on Evelyn Street right by the—'

'I know where that is,' I interrupted impatiently. 'There's a popular vampire club up there. It's a neutral zone, Derek. I have no power there at all.'

Derek was quiet and thoughtful for a moment.

'I'm surprised an upstanding coven prince, such as *you,*' he inserted, 'would know about a place like Warm Blooded.'

I was alarmed by his audacity.

'This is my city, Derek. I know who comes and goes, and I know where they hang out,' I assured him.

I wasn't about to tell him I'd frequented several of the clubs in that area before. My sexual appetite was just as strong as the next vampire's.

'Okay, fine,' Derek surrendered, but I could hear he was amused by my defensive response. 'I really do need your help with this one, though. Will you meet me?'

'I'm surprised you're not more concerned with Gwen's safety,' I stalled evasively.

'Charlotte just heard from her. I know she's safe. Not that I doubted you,' he added, and I scoffed in disbelief.

'I will meet you in half an hour,' I advised him sharply and hung up the phone before he could answer.

I slid the cell into my jeans pocket and went to the

closet. I was taking no chances this time, and I dressed only in clothing which I was unattached to.

Using backstreets, rooftops, and alleyways, it took me ten minutes to reach the Glen Park and Lawrence Heights area. I didn't go immediately toward Evelyn Street, however. The area was a neutral zone, with no presiding coven to enforce the Accords. I wanted an opportunity to scope it out to see if there was anything I needed to be particularly wary of before proceeding.

I'd learned my lesson from last time Derek had asked for my assistance.

Neutral zones were like the old American West where rogue vamps nested away from the influence of the Tribunal. Coven vampires frequently wandered through, looking to party, but I'd also encountered dryads, nymphs, witches, fey, and werewolves. They often resented coven royalty because they saw me as an enforcer of the Accords and an embodiment of vampire privilege. The only law they abided by was the law of nature, survival of the fittest, and sometimes the collective reign of nests or nightclub owners. Discretion was mandatory. Failure to remain tactful would attract the attention of human authorities and give a coven the excuse to police the area.

I hesitated as I heard the faintest step behind me. My shoulders tensed automatically, which alerted my stalker to my awareness before his scent came to me. I relaxed.

'What could you possibly be doing up in this part of the city?' asked Hudson as I turned toward him. He seemingly materialized out of the shadows.

'You're keeping an eye on me,' I assumed.

'Your dad says hi,' Hudson responded with a grin of satisfaction when my nostrils flared in annoyance.

'You told him I mentioned looking for evidence,' I guessed with disappointment. I turned from him to continue walking toward the deserted streets ahead. He was going to be following me regardless of whether I protested, so I decided not to make an issue of my father's order.

'What was I supposed to do? If you get killed while I'm in the city, Jaevus will blame me,' Hudson pointed out.

'I'm not going to get killed,' I chastised. He didn't know about the close call with the werewolf, and I wanted to keep it that way.

Hudson kept a respectful distance from me for some time as I continued to wander the dirty alleyways around Evelyn Street. Eventually, I made my way to the appointed meeting location where I knew I was in the right place when I saw police lights.

The alleyway in which the PSA agents were congregating was blocked off by police cars and yellow tape. There was no sign of Derek, and I couldn't see into the alleyway toward the crime scene. The longer I stood there analyzing the scents around me, the more certain I became my presence was unnecessary.

I waited impatiently as the police, obviously the first respondents, began to make room for the PSA agents. Many of them cast looks at me in my Tom Ford Military Jacket, and I guessed I stuck out a little.

'You can't stay here,' advised one of the older officers. 'There's a murder investigation.'

'I'm waiting for a friend,' I responded crisply and cursed Derek for calling me to an old-fashioned murder scene. The cop seemed prepared to give me more trouble.

'I'm here!' Derek huffed from behind me, and I turned as he reached my side. 'Traffic was terrible,' he apologized. Without a word to the cop, he flashed his badge, and the officer moved off with an unimpressed twist of his mouth.

'Derek, this is not a vampire kill,' I reprimanded Gwen's friend angrily once we were alone.

'But—'

'Or a werewolf's,' I added.

'I know, Miguel, but you should—'

'There is nothing here but humans,' I interrupted

again.

'Stop talking!' he commanded in frustration, taking us both by surprise. I glared at him and, looking a little nervous, he cleared his throat awkwardly. 'Come on,' he insisted.

I resented that he felt comfortable enough to become angry with me, but I followed reluctantly. The last time Derek had insisted I accompany him had been for good reason. Despite my irritation with his tactics, I was grudgingly prepared to respect his professional opinion.

He lifted the yellow tape, and we walked down the alleyway into a parking lot with two abandoned cars amidst the garbage. PSA agents, and a horde of forensic personnel in plastic suits, surrounded the vehicles. Based on the looks on some of their faces, I estimated that whatever lay between the two cars was positively grisly.

'Look out,' Derek shouted at them, and they looked at him with a familiar irritation I could relate to. Then they recognized me behind him, and they scattered to the sidelines with their heads together whispering. I could hear their disbelief that Derek had brought me to another investigation. I got the impression he'd gotten in trouble for it last time.

Derek halted immediately upon rounding the end of one car, and I saw his face drain of colour. I shouldered him out of the way and finally understood why he'd called me.

Between the two vehicles was a mess of gore and body parts, which loosely resembled an adult male. There was blood splattered on both cars and a large stain on the ground. I could see someone, or something, had attempted to lick it up. There were multiple bloody handprints on the dented car doors that disqualified it as an animal attack.

I had only ever seen this kind of thing once in my life. Now, with the covens on the verge of war with humans, it boded particularly ill.

'*Sanguinem furoris,*' I said with certainty.

'What's that?' Derek asked. His disgusted voice was muffled in his jacket collar, which he'd pulled up over his nose to ward of the pungent scent of human entrails.

'What are you doing, Agent Wells?' demanded someone, and I glanced aside to see his captain. I immediately recognized him as the man who'd given us a hard time previously and nearly gotten me killed.

'Sir, my friend thinks he knows what—'

'We were not asked to consult our liaisons on this one, Wells. Besides, you know that's Benet's job!' the captain interrupted.

I smirked at the thought of Benet requesting my presence in the field. The captain, who didn't know who I was, glanced at me, but he wasn't brave enough to challenge me directly. He glared again at Derek.

'You can't just bring any vampire onto a crime scene,' he growled. 'You should know better!'

'He's not just any vampire—'

'He's not cleared!' the captain reiterated.

'I have a higher clearance than the two of you put together, I assure you,' I interceded calmly after tiring of their banter. 'That is not important right now. *This,* however, is what you might call a very serious problem,' I admitted, trying to draw their attention back to the situation. The captain continued to glower.

'Who the hell do you think you are?' he asked me.

Derek stepped between us and leaned closer to his captain before I could respond angrily. I heard him whisper I was the Ambassador and I was "kinda... sorta... dating" his friend.

The captain looked shocked and then skeptical of this as he appraised me doubtfully over Derek's shoulder. I returned my attention to the scene before us.

'Humans who consume vampire blood do so under the illusion it will make them immortal,' I began. I saw both of their faces twist with shock at the direction I was going in.

'I take it that is not what it does,' Derek prompted.

'What it actually does is kill them very slowly. We call it "blood madness" because, as their brains deteriorate, the afflicted begin to crave blood and flesh. They tend to nest together in packs,' I said, and I turned my attention to the abandoned buildings around us. It was a prime habitat for the creatures.

Derek looked disturbed by what I was saying but his features hardened stubbornly as he prepared to deal reasonably with the situation.

'How do we kill them?' he wanted to know.

'The usual way you would kill humans, but they will be stronger and faster,' I admitted.

'Why would a vampire make them?' the captain demanded.

'It is illegal to infect humans, but rogue vampires, with nothing to lose, may fancy themselves the leader of the pack.'

Of course, there was a good chance humans had created the monsters using vampire blood, but I didn't bring that up. I didn't want to inadvertently plant seeds of inspiration.

Both humans were quiet as they considered what I had revealed. After a moment, Derek looked hopeful.

'Can you help us find them?' he asked, and I hesitated in consideration of a partnership with him. If this were humans experimenting with blood madness, it was likely connected to the reports Hudson had given me. I didn't want Derek anywhere near that. Not only could it expose my people to dangerous intentions from the PSA, but it could also get Derek killed. I knew Gwen would hate that.

I heard Hudson drop lightly from the rooftop behind the humans in anticipation of me. Neither of them heard his approach.

'Yes,' I finally answered, 'but I will need help. There is no way to know how many of them there are.'

'Help from us?' Derek asked in confusion.

'I assume he is referring to me,' said Hudson, and both

humans whirled in surprise.

'Hudson, Derek. Derek, Hudson.' I introduced them quickly.

'This was not part of the deal,' Hudson growled at me in Latin, and I shrugged smugly.

'You're the one who agreed to babysit,' I responded without hesitation, and he sighed reluctantly.

'Where do you wish to start, my lord?' he asked in English and with just the hint of sarcasm.

'Near,' I answered, glancing around at the dark windows of the abandoned buildings. 'They don't like the sunlight, so they will not wander far from their nest. It will give us the advantage.'

'Wait just a minute!' the captain interrupted with frustration. 'This is a PSA investigation. You can't just walk in here and start calling the shots,' he complained.

I saw one of Hudson's brows lift ever so slightly and his unnaturally blue eyes met mine questioningly.

'Cover me,' I directed, and Hudson nodded. He jumped back up the wall, and by the time the humans had turned back toward him, he was gone.

I ignored the captain's furious promises to call his superiors and walked toward the other side of the parking lot. Derek fell into step beside me.

'Your friend's eyes—'

'Don't mention it,' I warned him seriously. Hudson was extremely sensitive about his mutation, and bringing it up to him was a good way to get killed.

'Okay, noted,' Derek acknowledged grudgingly. 'So, what's the plan, Miguel?'

'The plan,' I said abruptly, stopping to glare at him 'is for you not to get killed. Got that?'

He appeared shocked at first, as though confused where my newfound compassion was coming from. Then he seemed to understand.

'That need to protect her will only increase,' he promised enigmatically. I frowned forbiddingly at him, but he seemed ashamed enough of his impulsive response

that I didn't bother to berate him further for it. 'I'm sorry.
Just let me help you!' he insisted.

'You want to help? Stay back, and get the biggest gun
you can find' I suggested before resuming my path
toward the abandoned buildings. Thankfully, I heard him
go to do as I said this time.

I reached the end of the parking lot and began to
consider the windows above me with some thought. I
quickly noticed one of them, on the third floor, was
broken and covered in dirty cardboard.

I leaped up, catching the edge of the sill thirty feet
above, and I breathed in the scent from inside. It was the
entrance to their nest; I was sure of it.

'You had to accept the invitation to help, didn't you?'
accused Hudson from ten feet above me on the roof.

Ignoring him, I glanced down to see Derek had parked
a black Dodge Charger horizontal to us about fifty feet
from the base of the building. There was another agent in
the passenger seat with him, and they were both holding
enormous rifles.

'He is Gwen's friend, Hudson. He does not die today,'
I cautioned him, and Hudson sighed half-heartedly.

'What about the rest of them?' he asked with
resignation.

'I don't give a shit about them,' I answered promptly
as Derek gave me the thumbs up from below.

I turned and pulled the cardboard down from the
window before climbing inside. Hudson swung down
after me.

The building smelled strongly of mould, wood, and
dust, but there were also trace scents of blood, human
filth, and sickness. The floorboards creaked threateningly
under our feet as we moved cautiously through the dark
room. All the windows were boarded up except the one
through which we'd come. The single shaft of light
caught dust glittering through the air, and I could see
tattered, bloodstained mattresses in the corner. There were
human bones, strewn about the floor, which had been

vigorously gnawed on. Nearer the back, I saw holes in the floor which were quite worn around the edges, and I knew the creatures had been living here for some time.

'Beneath us,' guessed Hudson softly, and I nodded.

'They know we're here,' I promised him.

Suddenly, the entire floor began to shudder with impact, and the silence was shattered by shrieks of outrage. Ragged, bloody humanoids erupted from the holes in the floor and from the rafters of the ceiling. Their faces were ashen and moist with sweat. Their yellowed eyes were dazed with fever and splotchy with broken blood vessels from violent vomiting. Their teeth were broken from gnawing on bone and were falling out of their blackened, bleeding gums. Most of them had lost their hair or had clumps of it coming out in patches all over their heads. They all had broken limbs or infected wounds because they could no longer feel pain. Though the vampire blood had made them strong enough to jump from a building, their human bodies remained fragile.

Hudson grabbed the first one to reach us, and he quickly twisted her head off her shoulders.

'Too many!' he shouted over the horrible chorus of screeching.

I grabbed the next man, revulsion coursing through me at the sight of his gaping, bleeding mouth and wide, bloodshot eyes. I crushed his skull between my palms and wiped the gore off my hands on his shirt with deep aversion.

'Agreed,' I responded. 'Let's take this outside so Derek can finish them off.'

We darted to the opening where Hudson went up, and I went down. The guns started going off, and I looked up to see the infected littering the ground with bullets riddling their corpses. Hudson and I quickly picked off any that were either still alive or which managed to escape the window unscathed. Fifteen minutes later, there were almost fifty dead bodies in the parking lot.

I saw a female crawling along the ground with

shaking arms. Her legs had been shot to hell, but she was still trying to reach the body of a male lying close to her. I'd seen them eat each other before so, disgusted, I stepped on her foot to prevent further cannibalism. I was shocked when she gave a cry of desperation, which sounded suspiciously genuine. I looked toward the man I had thought was dead, and I saw his hand outstretched toward her.

A sense of dread consumed me as he died, and the woman at my feet gave a hollow howl. Her filthy frame began to shake as she cried.

Derek had put his gun in the car, and I could hear him approaching. I didn't want his sensibilities to hinder me, so I acted quickly in flipping the woman over onto her back. She met my eyes in surprise, which quickly melted into hatred.

'Let me go!' she screeched and struggled uselessly.

'Who created you?' I questioned her, and she spat in my direction. Luckily, she missed me with her bloody spittle. 'Who created you?' I demanded more insistently, and I gave her thin arms a shake.

'Fuck you, leech,' she snarled loathingly, and my patience evaporated. I stood, detesting that smug expression on her ugly face, and I smirked at her.

'You don't think I can make you feel pain,' I guessed, and I walked by her. Her eyes widened in realization when I approached the body of the man lying near to her.

'What are you doing?' she hissed nervously.

'Who created you?' I asked again, and I put my foot over the dead man's skull. She looked up at me, and I could see the madness blooming in her eyes.

'*Don't!*' she screamed.

'Who created you?' I snarled, my voice shaking with the force of my frustration.

'I don't know! They said we'd live forever!' she bawled.

'Were they vampires or humans?' I pressed, and she shook her head desperately.

'I can't—'

Using just a bit of force, I put pressure on the skull beneath my foot. It made a creaking sound, which had her suddenly screaming in horror.

'Human!' she screeched, and I took my foot away from the body on the ground. I walked back to where she was laying, her violent sobs shaking her skeletal frame, and I did the merciful thing. I snapped her neck.

I rose and looked up to meet Derek's wide eyes. I could sense so many emotions in the air it was difficult to know how he felt about what he'd just seen.

'Those infected with blood madness are not curable,' I tried to explicate. 'She was dying a very slow and painful death.'

I was uncertain why I felt the need to explain myself to him or to erase that accusing expression on his face. I was even more troubled when his nod of understanding succeeded in easing my guilt.

'I know,' he assured me reluctantly. 'Remind me not to piss you off,' he added, and I knew he was trying to lighten the mood. I chose to embrace it.

'You should already know that,' I reprimanded him as Hudson joined us.

'It's been a while,' my friend commented. There was a familiar excitement in his strange eyes that had brightened to an alarming white-blue. 'The truce between the covens has made things boring.'

'You enjoy fighting?' Derek asked with disbelief.

'Hudson is Roman,' I clarified dismissively.

'Etruscan,' Hudson inserted sharply, and his good mood ended abruptly. He knew I knew better than to call him a Roman.

Derek looked both incredulous and awed as he realized how old my friend was.

Gwendolyn

Chapter Eighteen

Work was brutal when all Gwen could think about was the night she'd spent with Miguel. She couldn't help recalling the sensation of him against her and his soft lips on her skin. The memory of the expression in his erotic eyes had been distracting her all day.

She grew increasingly anxious that he hadn't offered her a means of communication although she knew Charlotte was right. He didn't seem like the texting type. It still would have been nice to let him know she was thinking about him, though. The nagging suspicion he hadn't given her his cell because he didn't intend to see her again scared her.

Then he walked through the door five minutes before she was finished work, and she had to bite her lip to keep the grin off her face.

After removing her apron, Gwen got the bag Sandra had left her and signed out. When she got back to the front, Miguel was waiting near the door.

'I missed you,' he greeted her and immediately pulled her near enough to kiss her before she could respond. She was craving him again and desperately wanted to deepen the kiss, but she managed not to do that in public.

'I missed you too,' she promised him when their lips parted. He seemed happy to hear it as he wrapped an arm around her to steer her toward the door.

'Come for dinner with me,' he bade once they were outside, and she laughed, secretly thrilled by his demand.

'Miguel!' she protested. 'I *have* to go home and change. I need to shower,' she insisted.

'I'll walk you,' he offered.

'Why don't I meet you somewhere?' she proposed, but he seemed to have seen through her. He looked suspicious.

'Do you still not trust me?' he asked, and she sighed.

'It's not that! I guess I just don't want you to see where I live. It's... awful,' she explained. Miguel looked surprised by this.

'You think I care about that?' he asked in confusion.

'Most people do,' insisted Gwen defensively.

'Gwen, I told you I was born on the street, remember?' Miguel reminded her gently. 'I hardly think your apartment will frighten me away. Besides, despite what you might think, the things I value most are not materialistic. You are one of them,' he assured her with such sincerity she felt ridiculous for worrying otherwise.

'Yah, of course,' she acknowledged.

They arrived at her building and rode to the second floor in the smelly elevator. She kept her eyes away from Miguel as they walked by what sounded like a domestic on their way to her door. She unlocked it and jerked the door up on its hinges to step inside.

'*Where* have you been?' her roommate demanded immediately, taking Gwen by surprise. Sandra hit pause on the TV remote and rose from the couch.

Melisandre Moore was a slender woman of impressive height with a tattoo sleeve on her right arm. Her short, white-blonde hair was longer on one side and frequently subjected to colourful dye. There was a smudge of blue pastel on one cheekbone, and Gwen saw an easel in the corner with the unfinished piece on it.

The girls had met years ago at an indoor art show Sandra had been showing at in Garden Park. It had been immediately clear that it wasn't just Sandra's ripped jeans, purple hair, and band shirt setting her apart. Her artistic style and technique were unique, and Charlotte had invited her out for a drink with them after the show. They'd all been friends ever since.

Mr. Moore was a serious man and an English professor at the University of Toronto. Like Gwen's father, he was stern and had high expectations for his daughter's future, which were not congruent with what she'd envisioned for herself. Gwen had conformed, but Sandra had refused, and her father had effectively cut her off.

'All I get this morning is a vague text begging me to drop off some stuff for you and *no* explanation as to why you never came home last night! Not like you,' Sandra berated her.

Gwen opened her mouth to explain herself, but Miguel stepped through the door behind her. Sandra's attention was immediately distracted.

'You can blame me for her absence last night,' he informed her roomie. Gwen was embarrassed as she noted Sandra's gaze becoming wild with disbelief. Her stance shifted from confrontational to loose, and her hands slowly slid from her hips. Her gaze was drifting in confusion back and forth between them.

'This is my roommate, Melisandre. Sandra, this is my friend, Miguel,' Gwen introduced them. Sandra seemed to remember herself, and she came forward quickly to shake Miguel's hand.

'*Pleased,*' she assured him with enthusiasm. 'It's not often *I'm* the one worrying about *her.*'

'Yah,' Gwen reminded her subtly, but Sandra looked only mildly apologetic.

'Well, Gwen, just so you know, your little homeless ball of joy pissed in the bathroom. He scratched me when I tried to put him outside and attacked me when I kicked him off the couch.'

'Tabby is a girl,' Gwen reprimanded Sandra. 'Where is she?'

'Guarding your bed like the House of Bastet,' Sandra responded sarcastically. Gwen looked at her curiously.

'I don't know what that means!' she exclaimed.

'Temple of the ancient Egyptian goddess of cats,' Miguel supplied helpfully. Sandra looked at him with new appreciation.

'Not just a pretty face. I like it,' she told Gwen.

'Okay!' Gwen intervened, and she took Miguel's arm to drag him toward her bedroom. As promised, the cat was lying on her comforter in utter contentment and started to purr when she saw Gwen.

'I guess that makes you Bastet,' Miguel teased her.

'Lovely. You know, most women detest any label associated with cats!' Gwen protested. She began to go through her closet for clothing while Miguel stood silently behind her.

'These are stunning,' he said softly, and she glanced back to see he was gazing up at all the paintings on her walls.

'Thanks. I haven't painted in a while. Since before school, I guess,' she admitted.

'You should start,' he advised her, but she said nothing as she returned to her closet. After several moments, Miguel sat next to the cat on the bed. She continued to purr as he stroked her.

'Cats are fierce, independent hunters that do not require anything from anyone. They thoroughly enjoy all the simplicities of life,' Miguel said fondly. 'Why should that be an undesirable association?'

It took Gwen a moment to realize he'd returned to her earlier comment about cat lady labels.

'It's lonely,' Gwen explained reluctantly. 'Usually, women who have failed miserably in their love life have a million cats.'

Miguel grunted in dissatisfaction, as if that made little sense to him, and she was confused he seemed unfamiliar with the stereotype.

'Are we going anywhere tonight?' she asked.

'Let's eat in,' he proposed, looking up to meet her eyes.

'So I can wear jeans?' Gwen verified, and he laughed.

'Yes, and bring a change of clothing for tomorrow,' he recommended significantly. She grinned knowingly.

'I have tomorrow off,' she recalled aloud as she pulled her overnight bag out of her closet. 'I won't have to rush out like this afternoon.'

'Perhaps you should bring more than one change of clothes. You're going to Trolley's Accounting on Monday morning,' he reminded her, and her eyes widened with realization. She couldn't believe she'd forgotten in all the excitement of the night before.

'Um... do you think we could actually exchange numbers?' she asked hesitantly. 'So we can keep in contact' she clarified. Miguel looked concerned by the tone of strain she'd tried really hard to keep out of her voice.

'Is something wrong?' he asked.

'No! It would just be nice to talk to you during the day,' she professed. She kept her eyes on the bag.

'I won't lie. I don't do this texting thing,' he informed her.

'That's okay!' she insisted, feeling ridiculous. She only became more uncomfortable as he continued to stare at her. Finally, he got up and walked around the bed to pull her into his arms.

'I'd be happy to make an exception for you,' he assured her. 'You will need to be patient with me,' he admitted, and she nodded in relief.

She'd been longing for him all day, and when he kissed her, he felt as incredible as he had that morning. Before she knew it, she was on the bed beneath him, and his hands were under her shirt. She couldn't help arching up against him in wordless invitation.

The cat growled when they came too near her, and Gwen laughed, having forgotten about their audience.

'Sorry, Tabby,' she giggled as Miguel reluctantly let

her up. 'Guess I'll go have a shower.'

'No,' Miguel groaned. 'You should wait until we get back to my place. I have a custom shower that's big enough for both of us.'

Gwen had never showered with another person, but she knew couples did it all the time. She wondered if it was going to be awkward the first time.

Once she was ready, Miguel took her bag, and they walked to the front door. She told Sandra she was leaving for the night.

'Wait! What about the cat?' Sandra demanded as she sat up on the couch again.

'Leave her in my room. There's food and water in there for her, and the window is open so she can get outside,' Gwen recommended. It wasn't like she paid the utilities. Fuck the lazy landlord.

The half hour walk to Yorkville was brisk and refreshing. When she asked him what he'd been up to while she was at work, Miguel shrugged nonchalantly.

'I have my own work,' he said enigmatically. Gwen felt skeptical, but she decided not to push him yet.

They reached the Royal Alton where Carlton greeted them cheerily. He had exchanged his red jacket for a heavy red coat and black mittens as the cold weather began to set in.

They got up to the suite, and Gwen saw immediately the *La Dame en Rouge* painting was gone from the living room.

'Did you hang it?' she asked excitedly, barely allowing Miguel to take her coat, before she walked toward the bedroom. Sure enough, the painting was across from the bed. It was the only one in the room, and it seemed like the perfect place for it.

'You approve?' he teased her, and she nodded quickly as he set her bag down on the floor. He came up behind her, and the heat of his body made her melt into the strength of his chest. His arms wrapped around her as he kissed her neck and shoulder.

'Come on,' he urged, and he pulled her toward the open door of the ensuite. She had been in to use the toilet, near to the door, but around the corner she saw an enormous, walk-in stone shower.

Miguel reached to her waist from behind, and she let him peel her blouse over her head. He unhooked her bra, and she turned toward him as he pulled the straps down her shoulders. It came away from her and was tossed into the corner with her shirt.

Gwen groaned when he took one breast in the palm of his hand before leaning down to kiss her. His tongue stroked hers in time with his thumb circling her nipple.

Gwen reached up to unbutton his shirt so she could feel his bare chest against hers. He obliged her in stripping it off and dropping it to the floor. Gwen's hands eagerly found the familiar contours of his stomach and back. The man was seriously gorgeous and touching him was captivating.

He pressed her backwards against the cold glass of the shower. The sensation of his heat contrasting with the cold bite of the unyielding glass was deeply arousing.

Miguel stepped back, quickly unbuckling his pants, and he reached up toward a touchscreen on the wall. He tapped it, and the shower came on along with the bathroom fan.

He returned to her and smiled at the hunger in her eyes as her gaze swept over his chest. She quickly finished unfastening his jeans so she could wrap her hand around his erection. Miguel grunted, and the low sound became a growl of pleasure as she stroked him hard.

She felt his body become very tense, and she could once again sense the wild thing beneath the gentlemanly exterior. It was what intrigued and frightened her most about him, and she still wasn't content she'd fully exposed that part of him yet.

Miguel's stubble scraped against her cheek as he lowered his lips to her neck, and something within her wanted more. Some part of her longed for him to abandon the facade and unmask whatever true savagery thrived inside him. It was such a strange and frightening desire, but its potency was undeniable.

The room was filling with hot steam from the shower running behind her, yet the glass at her back was still freezing cold. The mist clinging to their bodies made them damp and hot.

Miguel pushed her pants down her thighs, and he put his shoulder against her to force her more fully against the cold glass. Her feet slid willingly apart so he could touch the throbbing folds of her body with a familiar confidence. Her head sank against his shoulder as she succumbed after a moment, and she cried out as the wave of intensity crashed through her.

She heard his low chuckle that betrayed how much he enjoyed her submission.

'You're perfect,' he said into her hair before abruptly lifting her up. Gwen gasped, instinctively wrapping her legs around him, and he carried her into the shower. She felt as though she should have been at least a little self-conscious of her weight, but his strength was reassuring.

Warm water soaked them immediately from multiple showerheads as Miguel pinned her to the warm stone. He gradually lowered her hips against him until he'd impaled her on his cock.

Gwen gasped at the forceful thrill of him sliding into her. She even stretched backwards against the wall in an effort to take him as deep as physically possible. They groaned deeply in unison again and smiled at each other knowingly.

'I can't get over how unbelievable that feels,' she sighed.

'I hope we never do,' Miguel responded huskily before kissing her hungrily. He began to pump his hips up against her while suspending her weight with just his arms. Gwen was initially astounded by the feat of strength, but she quickly forgot about it as he continued to drive into her.

She screamed and writhed helplessly when she climaxed, but he held her safe. He increased the power of his thrusts until he was crying out with her and then lowered his head against her chest. His breath felt strangely cool on her skin in the hot mist of the shower.

He groaned deeply with some frustration.

'I will never get enough of you,' he whispered just loud enough for her to hear over the spray of the shower.

She giggled as he reluctantly let her down so she could stretch her legs. She could feel the warmth of his semen running down her thighs, so she stepped into the spray of the water to rinse herself. She decided she liked shower sex. It wasn't as messy.

After a moment, she felt the gentle scrub of a soapy cloth against her back, and she moaned appreciatively.

'You're amazing,' she laughed as he lathered her.

'The shower is not just for sex, Gwen,' he said with teasing chastisement.

They took turns scrubbing each other down, and then Miguel left her alone so she could attend to herself with some privacy. When she got out, there was a warmed towel waiting for her. Having rubbed it through her hair, she wrapped it around herself and went into the bedroom.

Miguel had just gotten into a pair of jeans, and there was a shirt in his hand. He dropped it on the leather wingback chair beside him when he saw her.

She watched his gaze sweep from her exposed thighs to her cleavage, her bare shoulders, and up to her eyes. The renewed hunger in him seized her again with longing. The power of the feeling was implausible considering they'd *just* had sex.

A slow smile crossed his face as he stalked toward her.

Miguel

Chapter Nineteen

The sight of her damp and naked, under nothing but a towel, returned me to that state of near desperation. In spite of having been sated not long before, I was hard and ready for her. There were no words to explain, but I needed her all over me, and I wanted my scent all over her. The thought that she meant to wash away all traces of my claim to her had been unbearable. Now she smelled of soap and cream, there was nothing else to do but ensure there could be no mistake about her.

She was *mine*.

I crossed the room, and my eyeteeth lengthened even before I'd touched her. When I reached her, it was all I could do to prevent myself from slinging her across the bed and biting her. Charlotte had said that, for the Dowrra, bloodlust became part of the erotic experience. I just hadn't anticipated Gwen becoming victim to it in a way similar to myself. Obviously, she had no idea what her strange desires meant, but I could sense the budding violence within her. The Dowrra, like their vampire lovers, were meant to experience a kind of passion unknown to humans. I just couldn't show it to her yet.

She seized me and allowed the towel to slide to the ground as she went to her toes to meet my kiss. Her skin was cool from the dampness of the water still clinging to her, and her red hair was dark and wet in my hands.

Gwen pulled hastily at my belt with eagerness rivalling my own impatience to be inside her again. I helped her by twisting the belt, and luckily, she didn't see it rip in half.

Once both of us were naked, I was about to pick her up and throw her onto the bed, but she shoved me first. I was surprised when she succeeded in making me stumble back a step. My knees hit the bed, and I sank down onto the mattress.

I'd been impressed with the resilience surfacing in her since the force of my hands on her should have bruised her by now. The power behind some thrusts had been enough to break her spine, but she'd bucked against me and urged me harder and faster.

I still couldn't hide my shock when she mustered enough effort against me to actually push me backwards. She didn't know I was strong enough to bring down a building with my bare hands, so she misunderstood and laughed. She looked rather proud as she crawled into my lap with her legs wrapped around me.

'Don't look so surprised! You wanted me to be bold,' she chastised me, and I quickly took control of my expression.

'I certainly did,' I said and pulled her against me for a rough kiss.

She was already wet and ready for me, which only heightened my insane need to be in her. Usually, I would have enjoyed teasing and tasting her, but it seemed imperative I claim her quickly. It was such a primitive and instinctual sense I didn't bother to question it.

I lifted her, and she giggled as I carried her up the bed on my knees. I set her down, turning her so her back was to me, and I bowed her forward onto her hands. She complied without hesitation and arched her hips for me. The sight of her bent over, with her ass in the air and her sweet depths exposed, was almost too much. I ran my hand up the inside of her thigh until my fingers found the slick heat of her sex. Each stroke ended carefully nudging her already swollen clit, and she groaned as her head lowered into the sheets. Her hips moved against me in encouragement.

'Is this okay?' I asked, feeling breathless with the anticipation when she nodded quickly. All shame and modesty seemed to have left her, and I loved it more than anything.

I knelt behind her and guided myself against her.

'*Oh, yes,*' she breathed as I pressed inside. I echoed her sentiment with a groan.

Sheathed deep, I reached forward under her belly so I could stroke her clit in time with my thrusts. Soon, she was thrusting back, and it was all I could do to focus on pushing her toward climax before succumbing myself. Once she was nearly there, I gave her what she was dying for.

A darker part of me was curious to see just what my Dowrra lover could handle.

I took her hips in both hands, and the front of my thighs forced hers wider apart as I began to strengthen and quicken my thrusts. Her encouraging groans fuelled my frenzy until she was sobbing and writhing in enthrallment to an imminent orgasm. Once again, I was grinding into her with enough strength to have snapped a human spine. She climaxed, and she screamed my name for the first time. Her voice was strained with ecstasy, and it pierced me with an alien sentiment to hear my name on her lips.

'Scream for me, Gwen,' I growled as my body threatened to succumb with her. The sound of her cries, along with the sensation of her orgasm, was overwhelming. I released more powerfully than ever, and it was very nearly painful.

I bent over her with my forehead resting against her damp back while I caught my breath. She groaned as her sex continued to clench me.

'Please don't move yet,' she breathed, and I grunted in agreement. I waited until the quiver of ecstasy was done before I pulled away from her.

'My bag,' she said softly, and I responded without

question. She fished inside the overnight bag she'd packed for damp napkins.

Once she was clean, she collapsed down against my chest, and we lay contentedly with our damp skin sticking together. Her wet hair was cool against my shoulder.

Derek had been right. The bond between us was only strengthening with time. The idea of leaving Gwen behind seemed impossible now.

Thinking of the human and his Dowrra wife led me to wondering how a human man would ever satisfy a Dowrra. Gwen's budding appetite and strength were so voracious I couldn't imagine it.

'I love that,' Gwen whispered, and I noticed that my hand had begun to trace unconsciously along her spine. I kissed her forehead just as her stomach growled so quietly not even she heard it.

'We should order some food,' I suggested, and she looked appreciative when she sat up to kiss me. It was just on the verge of deepening before she pulled away and slid off the bed. I rolled over onto my side to watch the grace of her swaying hips as she walked into the bathroom where her clothing was.

We both got dressed, and I went to the living room to order the Chinese food she'd requested. I knew very little about human food, so I ordered two of everything she'd asked for. Ainsley set up the dining table with candles and roses, so all I had to do was put the food on plates. By the time Gwen had finished brushing and drying her hair, there was a romantic dinner waiting for her.

I held her chair for her as she sat down. I could feel her eyes on me as I took my seat at the head of the table with her on my left.

'Thank you,' she said, and I squeezed her hand with a smile. Then I turned my attention toward mentally preparing myself to eat the noodles and chicken in front of me. It didn't smell or look appetizing in the least.

'So, you really think I can do this job at Trolley Accounting?' she asked me anxiously.

'Absolutely,' I responded without hesitation.

'I didn't even give notice at The Diner. My boss is going to kill me,' she muttered guiltily. She began to rub her temple with one hand while swirling her wine around the glass in her other.

'It's charming you care about someone who treated you so unfairly,' I told her ironically. I remembered more than a few rants about The Diner owner. 'You owe him nothing.'

'He gave me a job when no one else in this city would,' Gwen pointed out reluctantly.

'A minimum wage job, which he will fill in a week,' I dismissed. 'I wouldn't miss this opportunity for something you obviously hate doing.'

She nodded thoughtfully although I could see the idea of leaving her boss high and dry was still not something she relished. I hoped her ability to forgive would prove versatile.

'You're right,' she decided, and she lifted her glass determinedly toward me. 'To new beginnings,' she proposed, and I gladly tapped my glass against hers.

'To new beginnings,' I agreed.

We spent the night discussing her new job between bouts of lovemaking and episodes of a few of her favourite TV shows. It was past midnight, and Ainsley had retired, so we lay naked and tangled in a blanket on the floor in front of the hearth. The bottle of wine and our empty glasses were sitting on the coffee table, and we'd turned off the TV.

'You're too good to be true,' Gwen breathed with her head resting on her forearms. I tugged the blanket down on her back so I could kiss her shoulder. Goose bumps rose across her skin under my mouth and fingertips.

I could tell she was tipsy, and she was being a little more honest than usual. There was a suspicious hitch in her voice.

'I'm not going to disappear in a puff of smoke,' I teased.

'I hope not,' she whispered as her eyes closed drowsily. I rolled her over beneath me, and the blanket tented around her over my shoulders. She watched raptly as I kissed each hand gently.

'Not. Going. Anywhere.'

She smiled finally, and I leaned down to kiss her. I could feel a great surge of emotion within her, and I wondered if I had enough energy for one more bout before bed. I could tell something was still nagging at her when her lips parted distractedly from mine.

'What is this, then?' she whispered reluctantly, and I sensed it irked her to make herself so vulnerable.

'Do you mean this relationship?' I verified, and when she nodded, I kissed her hand again. 'I want as much of you as you will give. Whatever that means for you,' I told her.

'Like... a boyfriend?' she hedged in determination to hammer out the label. The concept seemed ridiculous to me, but I conceded, which seemed to make her happy. It was the first time in my incredibly long life that I had made any semblance of a commitment to any one woman.

When we made love again, it was poignant and filled with a vast amount of unfamiliar emotion. When she uttered my name for the second time, it went right through me. She fell asleep in my arms on the floor afterwards, so I picked her up and carried her to bed. I tucked her in and smiled as she wiggled into the covers to get more comfortable.

A dim light caught my attention on the bedside table, and I saw my father had tried to call me. All joy evaporated.

He would have heard that I'd evacuated all Wayside vampires and strongly recommended all nonhumans leave the city too. He would want to know why I'd not consulted him or the Tribunal. He'd want to know what circumstances had suddenly changed and when I was coming home.

I looked back at Gwen and sighed, releasing all the

tension as I climbed into bed with her.

I'd deal with him and our situation in the morning.

x x x

Gwendolyn

Gwen woke to the naked sensation of Miguel wrapped around her, and her heart ached at the memory of him the night before. She turned toward him to kiss his cheek and chin, and he squinted down at her before smiling.

'Morning,' he said sleepily.

'Morning,' she responded as she snuggled into his chest. When he put his arms around her, nothing had ever felt more right.

They ordered breakfast and went for a walk. It was a little chilly for mid-October, so Gwen was wearing one of his leather jackets with the sleeves pulled down over her hands. The city was beautiful with just a bit of frost on the trees that winked red in the morning sky. Her breath hung on the air in front of her although Miguel didn't seem cold at all. The streets were relatively quiet because it was Sunday.

Gwen hadn't noticed the direction they'd been walking until she suddenly recognized the Trolley building ahead of them. She turned to look up at Miguel. When he smiled knowingly, she knew he'd taken her that way on purpose.

'What do you think?' he asked, and she grinned at him.

'I think you're amazing,' she answered, and she leaned up to kiss him. He wrapped her up in his arms, and it almost felt like the world fell away around them so they were the only two in it. He stepped back with a laugh just before it was about to get too heated.

'You're going to make me undress you in front of your future place of employment,' he informed her teasingly, and she laughed. She was about to tell him she didn't mind when a limo pulled up to the sidewalk. Gwen's smile faded when the back window began to roll down.

'What could you possibly be doing in front of Trolley's new building?' mused a nasally voice from inside. She knew who it was before Jonathon Welford leaned forward.

His nose and the wells under his eyes were purple. He looked like he'd been hit by a bus, and he became strangely anxious when she failed to respond to him.

'Don't think you'll ever get in there,' he advised her sneeringly. 'After I talk to Trolley, she won't hire you as a janitor.'

Feeling a little smug, Gwen laughed at him.

'You're a little late,' she advised him. Her satisfaction was short-lived, and she regretted goading him even before Miguel stiffened defensively. Her dread only deepened when Jon's eyes widened with scathing hatred.

'You'll be sorry you ever crawled out from under the rock where we put you!' he promised her before the limo tires squealed. The car shot back into the road, and Gwen sighed.

'I don't want you coming alone on Monday,' said Miguel firmly, and she looked up at him in surprise. The carefree expression he'd been wearing all day was gone.

'He can't do anything to me now,' Gwen dismissed, but Miguel didn't seem to share her opinion.

'I don't trust him,' he insisted, but then he saw her look of concern, and he seemed to sober. 'We should celebrate. Why don't you invite Derek and Charlotte to come over for that hot tub?'

'You remembered,' she said in approval. She'd completely forgotten Charlotte's drunken demands.

'Charlotte Wells is not a woman I wish to disappoint,' Miguel pointed out, and Gwen nodded to agree with him.

Back at the hotel, Miguel told Ainsley of their plans for the night so he could make the appropriate arrangements for dinner. Gwen went ahead to the room to put away his jacket, but the sight of the rumpled bed made her hesitate and smile.

She knew something was coming over her with Miguel, and she could no longer account for the blind desire she felt for him. The truth was she wasn't looking forward to her friends intruding on their time. Thankfully, it turned out sharing their new relationship had its own kind of ecstasy.

'You're *glowing,*' Charlotte gushed happily when the women were alone in the bathroom putting on their bathing suits. Gwen smiled proudly.

'I'm happy,' she defended.

'I *know*!' Charlotte assured her.

They went out to the balcony where the men were enjoying cigars next to the open hot tub. Gwen could see Miguel's dark eyes on her as she folded her towel before climbing into the tub behind Charlotte. She tried not to let the sensation of his gaze distract her too much

The men joined them once they were finished their cigars. Miguel peeled his shirt off over his head, and Gwen smiled when she heard Charlotte's soft hiss of appreciation. She understood. It was wildly riveting to watch him strip.

'So, what's the news you had for us?' Derek asked Gwen.

'I may have a new job,' she advised them hesitantly.

'A new job?' exclaimed Charlotte excitedly.

'With Trolley Accounting,' Gwen revealed. 'Ms. Trolley wants to make me the executive assistant to her CFO. I start tomorrow.'

'That's incredible!' Charlotte shrieked in amazement.

'This is great, Gwen! This is what you deserve,' Derek congratulated her with a smile.

'*Oh*, just wait until Jon figures out who his new competition is,' giggled Charlotte with wicked delight.

'He already knows,' said Miguel, and Gwen could hear his voice deepening. 'I don't trust his next move.'

'Really, why?' asked Charlotte with concern. Gwen

glanced at Miguel guiltily when he made a sound of surprise.

'You didn't tell her,' he guessed, and she shook her head.

'Been a little preoccupied with all the things going great right now,' she assured him.

'What happened?' Derek asked worriedly.

'He was at the ball,' Gwen admitted. 'He tried to get me to leave, but Miguel stopped him. He, uh...'

'I punched him in the nose,' Miguel finished blatantly, and Charlotte whistled in admiration. She and Gwen shared a smile over Jon getting punched in the face.

'I don't blame you for not trusting him,' Derek told Miguel seriously. 'The guy's an egomaniac.'

'How did the conversation about my success turn into a discussion about Jonathon Welford?' Gwen demanded in disappointment.

'Gwen, this could be serious—' began Derek.

'I'm sorry,' Miguel cut in. Derek sighed in protest, but Charlotte looked enamoured of Miguel's sensitivity.

Gwen knew he was a good man, but it was nice her friend saw it too. She welcomed anything that helped her ignore the nagging voice that was suspicious about him.

After the hot tub, they changed and went into the games room. Gwen was as compelled by her partner as she'd been the first night they'd played pool. Watching his talented fingers dance across the piano keys was even more erotic now that she knew them more intimately.

This time she wasn't going home with a chaste kiss that haunted her all night. This time, she'd be crawling into his bed with him at the end of the night.

Miguel

Chapter Twenty

Derek had been looking for a private audience with me all night. He took the opportunity to corner me after the women went to the bathroom.

'What is it, Derek?' I hissed unwillingly. He looked incensed by my tone.

'You bail after having uncovered freakish monsters, with no explanation for them, and then wonder why *I'm* moody?' he responded sharply. 'This city is falling apart!'

'I told you I'd handle it,' I reminded him grumpily. I still hadn't called my father, and the man had as little patience as I did. He was going to be seething.

'She said they were made by humans,' Derek insisted seriously. 'How is that even possible?'

'Look, Derek, things are not good right now,' I finally relented. 'The covens are almost always on the verge of war with each other over how to handle the given situation. Now we are obviously about to be at war with humans too. You work for the PSA. Can you not understand why I might not trust you completely?' I demanded.

'Trust me?' Derek muttered with barely concealed offence. 'Miguel, I might work for the PSA, but I was born among the Dowrra. My mother, my wife, *and* Gwen are all Dowrra, and their protection will *always* be priority one. You don't think I'm aware of where they will fall on the PSA's radar if war breaks out?'

Reluctantly, I conceded his point.

'The timing of Dr. Anita Johansson's death was very suspicious. Humans killed her, but they attempted to make it look like a vampire attack. Then we got reports humans had been experimenting with blood madness. In our experience, this kind of testing often precedes attempts to overthrow us. The Church tried for centuries and often with terrible results,' I revealed. Derek looked stunned as he processed my words.

'So, this could be an old enemy resurfacing?' he pointed out thoughtfully. I was careful not to betray my fear of that exact thing. I didn't even want to think about a rebirth of the greatest foe my people had ever faced.

'We destroyed the Angeli Mortis a long time ago, but it *could* be a new enemy trying to recreate their work.'

'Well, Charlotte heard from the Dowrra Matrons. They won't awaken Quinn O'Connor,' Derek told me. 'They say he is too dangerous. He could threaten all humankind.'

'They care?' I asked in genuine surprise.

'They're not wrong. O'Connor could send us back to the Stone Age. *Again,*' he added pointedly. 'That's if he didn't wipe us out completely like he did the Indus Valley civilizations, the Olmec civilizations, the Mycenaeans, *and* the Atlanteans. Not to mention the Minoans, the Sumerians, the Etruscans, the Spartans, the Maya—'

'I see your point,' I interrupted him sarcastically.

'We can figure this out without resorting to awakening O'Connor,' he insisted. I felt compelled to nod despite my uncertainty. 'I will look into it discreetly and see if the PSA is involved at all,' Derek continued.

'Derek—'

'Then we can cross at least one potential enemy off a very long list,' he finished persistently. 'Besides, the Agency has a lot of resources. If the PSA could become an ally—'

'Humans have never sided against one another in favour of us, Derek,' I broke in bitterly.

'Then we eliminate one potential source for our

enemy,' Derek reiterated. Grudgingly, I agreed because ultimately, I knew the safety of the Dowrra needed to come first.

The women returned to the room, and neither of us said anything more about O'Connor or the PSA. By the end of the evening, I was eager to have my hands on Gwen. All the talk of imminent threats to her well-being was making me a little crazy.

'Finally,' I groaned once the elevator doors had closed. Gwen returned my kiss fervently, and I scooped her up to carry her to my room. Both of us had stripped before we even reached the mattress.

I picked her up to toss her onto the sheets, and she laughed. I meant to pin her under me, but she grabbed my shoulders and twisted me onto my back. She grinned at my expression of shock while eagerly straddling my legs. She knelt over me, and her mouth brushed down my stomach as I reached up helplessly to cup one of her full breasts. I revelled in the heaviness of it in my palm before she closed her lips around my cock, and then I lost my senses.

Groaning loudly, my hands fell to the mattress and twisted in the sheets. Her fingers stroked the base of my shaft in time with her tongue. It didn't take her long to get me close.

'You've got to stop,' I panted as I touched her hair. I saw her smile triumphantly as she rose over me again.

I tried to sit up, but she shoved me back down so she could straddle my hips. She guided the tip of me into her heat and sank down with one long stroke that made me gasp.

I'd never felt completely in the power of anyone else ever before, but I did at that moment. Instead of fighting her for dominance, the way I might have with another vampire, I found myself relinquishing myself.

Gwen drove me deep once more, but this time she was unable to help the groan as my thickness filled her to capacity again. She leaned back to get the most friction between us and then she began to ride me hard.

I wanted to sit up, but she kept me horizontal as she ruthlessly took what she needed from me. I'd never allowed a female to use me in such a way, and if she'd been anyone else, I probably would have hurt her. But watching her possess me, feeling myself succumbing to her, was freeing.

She came, and I sat up so I could continue thrusting into her and escalate her orgasm. I thought maybe she'd concede to me after that, but she didn't. Her fingers knotted in my hair, and she renewed her exertion over me while I was sitting up.

'Harder, Gwen,' I breathed pleadingly, and she happily complied until I succumbed loudly. She slumped against me, and it was some time before either of us could move. Then I wordlessly swung her into my arms and carried her to the shower.

X X X

Waking the next morning with Gwen nestled into my chest was easily the best thing I'd encountered during my long life. I just wished I could feel less helpless against her, but I already knew that was impossible.

I wanted nothing more than to be with her *fully* as both a man and a vampire and to show her the passion of bloodlust. I knew it was the reason for her aggression, but for the first time in my life, I was afraid to be insufficient. I was terrified she would walk away from me once she learned the truth.

Eventually, my fingers smoothing the red hair back from her forehead woke her. She nuzzled my bare chest with a contented kiss.

'Morning,' she whispered. Her hot breath tingled across my skin, and I knew it was time to feed before I became any cooler. She would know something was wrong.

'Good morning,' I responded, and I leaned down to kiss her cheek and jaw. She turned her head to capture my lips with hers, and I helplessly deepened the kiss.

'I have to go to work,' she mumbled in warning against my mouth. I smiled and nipped at her bottom lip.

'You kissed me first,' I defended, and she grinned before sliding away from me to get up.

I watched her longingly as my concerns returned, and I wondered how I'd *ever* explain to her. She was so gentle and soft. She would think I was a monster.

Gwen changed into her work clothing while my mind was distracted by these dark thoughts.

'You okay?' she asked, and I nodded quickly.

'Will I see you tonight?' I asked her.

'Sure! Maybe we could spend some time with Sandra? She's feeling neglected,' Gwen told me.

'Certainly,' I agreed.

It didn't take her long to get ready. I kissed her one last time before she left with Ainsley, who would drive her to Trolley's. She didn't know it, but he would be watching the building until she was finished. Derek had warned me that keeping it from Gwen would piss her off, but I was willing to risk that. With Jonathon Welford becoming increasingly threatening toward her, the alternative was unthinkable. Not only that, but I was becoming more paranoid about our as-of-yet unidentified enemy.

As soon as she was gone, I called my father, and he answered after just one ring. He sounded irate, as expected.

'I'm sorry,' I assured him immediately.

'Explain quickly,' he recommended.

'Hudson and I destroyed a nest of afflicted. One of the subjects told me they were created by other humans,' I described obligingly.

'*Sanguinem furoris,*' he acknowledged in concern.

'That's not all,' I admitted hesitantly. 'The subject betrayed... the remnants of emotional attachments.'

I had not even discussed this with Hudson or Derek yet because I was too afraid of the potential consequences. Even saying it out loud now felt like giving my fears more merit than I cared for, but this was serious. The addition of empath genes was the only way to stabilize a human host for vampire DNA. It was the only way to successfully recreate the Angels. The fact that the female infected had seemed even to recognize someone from her life meant the humans were close.

I received dreaded silence on the other end of the phone as my father realized this as well.

'You think someone means to recreate the Angeli Mortis?' he guessed reluctantly, and I closed my eyes.

'The empaths are too few,' I reasoned. 'They will never find enough of them.'

'You were still right to evacuate,' he assured me. 'The Summons is not until All Hallows' Eve, but I will clarify the situation to the others. They will ensure your evacuation is enforced.'

'What do you want me to do here?' I asked.

'I want you to come home,' my father commanded unconditionally. 'I want you to ensure our people are safe, and then I want you to come home.' I had absolutely no intentions of leaving Gwen behind so I said nothing. 'Call me when it's done,' he added, and he hung up. I dropped the phone on the bed, which was still messy from the night Gwen and I had spent in it.

I'd never seen one of the Angels the Iscariot humans had created to hunt down their vampire brethren. The war had ended hundreds of years before I was born, but I knew how close the Angels had come to eradicating my species. If humans had found the ancient recipe for creating their monsters, it could mean extinction for vampires this time.

Feeling irritated, I took to the streets to find prey. It is, unfortunately, far more difficult to hunt in the daylight, but I was seeing Gwen again that night. I slipped unnoticed into the shadows of the alleyways that were my primary stalking grounds. Like most of nature's predators, I often took the weak and the outcast.

On my way back to the hotel, it became apparent

someone was following me. I could feel their eyes on me.

I didn't indicate my awareness as I moved toward a rusted metal door in the wall of the building next to me. I pushed through the spray-painted entrance into an old building that smelled of mould and decay. I left the door slightly ajar and jumped silently up to the rafters, which barely creaked under my expert grip. I was even more agile than a cat as I moved to the wall where I melted into the shadows to wait.

Beneath me, the long line of sunlight splaying across the old floorboards darkened. I waited patiently as she edged slowly into the building. Her keen eyes flitted over the old machinery cautiously. She was as stunningly beautiful as any of our kind with a slender body that was deceptively powerful. She was wearing leather pants and a white blouse with her long black hair swinging against her lower back. She slid into the room like a shadow, and I could see her scenting the air. Once she'd moved directly beneath me, I dropped down silently behind her.

She tried to spin, but I'd already wrapped an arm around her and pinned both arms to her sides. Her back slammed against my chest, and she sent us careening into the wall behind. The bricks crumbled, and the wooden beam snapped, but I kept my hold on her to prevent her escape. I quickly pulled her legs out from under her, slamming her down against the floor, and I straddled her. I clasped her hands down at her sides so she couldn't strike me. She tried to buck me off, but I was older and stronger. After a moment she finally submitted, and her dark eyes rose to meet mine. She smiled coyly.

'I guess I'm not going anywhere,' she said softly. There was a sensual slur in her tone.

'Guess not. You didn't make it very difficult,' I chastised her, but it wasn't her fault. The fact she couldn't so much as free her wrists meant she was very young. I would have been surprised to know she was over fifty. 'Why are you here?'

'I know who you are,' she explained humbly. 'I caught

your scent up in Lawrence Heights.'

She moved slowly, still demonstrating submission, as she carefully slid her wrists out of my grasp. She stretched suggestively beneath me, and her hands glided up my thighs so her fingers could curl around my belt. I could see her black bra through her silk shirt as she lifted her breasts up toward me in invitation.

Vampiresses may not be fertile, but like every species, they do come into heat every so often. When they do, it can be the most intense experience of a man's life. It was usually considered a great honour to be sought out by a female during this time, but I was a coven prince. I was used to it.

'I'm sorry to disappoint, but I was not the oldest vampire in the area. Hudson was,' I reminded her impatiently. She looked offended by my insinuation.

'You think you were my second choice? You weren't!' she growled.

Normally, I probably wouldn't have cared to come second to Hudson, but I was feeling reluctant. Looking down into her hopeful face, I suddenly realized it was *Gwen*.

'Damn it,' I hissed, and I rose off her to put some space between myself and the female.

'Did I offend you?' she asked in confusion.

'Hudson will be happy to see you,' I assured her.

'But I wanted—'

'Go!' I commanded, and without another word, she shot up to slink dolefully into the shadows. 'What is happening to me?' I asked before I made my way home again.

Gwendolyn

Chapter Twenty-One

Gwen looked up as she left the office, and she saw Miguel standing on the sidewalk waiting for her. She made her way eagerly toward him.

'Hey,' she said, and he returned her kiss eagerly. It felt as though he were more impatient than usual to kiss her.

'How did it go?' he asked as she linked her arm with his. They began to walk toward the hotel.

'It went really well!' Gwen promised. 'Mostly, it was orientation. Ms. Trolley wanted to see what I remembered. I think she was impressed with me,' she said proudly. 'What did you do?'

'I caught up with some business,' he said, and he winked. 'Maybe some sleep too,' he admitted.

'No sex in my apartment tonight, by the way,' Gwen warned. 'The walls are *way* too thin, and Sandra would never forgive me.'

'Has she had sex while you were there?' Miguel countered, and Gwen hesitated. Her cheeks reddened tellingly. 'Then consider tonight an opportunity for revenge,' he suggested wickedly.

'You're bad!' she chastised teasingly, and she playfully slapped his shoulder.

'You have no idea,' he said lightly, but she suddenly had the strangest sense he meant it. She was immediately suspicious.

'Are you okay?' she asked worriedly.

'Yes, I just ran into a—'

He stopped walking and stiffened so suddenly she was terrified he was in pain. His arm was linked with hers, and it yanked her roughly to an abrupt stop. It felt like catching her shirt on an immovable object.

'What's wrong?' she demanded anxiously. Miguel had turned his head and was staring toward the silver Mazda Sedan parked across the street. 'Miguel—?'

He dropped her arm and turned to walk across the road. Horns blared at him in outrage, but he didn't seem to notice.

'Miguel!' Gwen screeched when he suddenly smashed his elbow effortlessly through the driver's window. Her jaw dropped, and her heart started thumping wildly when he roughly dragged the screaming man inside through the small opening.

Gwen began to dodge vehicles on the street to reach them as Miguel jerked his victim to the sidewalk. She could hear the man protesting as Miguel shoved him to sit on a bench.

'Why are you following her?' Miguel interrupted once Gwen had reached them.

'I wasn't!' the stranger objected. He was bleeding from being pulled out of the broken car window.

'You were taking pictures of us,' Miguel growled.

'No!' the man shouted. 'I was taking pictures of the buildings!'

'Miguel, what the *hell* are you—?' Gwen began to yell.

'Gwen, bring me the camera from the passenger's seat. You'll understand,' Miguel promised. He offered her a smile that seemed so out of place it all felt surreal. The calm tenderness suddenly in his tone made a mockery of the demonstration of his anger before.

Gwen hesitated only a moment in uncertainty, however, because she realized she trusted him.

She retrieved the camera with an enormous lens from the passenger's seat of the Mazda. She turned it on and began to flip through the pictures as she returned to

Miguel. Sure enough, there were pictures of them walking down the street. She saw herself grinning while slapping Miguel's shoulder. There was a picture of her through the window at work and one as she'd arrived at the building that morning. She saw herself leaving the hotel with Ainsley.

'He's been following me,' she said in horror.

'That is what I thought,' Miguel said darkly to the man who was sweating on the bench. 'What I want to know is whether Jonathon Welford is paying you enough to risk your life today.'

Gwen looked up at him in shock. 'No, it can't be—' she stuttered.

'I will do whatever you want,' the man assured Miguel, and he held up his bleeding hands in surrender.

'Go back to Jonathon and tell him if he does not stay away from Gwen, I'm going to pay him a visit. I won't be wearing my expensive suit this time,' said Miguel seriously.

Gwen felt her pulse quickening again as she considered if her new boyfriend would carry out that threat. She reflected on the way he'd broken the window and dragged the photographer out of the car, and she knew he would. It was silly to keep trying to imagine him only as the thoughtful gentleman and thorough lover he was with her. Miguel had grown up on the street, and she had no idea what he'd been through or what he was capable of. She didn't know him as well as she'd thought. It was possible he *was* as dangerous as Derek had hinted to her on the night he'd realized who her date was.

Miguel stepped back and took the camera from Gwen when the photographer nodded in understanding. She watched as he removed the memory chip and tossed the camera back to the photographer. Gwen opened her mouth to say something, but Miguel took her arm, and they continued quickly down the street.

'Um... are you gonna tell me what just happened?' she demanded angrily.

Miguel stopped walking, and he turned toward her. She could see he'd anticipated her aversion.

'Jon may really have it out for you,' Miguel insisted. 'The man is a sociopathic egomaniac, and we've publicly humiliated him. Men like that can't stand to have their power taken from them,' he tried to explain. 'Now he's hired someone to watch you in order to learn your habits. He means to hurt you!'

'Miguel, you just broke a car window and dragged someone out of it into the street! I want to talk about *that*,' she advised him sharply.

He was frustrated with her, but she could see him willing himself to be patient.

'I'm sorry if I scared you,' he began more calmly. 'Gwen, Jon clearly wants—'

'Do you have experience with these kinds of things?' Gwen interrupted, and he sighed impatiently.

'I will make you a deal,' he suggested. 'You agree to a bodyguard, and I will tell you anything you want to know about my past, all right?'

'You want me to hire a bodyguard?' she exploded.

'*Yes,*' he growled unconditionally, and she laughed at him sarcastically with disbelief.

'You see the irony here, don't you?' she demanded as they resumed their walk toward the hotel. 'You nearly killed a man for following me just minutes ago, and now you want to have another one follow me permanently?'

Miguel rolled his eyes, and despite her aggravation, Gwen found it endearing.

'I have a man in mind already,' he admitted, and she could hear the finality in his tone suggesting the discussion was over. That irritated her all the more.

'This is *my* life you're talking about invading. I think I should at least get a say in who is hovering around me,' she objected.

'You won't even know he's there,' Miguel assured her. 'He's done this kind of thing before. He's the best.'

'Who are you talking about?' she snipped as they

reached the Royal Alton. Carlton held open the door for them.

'Hudson, the man from the NTM,' Miguel said, and Gwen glanced up at him in surprise. She remembered the one with the disconcerting blue eyes.

'What kind of name is "Hudson" anyway?' she berated in an attempt to hide how intrigued she was. Meeting someone from Miguel's past could be interesting.

'I don't know. Will you at least talk to him?' Miguel asked her, sounding hopeful, and Gwen sighed as they got into the elevator. After a moment, she nodded.

'Sure. It would be nice to meet one of your friends,' she pointed out, but he didn't respond.

She collected her things, and she and Miguel met Anthony at the front so he could drive them to Gwen's apartment. Sandra had dinner nearly ready, so there was just enough time for Gwen to shower and change. When she sneakily suggested Miguel join her, he declined explaining that he wanted to call Hudson to arrange a meet.

X X X

Miguel

Gwen left me with a glance I interpreted as further evidence of her uncertainty regarding my behaviour with the photographer. I'd been too rash, and I'd nearly exposed myself for the animal I was who was ready to defend his mate. I felt guilty about scaring her, but it was seriously outweighed by my determination to protect her.

I heard the shower start, and I pulled out my phone to dial Hudson. I waited impatiently as the phone rang for some time.

'Hudson,' he finally answered, sounding breathless and more than a little annoyed.

'What the hell are you doing?' I demanded, but then I heard a familiar feminine giggle. I remembered the black-haired vampiress from earlier.

'I'm *busy*! What do you want?' he snapped, and I smirked at him.

'Just remember who sent her to you,' I advised him. 'I need a favour.'

'*Christ,* Miguel,' he grated. 'What *is* it? Can't it wait?'

'It can wait until tomorrow, but it's important, Hudson. It's concerning Gwen,' I admitted, and there was a moment of silence before he sighed in resignation.

'Where shall I meet you?' he asked reluctantly.

'My place for dinner,' I answered. 'I will call you tomorrow with more details.'

'Fine,' he agreed and hung up.

I put my phone away as I continued to consider the threat that was Jonathon Welford. Normally, I would have killed him, but it was against the Accords to kill influential humans. His death would be too public, and there was no guarantee we could perfectly cover it up. There was always a chance someone might talk or a reporter might get a hold of the information.

So, I wasn't allowed to kill Jonathon Welford, but I *would* if he tried to hurt Gwen again.

In spite of the afternoon's events, we were able to have a nice evening with Gwen's roommate. After dinner, we watched a movie, and then I managed to seduce my lover. Gwen tried to be quiet, but it was clear in the morning Sandra had heard. We avoided her teasing expressions during breakfast, and I walked Gwen to work.

I stayed near her all day until Ainsley arrived to pick her up, and then I beat them back to the hotel.

'Is he scary?' Gwen asked after I told her we were meeting Hudson for dinner. She sipped her wine nervously as she watched me set the table for the meal I doubted Hudson would even pretend to eat.

'He can be,' I admitted.

'What kind of experience does he have? Has he killed people?' she asked, and I nodded. She was quiet for a long time, and I could feel her eyes burning into me. 'Have *you*?' she breathed.

I straightened and looked up at her. I had no idea how to respond, and thankfully, the elevator doors opened. Hudson strolled in without announcing himself, and I embraced the distraction.

'Hudson,' I greeted him, but he didn't take his eyes off my mate.

'I hear you have a dangerous ex-boyfriend,' he said. He only released her from his gaze when he turned to look upon my home with appreciation.

'I don't think he's dangerous. Miguel—' Gwen began.

'Miguel is a better judge of what is dangerous than you are,' Hudson assured her a little harshly before taking a seat at the dinner table. Gwen glanced at me, and I glared at my friend.

'There is no need to be rude,' I growled in warning.

'I merely speak the truth. Are you not a better judge of danger?' he challenged me, and I frowned harder at him. 'I will protect you,' he redirected us, and he looked back at Gwen. 'Unless something horrible happens, you won't know I'm there, but I do have one condition. If I tell you to do something, you will do it. No questions asked. Understand?' he demanded.

Gwen met my gaze apprehensively, but she saw I had faith in this strange and frightening man. She slowly nodded.

'I also have a condition,' she advised him, and I saw Hudson's brow rise ever so slightly in response. Like me, he was not used to being challenged by humans.

'Yes?' he prompted reluctantly.

'This is still my life, so I'll be calling the shots. You may work for him*,*' she acknowledged, and Hudson's hackles rose when she indicated me, 'but *I'm* your client.'

Hudson was deeply offended by the notion he was in my employment, but he was also impressed by Gwen. He even offered her a rare smile.

'You got it, sweetheart,' he agreed.

'One more thing,' said Gwen. '*Don't* call me sweetheart.'

x x x

Gwendolyn

As promised, Gwen was surprisingly comfortable with the level of privacy she still had with Hudson keeping an eye on her. The only time he made contact with her over the next couple of weeks was when she initiated it or when they were driving. Even then, Gwen got the sense he didn't particularly enjoy her attention, and most often he insisted on quiet in the car.

Her initial intentions to dig information out of him concerning Miguel were largely thwarted, but she remained determined. Her boyfriend's promised Q and A session had proved as inconclusive and disappointing as she'd feared.

'I was worried I wasn't going to be able to find someone suitable for the position. Welford Accounting has such a foothold here in Toronto,' said Ms. Trolley. She'd taken Gwen out for lunch to discuss the official terms of her employment. They were nearly finished.

Gwen nodded, but she became a little distracted when she saw Hudson wander casually into the restaurant. Usually, he stayed farther away, but he didn't indicate any looming threats, so she relaxed. He walked by her as though they were strangers and used those good looks to get himself a seat near the back.

'I'm confident we can give Welford a run for his money any day,' Gwen promised Trolley. 'I'm very familiar with their company, and I have some ideas for winning over some of their clientele.'

'That's what I was hoping,' Trolley assured her as she signalled the waitress for the bill. Like the rest of the cafe staff and even some passionate patrons, the woman was dressed for Halloween. Gwen was pretty sure she was supposed to be some kind of vampiress.

Gwen discreetly glanced back toward Hudson while Trolley paid. He seemed completely engrossed in his "witch" companion.

'Shall we get back?' Trolley asked expectantly.

'You go ahead, Ms. Trolley. I'm meeting someone,' Gwen explained. 'Thank you for the meal!'

'Very well,' Trolley agreed as she put on her long black coat. She nodded to Gwen and exited the restaurant.

Gwen sat alone for a moment and, before long, Hudson slid into the seat Trolley had vacated. He moved with the grace and silence of a cat.

'You're going to be late back to work,' he advised her. He was avoiding her eyes as usual.

'Why did you come into the restaurant?' asked Gwen suspiciously. 'You hardly ever get this close.'

'She was pretty,' Hudson said dismissively, referring to the woman he'd sat down with.

Despite that they were not related, Gwen had come to appreciate the similarities between Hudson and her boyfriend. She knew when they were not being completely truthful.

'Hudson,' she growled.

'What do you want me to say?' he asked, and he suddenly met her gaze with those strange eyes. 'The man in the grey coat has been watching you since you—*don't look!*—since you left the Trolley building. I wanted to be closer in case he tried something,' Hudson explained. Then he leaned across the table toward her as though they were having an intimate discussion. 'Now, pretend I'm hitting on you, so he doesn't know I'm shadowing you.'

Gwen tried to keep her eyes on Hudson's, but it was terribly difficult as a thrill of danger tingled along her backbone. She decided to distract herself with the first thing that came to mind.

'Your eyes are unique,' she said offhandedly. Miguel had warned her not to bring up the topic with her grumpy guardian, but it was a little late.

Hudson was obviously surprised by her bold

statement. His gaze hardened although his smile didn't falter.

'People probably ask you about them all the time,' Gwen acknowledged regretfully.

'Why don't you try being a little more original?' he suggested.

'Tell me about Miguel. How did you two meet?' she asked.

'He didn't tell you the brothel story,' he assumed drolly, and when Gwen's eyes widened, he smiled. It almost transformed his stony face, and she was blown away by how gorgeous the man was.

'No,' Gwen said, fighting her own smile when she realized he was joking.

'Haven't you asked him?' Hudson pressed.

'I did, but if you're going to be following me around, I figure we could at least pretend to be civilized,' Gwen hedged. She hoped Hudson might be more liberal with information if he thought Miguel had already told her. He saw through her, though, and he snorted.

'You know he isn't telling you something,' he guessed. 'You think you'll figure it out by interrogating me.'

Gwen crossed her arms over her chest and lifted her chin in determination. 'Give me some credit,' she grumbled.

'Anything he doesn't tell you is probably for your own good,' he advised her.

'He's not a bad person,' Gwen said defensively, and Hudson looked amused by her assertion.

'What if he were? How would that make you feel?' Hudson challenged her. Gwen gazed at him suspiciously.

'Are you trying to tell me Miguel is not safe?' she demanded.

'You already know that,' Hudson dismissed. 'You also know I'm dangerous. You can sense it.'

Gwen looked away from his piercing eyes as his words struck cords of truth within her. She remembered thinking they seemed like wolves in sheep's clothing. She'd been agonizing over how Miguel had failed to assure her he'd never killed people.

'Were you in the army or something?' she asked, sounding hopeful.

'The army?' he repeated in confusion.

'Miguel told me you... killed people before,' Gwen admitted hesitantly. She glanced down to avoid his gaze, and Hudson grunted thoughtfully.

'He didn't tell you about himself?' he verified, and Gwen looked back up at him. Her heart began to pound heavily with dread as she prepared to ask him her question.

'So, he *has* killed someone?' she guessed, and her voice waivered. Hudson looked very serious.

'He's killed many,' he revealed grimly. 'Now, I'm going to get up and move on to another table. You're going to go to work. I will be right behind you.'

Gwen nodded, feeling slightly panicky as he rose from her table and left her alone. She took a moment to reassemble her nerve and got up to put on her coat.

Hudson had told her not to look at the man who was following her, but she knew she needed to know what he looked like. So, once her coat was buttoned, she did a casual scan without looking at anyone in particular, and she saw the man in the grey coat.

He was enormously built with short dark hair, a square jaw, crooked nose, and dark eyes that met hers knowingly.

She looked away, trying to maintain calm as though she'd only met the eyes of a stranger accidentally. She tried not to glance over her shoulder the whole walk back to work.

Miguel

Chapter Twenty-Two

'There is a vampire following Gwen,' said Hudson when I picked up my phone.

'*What?*' I snarled.

'I had to stay close to her. He's been watching her for about two days. I'm certain I recognize him. Probably one of Judas's agents,' Hudson continued. I considered this thoughtfully for some time.

'You think Judas is trying to start a fight with me?' I asked. The idea was deeply concerning and very possible. Judas and I had never gotten along. He disliked human politics, and I was the representation of our truce with them. We rarely agreed on anything, and if his mate had been recently killed, there was a good chance I could become a target for his anger.

'Perhaps he knows Gwen is Dowrra, and he is looking to collect her,' Hudson suggested. 'Either way, the vamp now knows Gwen is under my protection.'

'Does she know?' I asked as I pinched the bridge of my nose with my thumb and forefinger.

'I told her someone was following her so she will exercise caution. I let her think the asshole was a stranger. Better she doesn't start asking all kinds of awkward questions,' Hudson explained.

'Keep me updated,' I advised, and he grunted before hanging up. I set the phone down on the table, and Derek, who was sitting across from me, cocked his head.

'Okay?' he asked.

'Gwen is being followed, so no,' I assured him. Derek's eyes widened, so I held up my hand before he could annoy me anymore with his concerns. 'I have a man protecting her.'

'Charlotte told me about her bodyguard,' Derek told me, his brow rising at me. 'I'm still surprised Gwen agreed to that.'

'Can we get on with this?' I demanded and drummed my fingers against the table. 'You called me here for something?'

Derek nodded before he pushed the stack of papers in front of him toward me.

'This is what I got,' he said a little proudly as I began to flip through the file dispassionately. My mind was still distracted by Gwen and her circumstance, but as I read, concerns for her immediate safety faded.

'Where did you get this?' I asked in disbelief.

'Let's just say I have a friend in parliament who likes to drink and gamble *way* too—'

'Derek,' I scowled seriously, and he cleared his throat in embarrassment.

'Seems the PSA is only a department of a much larger bureau for paranormal relations,' Derek admitted. He leaned a little closer to me over the table so other diner patrons couldn't overhear us. 'In addition are the Extraterrestrial Control Agency, the Bureau of Supernatural Investigation, and the Department of Research for the Paranormal,' he elaborated. 'I also saw something about a future Registry. It will identify someone's "human status," and all nonhumans will be required to carry ID,' Derek revealed. He reached across the table to flip through the stack to the place marked with a sticky note.

'Angeli Mortis,' I sighed with dread.

'There's a book, written by some Pope, about them. It talks about super soldiers they call "Angels" with the ability to combat vampires,' Derek described. 'Whatever "recipe" they have for them is still incomplete.'

'They need Aegian DNA,' I dismissed stubbornly. I didn't want to talk to him about empaths.

'Aegian?' repeated Derek thoughtfully. He looked at the stack of paper as if trying to remember whether he'd come across such a reference. I reluctantly flipped to a part nearer the beginning, and he leaned over the table to see. 'Aliens?' he gasped in surprise, and I nodded. He was thoughtful for a moment. 'Regardless, it seems they are coming after us. We should leave the city.'

'Take anyone with you who may be in danger,' I encouraged him.

'What about Gwen?' he asked hesitantly. 'She still doesn't know about any of this,' he reminded me unnecessarily.

'I need to call my father,' I said to myself, ignoring his words concerning Gwen. 'The Summons is tonight, and it is imperative the Tribunal know this evidence.'

'Miguel,' said Derek insistently. 'What about Gwen?'

I considered my options with a heavy heart pounding in my chest. 'I will find a way to tell Gwen. Tonight,' I promised.

x x x

Gwendolyn

Gwen was distracted all day as she tried to work through what Hudson had said. In the end, she was forced to admit the man had only confirmed what she'd feared from the beginning. Miguel was dangerous, yet she wasn't afraid, and she couldn't convince herself to *be* afraid.

Hudson opened the car door for her, and she slid wordlessly into the passenger seat of his red Ferrari 488 GTB. People around were taking pictures, but Gwen had become used to it.

She glared at Hudson when he got into the driver's seat, and he chuckled without even looking at her.

'Still angry,' he observed as he put the car into gear. It rumbled beneath them, and the crowd tittered in excitement as they pulled away from the curb.

'Wouldn't you be if someone suggested your girlfriend was a killer?' she snapped.

'No,' he assured her, and Gwen looked up at him in confusion.

'Well, I'm sure someone has given you information you wished were not true,' she insisted.

'You went fishing, and you caught something,' he pointed out firmly. 'I don't allow others to hold enough sway over me to influence my emotions. You should try it,' he informed her, and Gwen snorted in laughter.

'I call bullshit,' she advised him. 'Anyone who is as fucked up as you clearly are has been seriously hurt before.'

Hudson didn't say anything, but his hands tightened tellingly on the steering wheel. After a few moments staring out the window, Gwen turned back toward him.

'Was Miguel a solider?'

'Once or twice,' Hudson revealed readily.

'So, that's when he killed people,' she reasoned in relief. Hudson was too quiet, and she knew she was still missing the truth, but she was suddenly unwilling to pursue. She wasn't ready to risk what she had with Miguel.

'What are you doing for Halloween tonight?' she asked to change the subject. Hudson glanced at her dubiously.

'Nothing,' he assured her as if this were obvious.

'It's Halloween!' she objected. 'We're going to one of those masquerade balls. Miguel said they were really popular in the seventeenth and eighteenth centuries. Why don't you join us?'

'No,' Hudson said simply.

'Why not?' groaned Gwen.

'I haven't been to a masquerade ball since Venice in 1654,' he responded with what she thought was a poor tone of sarcasm. 'It did not end well.'

'You're so dramatic,' she complained and rolled her eyes, but it was the furthest thing from the truth. Hudson was the exact opposite of dramatic. Gwen had rarely seen him smile, and she had yet to hear him laugh. He hadn't told her anything real about himself because he always seemed to speak in exaggeration.

I haven't done that *since 1326 during the Raid of Brandenburg!*

I haven't done this *since the earthquake of Ierissos in 1932!*

He was always so specific with the dates, events, and the places. She'd even researched some of the random things that came out of his mouth. His details were always painstakingly accurate, and it always made Miguel uncomfortable.

'Where else did you go in 1654 that you hated? Just so I know not to ask,' she mumbled cynically.

'I mostly stayed in Venice for the Battle of Dardanelles when the Ottomans were trying to capture Crete,' he responded. His voice was smooth and without a hint of apology.

'Really?' sighed Gwen as she discreetly typed this information into the search engine on her phone. 'Who was the commander?'

'Giuseppe Delfino was a moron,' Hudson responded as they turned into the hotel lane. Gwen's mouth twisted wryly as she read the name. 'His sixteen ships were outnumbered by the Kapudan Pasha's thirty. They lost the battle when Delfino tried to let the Ottomans pass and sailed too soon. He left some of the fleet exposed without support.'

'How do you remember all this?' Gwen demanded skeptically. Hudson's hands tightened on the steering wheel again.

'There are days I wish I could forget,' he assured her

enigmatically as they pulled up to the hotel. Before she could ask for clarification, he got out of the vehicle.

They went upstairs, and Gwen saw Miguel was on the phone. She rarely saw him talk to anyone because he politely excused himself or would call them back later. This time he was pacing the reception area, and he looked as if he wanted to throw his cell through the wall.

'No, Mackayla! Don't come here!' he said in frustration.

'His lovely sister,' Hudson informed Gwen before he walked into the kitchen.

'I understand—' Miguel began, and then he was cut off. He swore under his breath. 'Yes, I know—' He was cut off again, and she saw his hand tighten into a fist.

Gwen slowly sank into the couch, which seemed to finally get his attention, and he turned to look at her. She saw the anger melt from his expression, and he smiled at her.

'Mackayla, I have to go,' he said sternly, and he ran a hand through his hair the way he did when he was anxious. 'Yes, tell our father I will see him soon,' he said grudgingly, and Gwen's brows rose in concern. 'No, I'm not doing that. No!' he snapped. 'Goodbye,' he hissed, and Gwen could still hear a woman's desperate voice on the other end before he hung up.

'Hi,' she greeted him, and he sighed in relief.

'Hi,' he responded, and he leaned over her to kiss her.

'That sounded as charming as ever,' commented Hudson as he came back into the room. Miguel leaned away from Gwen to give Hudson a dark glance before he slowly took a seat next to Gwen on the couch.

'She wants me home. Now,' he revealed.

'Not surprising,' Hudson acknowledged.

'Are you leaving?' Gwen asked. 'Are we not going to the ball?'

She saw immediately Miguel had forgotten about their plans by the widening of his eyes. He did an admirable job of covering his surprise, however.

'We can still go to the ball,' he promised her. 'I know you were excited about it.'

'I've never been,' Gwen reminded him sounding hopeful.

'Overrated and overdone,' Hudson dismissed.

'Didn't you used to date Miguel's sister?' Gwen shot back, and she was satisfied when Hudson's expression darkened. He nodded wordlessly at Miguel, and he retreated. Once the doors of the elevator closed, Gwen turned toward Miguel, who looked disbelieving. She rolled her eyes.

'Hudson is not as scary as he wants everyone to think,' she dismissed.

'He really is, Gwen,' Miguel assured her nervously.

'Is something wrong?' she redirected him. 'We don't have to go tonight.'

'Something is wrong,' Miguel admitted delicately, obviously looking for a way to enlighten her. 'There's… something I have to tell you,' he said, and she could see a great deal of reluctance in his eyes.

'Okay,' she agreed as he took her hand. He lifted it to his lips and kissed her skin.

'It's about my family and where we come from,' he explained, and Gwen knew instinctively this would be the answer to all her questions. She would finally understand what he was holding back.

'You're part of the mob, aren't you?' she blurted, and her eyes widened after it slipped out. Miguel gazed at her as if gauging her reaction, and he nodded.

'Something like that' he began. 'We—'

Gwen's phone rang suddenly between them and cut him off.

'Sorry!' she exclaimed. 'It's probably Charlotte. She'll want to know where to meet us. Should I tell her we aren't going?'

Miguel looked thoughtful. She could tell he was locked in an internal debate about what he had to tell her. Finally, he shook his head.

'Tell her Anthony will pick them up at their house in forty minutes,' he said, and she nodded before answering the phone. Miguel rose from the couch and walked toward the enormous windows overlooking the autumn trees behind the hotel. It was getting dark earlier, so the solar lights had come on in the garden. There was a shimmer of snow in the air.

Gwen hung up with Charlotte, and she got up to come toward him. She wrapped her arms around him and leaned her head against his back.

'What were you going to say?' she asked, and she loosened her hold on him so he could turn toward her. He leaned down and kissed her with a surprising amount of emotion. It felt suspiciously like a goodbye.

'I don't want to ruin the night,' he confessed. 'Perhaps we should talk about it in the morning?'

She'd been waiting to know what it was about this man that made him different. She got the sense it was not going to be as blissfully enlightening as she'd fantasized, however. There was a possibility she wouldn't like what he told her and it would, in fact, ruin the night. So, she nodded.

'Sure. We can do that,' she promised.

x x x

Miguel

Gwen had bought herself a black and silver masquerade ball gown and matching mask for the Halloween party. She came out of the bedroom, and she nearly took me back to Venice in 1654 after Hudson's mishap at the Palace of the Doge.

The dress rippled in layers of black lace to the floor with intricate silver designs sewn into the fitted bodice. The silver mask was covered in black lace and spanned her upper face like bird's wings. It had a black feather on the right, and silky strands of black ribbon hung down to caress Gwen's bare shoulder. There were black pearls hanging from the nose and cheeks that wiggled when she smiled.

'You like it?' she guessed. 'Me too,' she added, and she gestured with her fan to my waistcoat.

I stepped forward without a word. I had to be careful not to disrupt the messy bun she'd piled her hair into or her red lipstick as I pulled her in for a quick kiss.

Anthony was waiting for us downstairs with Charlotte and Derek in the back of the limo. The women gushed excitedly over their costumes, but Derek was watching me with his mask held distastefully in his lap. I could tell he was trying to determine whether I'd told Gwen about myself as I'd promised.

'Miguel, you look good!' Charlotte complimented me, and she turned toward her husband. 'Miguel is wearing *his* mask.'

'Miguel has been to plenty of these kinds of parties,' Derek dismissed quickly. He glared at me resentfully for the example I had set.

'Have you?' asked Gwen eagerly, and I saw Derek watching us with a little more interest.

'A few,' I confessed, giving him a discouraging glance. He frowned knowingly.

The women became immersed in a conversation about their dresses. Derek slid discreetly from Charlotte's seat so he was on my side of the car.

'Why didn't you tell her?' he hissed.

'I didn't want to ruin her night,' I admitted without looking at him. He snorted.

'As opposed to her day tomorrow?' he demanded mockingly.

'She was excited for this,' I defended. 'I didn't want to disappoint her.'

'Kinda hard to avoid, don't you think?' he asked. He looked immediately apologetic when I glared at him. 'Sorry.'

I turned my face from him and resolved not to speak to him for the rest of the night. Gwen was oblivious to my mood and enjoying herself with Charlotte as they fawned over the costumes of others upon our arrival.

Palazzo di Giustiniani was the large estate where the party was being hosted. It had been previously owed by a Venetian family now extinct and had been sold to Niccolò Boerio. He'd converted it into a popular tourist destination. Boerio would not be there, of course, because he was no longer in the city. He'd been one of the first vampires to leave after my recommendation.

We were escorted into the ballroom by men in Pantalone masks, and Gwen's arm clenched on mine excitedly. The room beneath us really did take me back to Venice.

'Must have been pretty cool,' said Charlotte conversationally although I could tell her comment was directed at me.

'I'm sure it was,' I responded ironically, and she smiled.

'Wine!' she suddenly exclaimed, and she tugged Gwen away from me and toward the bar.

'Did you call your father?' Derek asked me, following after me as I led the way down the stairs. The man had a knack for making me feel like a child although I was old enough to have been his great-great-grandfather's great-great-grandfather.

'I did,' I said just before catching a familiar scent.

I stiffened and turned to meet the dark eyes behind a red and gold Bauta mask under a Venetian highwayman hat. His red waistcoat was embroidered with gold, and there was a stunning vampiress on his arm as usual. She was wearing a white downy dress and a silver and gold Colombina mask. She smiled wickedly at me when I glanced at her.

'Anatolius,' I greeted one of Hudson's infamous five-thousand-year-old big brothers. He and his twin were the second eldest vampires in the world. I did *not* want to piss this guy off.

'Miguel, you know to call me Liam,' he chastised me.

His tone still betrayed just the hint of an ancient Minoan accent.

Liam Demetrius was like a god among vampires. Women couldn't resist him, and men wanted to *be* him. It was said he'd seduced Aphrodite herself and she'd cursed him with an insatiable lust so he would never find love. Whether it was true, I didn't know, but his wildly decadent lifestyle was legendary.

'Should you not be at the Summons tonight?' I remembered belatedly. I couldn't see his mouth, but I could tell he smiled.

'Who is this hanging about your shoulder?' he asked instead of answering my question. He indicated Derek with an incline of his masked face.

'Detective Derek Wells of the PSA,' I said. 'Derek, this is Liam Demetrius. He is the Lord of the Redemption Coven.'

'PSA,' repeated Liam, and his eyes slid to me curiously. He would have heard about the imminent implosion of our human relations.

'One of the good ones,' I assured him.

Thankfully, Derek knew better than to step forward for a handshake. In fact, he looked a little like he couldn't breathe. I assumed he must have known to whom he was speaking. Liam had a hell of a reputation.

'It's a pleasure to meet you,' Derek said, although I doubted he thought so.

'I'm sure it is,' Liam responded with characteristic arrogance, and his pretty guest giggled as she glanced up at him appreciatively. 'Who are these lovely things?' Liam asked when Gwen and Charlotte rejoined us. Gwen balked a little at being called a "thing," but she was polite enough to smile patiently at my companion.

'Gwendolyn Rhys is my date, and this is her friend. Charlotte is Derek's wife,' I explained, and Liam cocked his head.

'Rhys,' he repeated, and I knew, immediately, I'd probably made a mistake in revealing her name to him.

Liam kept track of the Dowrra bloodlines to actively avoid coming into contact with potential mates.

'Perhaps you knew her mother,' Charlotte cut in quickly before Liam could say anything incriminating. 'Maria Rhys was an artist.'

Liam's dark eyes met mine suspiciously, and I saw him become skeptical as he recognized the situation. 'That is possible,' he agreed, deciding to humour us.

'Gwen, this is Liam Demetrius,' I said to my mate.

'It's nice to meet you,' she told him, and she held out her hand. 'I don't suppose there is any relation to Leonardo Demetrois? The French artist, who painted *Filles Francaises* in 1838,' she clarified.

My heart jumped into my throat because I knew all about Liam's supposed weakness for an educated woman. I imagined he'd be all the more intrigued by a woman who knew anything about one his aliases from over the millennia. There was absolutely nothing I would have been able to do if he decided he'd rather have her on his arm for the evening. It was a switch he'd been known to make before.

'You might say there is a relation,' said Liam with a newfound fondness for my mate as he took Gwen's offered hand. Instead of shaking it, as she'd intended, he turned it over so he could kiss her knuckles. The skin on her arm rippled, and Charlotte's eyes widened as Gwen swallowed nervously. Both women glanced at me in question, but I was thankful the man was wearing a mask. Hudson had frequently complained about how painters had always begged for the opportunity to capture his brother's features on canvas. Due to Liam's longevity, they'd all been denied, of course.

Liam straightened, looking like he had no idea about the kind of effect he had on people, and he looked at me more seriously. 'Where is my brother?' he asked.

'You know Hudson hates masquerades,' I reminded him.

'You're Hudson's brother?' Gwen asked in surprise,

and Liam cocked his head at her.

'Can't you see the family resemblance?' he asked teasingly, and I was dismayed when her cheeks coloured just a little.

'Now that you mention it,' she laughed as she gazed up at his mask in curiosity. I knew she must have been wondering just what the enigmatic man with the sexy voice looked like.

'Miguel, I would like to speak to you alone,' Liam advised me abruptly. Evidently, he'd tired of my guests, so I nodded.

Chapter Twenty-Three

Gwen looked suspicious, but she handed me the glass of wine she'd brought for me. She followed Derek and Charlotte toward the live band on stage, and Liam's date joined a group of vampiresses from their coven.

'You have heard about the PSA,' I assumed.

'We always knew it would come to this,' he dismissed. All pretense of seduction was gone from his tone now that we were alone. 'What concerns me is the neglect on the part of the Dowrra Matrons to awaken my brother.'

I sighed and nodded. Hudson had not been happy about that either. In fact, I was not so pleased.

'In their mind, he is too much of a threat. If we can deal with the situation—'

'The situation has potential to become far worse than anything we've faced before,' Liam interrupted me. 'It might soon be too late to realize that.'

'It is unlikely they will ever find enough empaths,' I reasoned, but Liam didn't seem to agree. His gaze darkened, and my heart felt like it slipped into my stomach. 'Do you know something?' I demanded.

'I'm confident they will have what they need,' he admitted. 'They have only to determine how to put it together.'

'Are there more empaths than we thought?' I asked in shock.

'Worse,' Liam assured me. 'The Aegian aliens were not all gone. Quinn bound Attula here in a tomb when he sank Atlantis,' Liam confessed. 'The humans are using an empath to get him.'

Hudson had never been forthcoming regarding his eldest brother, who'd gone to sleep hundreds of years before I was born. All I knew about Quinn O'Connor was he'd been imbued with the dark power of a Destroyer. This entity was feared by the gods because it was the only force which could control them so they'd come after him. To protect himself and his family, he'd bound them in mortal forms. That was the second time he'd destroyed the world, which I knew, logically, meant he was far older than anyone knew.

When Attula had come from the world of Aegea, he was the only unbound god in our universe. Hoping to finally attain the means to Quinn's destruction, the gods had stolen the power of the Aegian Crystals from Attula. During their attempts to bind Quinn's power, the gods had murdered his lover at the time. This had driven Quinn to the edge of perhaps the third worst catastrophe in his long history of destruction. In a fit of rage, he'd sunk Atlantis into the Aegean and forced the Aegian aliens who'd built the civilization to return to their world. Their surviving human ancestors, who possessed the empathic abilities of their alien sires, had been scattered. A thousand years later, they'd been rounded up and used by the Church to create the Angeli Mortis. Vampires had hunted empaths down and exterminated them to prevent that from ever happening again.

I'd thought all the Aegian aliens had left our world. It turned out one of them, the most powerful among them, had remained.

'Attula is here because of Quinn!' I hissed, forgetting my place for a moment. 'Whatever the humans make next will be ten times more powerful because of it!'

'An excellent reason to wake him so he can send Attula home' Liam pointed out impatiently. 'My brother might have a reputation, but you cannot argue with his results. Humans have survived his wrath before. They can do it again,' he assured me.

I raised my brows at him in disbelief, but he turned away toward my companions, who were watching the band.

'I might understand the source of your sympathy,' he admitted. 'She makes you weak, Miguel.'

'She makes me *happy,'* I corrected him sharply, and his interest was piqued.

'For now,' he shrugged. 'But you're a vampire, and you were born with the world at your feet. Why would you give it up?' I didn't sense that he was berating me but rather he was genuinely curious. I decided to humour his question seriously.

'I suppose even the whole world means nothing if you can no longer appreciate it,' I mused thoughtfully. 'The truth is she fills a void I didn't know I had. A void which not even everything could satisfy,' I clarified. He made a sound of interest and inclined his head.

'Get out of the city, Miguel. While you still can,' he advised. Then he turned back for his female companions.

Feeling burdened by the knowledge he'd imparted, I turned toward Gwen. She caught my eye at the same time, and when she smiled, my weary heart was full.

I knew in that moment I'd do whatever it took to protect her from whatever was coming for us. I just wished there was not this part of me afraid she could never love me for what I really was.

X X X

Gwendolyn

'*Who* was *that*?' hissed Gwen as soon as they were out of earshot of Miguel and his strange companion. She wondered if perhaps Hudson and his brother were a part of whatever organization Miguel was.

'You might call him Miguel's superior,' Derek confirmed a little smugly. Gwen frowned at him.

'You tried to warn me he was dangerous when we first

met. Have you dealt with him in your line of work before?' she demanded. Derek looked shocked and deeply uncertain how to respond.

'Gwen, this is *really* something he needs to tell you. I will say that I do deal with his… kind all the time,' he admitted. Charlotte bunted him less than discreetly in the ribs, and he rolled his eyes. 'I will also say that whatever you might think of him after tonight, he's… a good guy,' he assured her haltingly.

'Thanks,' she muttered in disappointment that not even her own friends would tell her what was going on. She glanced back at Miguel to see his companion returning to the gaggle of women who were eagerly awaiting him. Miguel looked at her, and they shared a smile before he came back toward her.

She consoled herself with the knowledge she would have her answers tomorrow.

The remainder of the night was salvaged once Liam and his obnoxious fangirls left the party. Miguel had sensed her anxiety, and he gave her the odd comforting squeeze in just the right place to release her tension. They'd never danced to anything with a bass before, but he surprised her with an excellent rhythm to grind against.

Gwen looked up into his masked face and wondered how deep the disguise really went. She was growing suspicious about how much she didn't know about him.

Miguel's full lips were even more sensual when they were the only part of his face she could see. They trailed soft kisses down her arm and skipped across to her bare shoulder. She closed her eyes as he leaned against her and wrapped his strong arms around her for a slower song.

'Miguel, tell me who you are,' she whispered.

'Tomorrow,' he murmured. 'Give me one more night.'

She wanted to promise him that whatever it was, it wouldn't change anything, but she knew that might not be true. So, she nodded grudgingly and he kissed her shoulder.

Her phone vibrated in her bust, and Miguel glanced down in confusion before she pulled it out for him to see. She laughed at his expression and checked the message from Sandra. Her smile faded as she read.

Com 2 apartment need 2 see u

'That's cryptic and terribly written,' Gwen muttered as she texted back to see if Sandra was okay.

'Is everything all right?' Miguel asked, and Gwen shrugged as she looked down at Sandra's reply.

Fine but need 2 talk plz hurry. Its about Henry.

'Can we swing by there? I think something happened with her weird boyfriend,' Gwen said to Miguel, who nodded quickly.

'Of course,' he agreed, and he took her hand to guide her off the dance floor. Charlotte insisted on accompanying them, and Gwen texted Sandra to tell her they were on their way as everyone got into the limo. Sandra's reply was almost immediate.

Don u dare bring evry1 up here! Im crying

Gwen cocked her head, feeling just a little wary of her roomie's uncharacteristic response.

Are you sure? What about Charlotte? she texted back.

Can u just com up plz?!

Gwen sighed and typed that she would come alone.

They got to the building, and Gwen put a hand on Charlotte's shoulder to stop her from getting out of the car.

'Let me go up first. You guys come up in a minute. She sounds really upset,' Gwen described. Charlotte looked indignant, but she was a good sport and nodded. Gwen kissed Miguel and got out of the car.

An elderly lady in the elevator cooed over her dress and mask. Gwen smiled and got off eagerly on her floor. She opened the door to her apartment and found it almost completely dark.

'Sandra!' she called as she closed the door behind her. She flipped on the lights and saw the little table by the door on which they kept their keys had been overturned.

The contents lay on the floor. 'Are you drunk?' Gwen groaned as she righted the table. It would explain the weirdness of the texts.

Gwen stood and peeled off her coat to toss it on the couch as she walked toward the hallway where their rooms were. She heard frantic scratching and meowing coming from the bathroom, so she opened the door. Tabby rushed out, but she didn't go toward Gwen's closed door as usual. Instead, she ran into the living room, and Gwen could hear her meowing at the sliding door.

Gwen turned to go toward Sandra's open bedroom door, but her eye caught Sandra's limp body in a heap in the tub. Her bleeding head was sprawled over the edge.

'Sandra!' screeched Gwen as she turned on the light and rushed inside to her roommate's side. She touched Sandra's neck gently and was thankful to find a pulse.

'Gwen,' her friend breathed weakly.

'Did you fall into the tub?' Gwen demanded. Her friend was still in her sparkly flapper Halloween costume.

'Jon... Jonathon,' Sandra hissed in warning, and Gwen's heart nearly stopped. For a half a moment, she couldn't move or think beyond the fact that her cellphone was in her coat pocket on the couch.

'Is he still here?' she asked, but Sandra seemed to have lost consciousness again.

Gwen rose, debating whether to run for the living room or to stay with her friend. Looking down at Sandra, Gwen knew she needed medical attention ASAP, so she took in a deep breath. She quickly kicked off her heels and hitched her ridiculously enormous dress up around her thighs. Her muscles twitched in frightened readiness as she prepared to run and to fight for her life if necessary. She lunged forward out of the bathroom door and ran right into Jonathon Welford. He was waiting in the hall, and he wrapped his arms around her so tightly that at first she couldn't even scream.

'Gotcha, you stupid bitch!' he snarled.

Gwen screeched and twisted violently in her efforts to

free herself as he dragged her backwards toward her room. The door was now open, and she realized he'd been waiting in there. She tried to hook her heels around the doorframe, but he roughly jerked her through. Gwen glanced around to see her room had been ripped apart. Her closet doors and dresser drawers had been torn off, and the bed was overturned.

Gwen lifted her foot and was able to kick against the dresser, which knocked Jon back into the wall. She heard his breath blasted out of him as her weight hit him, and his grip on her weakened. He grabbed her hair before she could bolt for the door, and Gwen cried out in pain as he heaved her to the floor. He collapsed on top of her, and his weight knocked the air out of her.

'*Get off!*' she shrieked and began to kick and punch in desperation to get him away from her. He used his knees and her skirts to hold down her legs while his hands restrained her arms at her sides. His laughter, and the familiar scent of whisky on his breath, twisted her gut with disgust.

'Just stop!' he shouted. 'You never were very smart.'

He leaned down toward her, and she knew he was going to try and kiss her. She head-butted him, and her forehead connected with a crack against his recently healed nose. Fresh blood erupted from his nostrils and dripped all over her dress as he sat back to howl in pain.

She tried to shove him off her when he released her arms, but his weight on the dress was still holding her down. She could only hold her arms up uselessly when he grabbed a heavy wooden sculpture that had been knocked off her dresser. She didn't hear the *thunk* when he hit her, only the ringing in her ears.

'You're going to pay for everything!' he insisted. She was suddenly numb as she felt the wet warmth of blood leaking down her scalp and spreading through her hair. All she could think was this was not the way the night was supposed to go.

'Miguel... downstairs,' she said in an attempt to scare

Jon and make him stop. Anything to make him stop...

'Shut up!' he shouted, and Gwen felt him roughly tear off her mask. Then she heard him start ripping at her dress.

Miguel

Chapter Twenty-Four

A sudden chill ran down my spine, and made my incisors lengthen immediately. My pupils dilated, and blood pooled under my eyes. We'd turned on the interior lighting, and I'd taken off my mask so Charlotte saw my face change.

'Holy mother of shit!' she cried.

'Are you all right?' Derek demanded.

'Something is wrong,' I hissed. I was humming with the need to tear something apart, and Charlotte's eyes suddenly widened with understanding. She looked toward the roof of the limo, but I knew she was glancing toward the building outside.

'Gwen,' she guessed, and I didn't wait for any more information.

I heard them gasp at my speed when I opened the door and leaped onto the sidewalk. By the time they'd gotten out of the car, I'd determined the elevator would be too slow, and I'd circled the building. I saw a light on in Gwen's window, which was cracked so the cat could enter from the pine tree next to the building. I jumped, catching the ledge, and pulled the window open more. I heard it creak, and the hinges broke, but I didn't care.

Jonathon Welford was kneeling over Gwen, who was bleeding and nearly unconscious. He was ripping at her dress and trying to find his way between her thighs.

I smashed the rest of the window out of my way so I could climb into the room. Jonathon looked up in shock, which turned quickly into horror.

'You,' he said, and I saw his eyes go to the window in misunderstanding as Gwen's head lolled toward me. Her eyes were blank when she looked up at me, and I knew she was hurt.

'Miguel' she sighed with relief as my nostrils flared, and my lips lifted in a snarl.

Jonathon realized he wasn't facing a human, and he scrambled to his feet to flee. I was across the room in the blink of an eye, and I snatched him by the neck with one hand as he started to scream. Bashing his skull on the wall silenced him, and he crumpled to the floor.

I grabbed a handful of his dark hair and lifted him with one arm. He squealed and thrashed with his hands covering mine while I pulled him to me. I broke his arm in my hand, and he screeched again before my long teeth sank into his neck with ease. He choked on his own scream and began to spasm vigorously against the paralyzing effects of the vampire venom. Blood leaked down his throat because I was shaking in my fury, but normally I abhorred the wasting of blood. I finished and dropped him onto the floor with a dull thud.

My body was throbbing from the adrenaline. It took me some time to get myself back under control and force the predator back down to his place. I opened my eyes once my teeth had receded, and I saw his lifeless eyes staring up at me.

I turned away from him in disgust and became immobile when I saw Gwen was sitting up and holding the side of her head. She was staring at me with the same horror Jonathon had experienced when I'd come through the window.

'Gwen—'

'Stay back!' she cried when I stepped toward her, and she threw out her bloody hands to ward me away. Her terror pierced me with a physical pain, and my chest seemed to swell with dread. I obliged her and took several steps away from her.

She watched me until she thought I was far enough, and then she got unsteadily to her feet. She staggered and tripped over her ruined dress toward the doorway.

'Don't,' I said softly. 'You need to sit down.'

'Stay there!' she yelled at me, but then she got suddenly dizzy and stumbled. I was there immediately to catch her before she hit the floor. 'Stay away from me, please,' she wept, and her hands began to push at me uselessly as I guided her down to the floor. I knelt with her and held out my hands in a gesture of peace.

'Gwen, you know I'd never hurt you,' I reminded her.

We sat there together as she sobbed, and I tried to stem the ache of her rejection. I could see her glancing at Jonathon's motionless body. Finally, after several moments, she looked up at me. There were tears running down her cheeks leaving bloody tracks.

'What are you?' she breathed.

'Gwen, I don't—'

'What *are* you!?' she yelled.

Looking into her frantic eyes, I saw Hudson was right. What we'd had was over now that she knew.

'What. Are. You?' she grated again when I said nothing, and I sank fully to the floorboards as the fight went out of me.

'Please,' I said softly, lowering my eyes from her scathing look, 'just listen to—'

'*Tell me what you are,*' she insisted with angry anguish.

'I'm *me*, Gwen!' I shouted back. 'Trust me, I'm as terrified as you are right now,' I promised her.

'Why?' she snapped, and I looked down again as a great wave of humility crashed through me.

'I don't want to lose you' I admitted, and when I glanced up her eyes had softened but only a little.

'I don't understand,' she whispered. I inched nearer to comfort her, but she pulled away from me. My hands lowered to the floor between us.

'I'm not human,' I said finally. 'I'm sorry.'

She looked even more confused as the front door opened, but she didn't seem to hear it. She was intent on me until Derek entered the hallway between the two bedrooms.

'Derek!' she cried in relief as he came very slowly into the room. He took in Jonathon's body and Gwen's ruined dress.

'Oh no,' he sighed.

'Derek, what's going on?' Gwen shrieked at him as Charlotte appeared and rushed to her side. Charlotte hadn't seen Jon's body before entering the room, and she froze next to Gwen. Then she looked up at me with understanding.

'Are you okay?' she asked, and there was this part of me that really appreciated her for that. I nodded wordlessly and inched away from Gwen, who watched me cautiously.

'Sandra!' my mate suddenly remembered, and she began to struggle to get up. Luckily, Charlotte held her down.

'Where is she?' Derek asked.

'Bathroom,' said Gwen quickly, and he nodded before going to see about Gwen's roomie.

I turned toward the window, but I could feel Gwen's eyes burning into my back. I texted Hudson and asked him to meet me.

'Did you come through the window?' Charlotte asked with her typical talent of lightening the mood.

'Yes,' I answered without taking my eyes off the city lights outside. It was starting to snow harder.

'It's two storeys,' Gwen reminded us.

'Yes, I know,' Charlotte assured her. 'I'm sorry, honey. You were not supposed to figure this out this way.'

'Figure out what?' Gwen demanded, and I looked over to see Charlotte was dabbing at her head wound with a pillowcase.

'That your boyfriend is a vampire,' Charlotte explained calmly, and Gwen looked at her with wild disbelief. Then she glanced at me, and I could almost see her putting all the clues together in her mind before she glared at her friend.

'You *knew*?'

'Knew the first night we met him,' Charlotte informed her honestly. 'It's what Derek does. It's why he didn't like Miguel at first, remember? But he does now,' Charlotte added meaningfully. 'Miguel is a good person.'

'This… is impossible!' Gwen rejected.

'Sandra is fine, but she needs stitches,' said Derek. 'I can take her to the hospital.'

'What are *you* going to do?' asked Charlotte, and I looked back to see she and Derek were looking at me. Gwen was avoiding my eyes.

'Hudson will be here soon. I will have him deal with the body,' I advised them. Even to my own ears, my voice was devoid of emotion. 'Then I will go.'

'Don't you think you should talk to Gwen a little?' Charlotte asked hopefully, and I looked at my lover. I didn't know if I could face all the hatred brewing behind her gaze, and I turned away before emotion could breech my expression.

'We need to go,' Derek said softly. 'Charlotte and I will take Sandra to the hospital.'

'Don't leave me alone,' pleaded Gwen quietly, and Charlotte scoffed at her.

'Don't be silly! Talk to him,' she insisted.

'He's not—!' Gwen broke off in uncertainty. 'He's not human. There is nothing to talk about,' she finished.

Those were the *very* words I'd been dreading. They lanced through me more painfully than I'd anticipated they would.

Hudson had been at Liam's apartment nearby, and he drifted silently into the room. He slowly took in his surroundings.

'Are you all right, Gwen?' he asked softly.

'Are you… like Miguel?' she asked instead of answering.

'Yes,' he responded without hesitation. 'Shall I take care of that?' he asked in my direction. I knew he would be indicating Jon's body, so I nodded wordlessly.

Hudson picked up Gwen's wool throw blanket and wrapped it around my mate's shoulders as she leaned away from him. He turned to strip the sheets off the mattress. There was an awkward silence as he roughly wrapped the body and threw it over his shoulder. He stepped up behind me, putting his hand briefly on my shoulder, before slipping out the window.

Gwen made a sound of confusion, and I could imagine she was casting around for some semblance of sanity in the world.

'Derek, take them to the hospital,' I said without turning my head. 'Call me later, and I'll give you directions for the Dowrra Sanctuary. You'll be safe there.'

'Miguel, please—' Charlotte began, but I stepped through the window and dropped down to the ground.

x x x

Gwendolyn

'That could have gone better,' Derek observed, and Charlotte snorted.

'Why did no one tell me I was hanging out with *vampires*?' Gwen growled with absolute fury. 'I was surrounded by monsters, and no one said *anything*.'

She had never felt more betrayed, not even when her mother had died, and she was angry. She was angry because he'd been everything she'd ever longed for, and now he was *nothing*.

Charlotte looked uncomfortable as she looked up at her husband for guidance. He offered none.

'Why don't you take Sandra to the hospital? I'll stay and talk to her,' Charlotte suggested. Derek nodded, and he leaned down to touch her shoulder in support before he left them alone.

Charlotte fought with the overturned mattress until it

was flat. Then she sat down on it and studied her friend's angry eyes.

'No one said anything because you were never in any danger,' she told Gwen firmly.

'Never in any danger?' repeated Gwen in disbelief. 'I just watched him kill Jon!'

'Yah, I can't really defend him on that account,' Charlotte admitted reluctantly. 'Gwen, it's just nature! I don't know what else to tell you. He was born a vampire, and they hunt humans, but I don't think that makes him a monster. He also... loves you,' she said, sounding hopeful. 'Besides, Jon kinda deserved it.'

Gwen was silent as she clenched the blanket Hudson had wrapped around her tighter. Her mind was whirling with confusion.

'So... why didn't he ever kill me?' she asked. 'If it's their nature to kill humans, why would he and Hudson protect me?'

Charlotte sighed long and hard.

'This... is a long story. I'm going to go make some tea. When you're ready, come out to the living room with me,' she proposed.

Gwen nodded, and Charlotte got up. Gwen sat listening to her open and close cupboards in the kitchen in her quest for tea supplies. After a few moments, Gwen got to her feet with the blanket still wrapped around her, and she went out to help. Once the tea was made, they moved to the couch where Tabby had curled up.

'Miguel said Dr. Johansson told a story about the Dowrra?' Charlotte began. Gwen closed her eyes as she wracked her brain for the memory of their first date.

'Yes, she said there were vampires...' Gwen hesitated, and her eyes opened as she remembered that. 'Miguel lied!'

'Can you blame him?' Charlotte muttered sarcastically. She sobered, however, when Gwen glared at her. 'Tell me what she said about the Dowrra,' she redirected.

'They are women who fall in love with...'

Once again Gwen hesitated as she suddenly remembered Miguel's expression during Anita's speech. He'd been looking at her with such curiosity and wonder that she knew he must have realized what she was to him. She was suddenly conflicted.

Part of her was convinced Miguel was a monster. It would be easier to let him go if she could maintain he was evil, and he'd maliciously used her. But another part of her just wanted things to go back to the way they were before Jon's attack.

'Are you saying that he and I… are meant to be together because of some goddess feud?' asked Gwen doubtfully.

'I know it sounds crazy—'

'It *is* crazy!' Gwen shouted at her.

'I'm Dowrra too,' Charlotte continued firmly, and Gwen's eyes widened in surprise. 'Your mother was Dowrra. Your grandmother was Dowrra. Look, Miguel is the answer to why you haven't been able to lead a normal life until now. He needs you right now, and you really, *really* need him.'

'What do you mean?' Gwen asked suspiciously.

'Humans have always hated vampires for obvious reasons, but they also hate us. You and I are the reason vampires can even exist, so humans have spent thousands of years hunting us down. Two hundred years ago, they signed the Accords and made a truce with vampires, but now they might be able to fight back. If they can kill vampires, vampires can't protect us anymore. Which means you and I are in danger.'

Gwen sat there listening to the insane words but not really comprehending them.

'Is it *really* that difficult to understand?' demanded a voice from behind Gwen.

She turned in shock to see two men and a black-haired woman standing in her hallway. Gwen immediately recognized the man in the grey coat as the one Hudson had said was following her. More importantly, she registered that they all had the same dark eyes she now knew betrayed them for what they really were.

They were vampires.

Chapter Twenty-Five

Gwen shot to her feet.

'Who are you, and why are you following me?' she demanded.

'My name is Jacqueline Iscariot,' said the vampiress, drawing Gwen's eyes to her. 'This is Matthew Dentz and Ahren Schmidt. They have been following you to protect you, Gwen. I have wanted to meet you ever since my mother told me I had a sister.'

Gwen was taken aback, and she automatically began searching the stranger for signs of her suspicions. She wanted to deny the possibility, but it was too obvious to pretend otherwise. Jacqueline could have been her dark-haired twin.

Gwen glanced down to Charlotte for support. She was relieved to see her friend had discreetly pulled Gwen's cell out of her coat, which had been left on the couch. She had dialled Miguel's number, and it was ringing. She just had to wait, and Miguel would be back soon.

'Who is your mother?' Gwen asked in an effort to keep their unwanted companion talking.

'Maria Rhys,' said the vampiress knowingly, and Gwen immediately shook her head despite already knowing it was true.

'My mother died twenty years ago,' she maintained.

'Your father lied to you! She died two months ago,' Jaqueline informed her.

Gwen glanced down at her phone on the couch and

saw it was still ringing. *Why wasn't he picking up?*

'She was killed by humans. You need to tell your sympathetic boyfriend they've developed werewolf venom darts that can kill us. Many of my best agents have already lost their lives,' Jacqueline snapped. 'My father can't protect us all alone.'

'Who... *is* your father?' Gwen asked. She'd been bombarded with so much insane information, and she was at her limit. All she could wonder was the name of the vampire for whom her mother had abandoned her all those years ago.

'Judas,' responded Jacqueline. 'My father's name is Judas.'

'Jacqueline Iscariot, you said your name was?' asked Charlotte rather loudly. Gwen glanced down to see Miguel had finally picked up the phone, and Charlotte was discreetly warning him. 'Your father's name is Judas, and the humans have werewolf venom darts?'

'That is what I said,' Jacqueline growled with confusion.

'My mother... was she happy?' Gwen asked hesitantly, before realizing she didn't really want to know. Jacqueline looked sympathetic.

'She was very happy, but she always missed you. She even asked my father about bringing you to the coven, but it wouldn't have been fair to you,' she revealed. 'A coven is no place for an unmated Dowrra.'

'How did she die?' Gwen asked, and Jacqueline became hesitant.

'She was coming to warn you. She wanted to convince you to go to a Sanctuary,' Jacqueline admitted. 'I pissed someone off, and they came after her when she was exposed.'

Gwen noticed the blond vampire, Matthew, turn his head as though he'd heard something. Then he suddenly grabbed Jacqueline to throw her backwards into the hallway. The man who'd been following Gwen, Ahren, reached her and Charlotte in the blink of an eye. Gwen screamed when he suddenly put himself between her and the window just before the glass shattered. Two men wearing combat gear swung into the apartment on harnesses, and they opened fire the moment their feet hit the floor. Luckily, their bullets bounced off the vampire, whom Gwen realized was blocking her and Charlotte.

'*We have a VMP target! Switch ammunition*!' said a male voice over the radios in the helmets of their attackers.

Ahren abruptly turned while the men behind him switched their magazines. Gwen screeched when he grabbed her, and he threw her effortlessly. Before she hit the floor, Matthew caught her and pushed her to safety with Jacqueline. Gwen spun around and was relieved Charlotte was right behind her.

She looked toward Ahren as multiple darts struck him. They were red, and although the bullets had bounced off, they pierced his chest. He closed his eyes and stumbled to the floor.

'Ahren!' screamed Jacqueline, and Matthew grabbed her against his chest before she could run to their fallen companion.

'He's gone, Jackie. We need to move now!' Matthew urged as the anguish twisted her beautiful features. She grudgingly regained control of herself, and she reached for Gwen's hand. Before they could make a run for it, Matthew cursed, and he pushed them farther down the hall.

Gwen's room blew apart behind him.

The explosion sent all the women to the ground, and they covered their heads as bits of debris battered them. Gwen looked up to see Matthew had taken the brunt of the abuse, and he'd shielded them with his body from harm. He looked absurdly calm as he quickly patted the smoking parts of his clothing. There was steel stabbing into the concrete walls, yet he'd stood utterly unfazed.

'What the *fuck* is going on?' Charlotte screamed.

'We're surrounded,' Matthew explained curtly, and

there was brief silence.

'*We've got a VMP on the roof! Watch out!*' said the voice on the radio in the living room. '*Another one on the ground!*' screamed someone else.

Suddenly, the front door was blasted off its hinges. Gwen screamed and ducked instinctively before she turned hoping to see it was Miguel who'd returned.

A man more beautiful than anyone she'd ever seen was standing there with his auburn blond hair mussed from the wind. He was wearing a black shirt, stretched tight across his broad chest, and jeans although it was starting to snow outside. His angry eyes swept the room quickly, and when he spotted Gwen, he was relieved.

Gwen opened her mouth to warn him, but it was too late, and the men with guns started shooting. The stranger lifted his arm calmly, so the darts stuck into his forearm. Gwen expected him to go down the way Ahren had, but the shots seemed merely to irritate him. He casually examined the darts and then looked back up at the human men.

'I *really* hate it when people shoot me,' he advised them, and Gwen recognized his voice. It was Liam, Hudson's enigmatic brother in the mask, from the Halloween party.

Liam moved so quickly he seemed to simply appear in front of the two human men. He was even faster than the other vampires, and he grabbed both humans by their throats to lift them. They made strangled coughing noises and dropped their guns before he gave them a small shake. Gwen flinched when she heard both their necks snap, and then he deposited them on the floor.

Liam, who was clearly another vampire, suddenly took an unsteady step backwards. He gave his head a shake and turned toward them. Gwen thought he looked a little faint.

'They've… upped the dosage,' he noted.

'I see that,' said someone else, and Gwen turned with relief to see Hudson was standing in the doorway. He looked rather amused by his brother.

'Thank the gods, Hudson,' breathed Jacqueline.

'Where's Miguel?' Gwen asked worriedly.

'He called me. I was closer,' Liam explained, and he looked at Hudson. 'Who called *you*?'

'Jacqueline,' said Hudson with his hands tucked casually into his pockets. He leaned against the doorframe and inclined his head toward Gwen's sister, who winked at him suggestively.

Liam grunted, and he gave his head another shake. 'They *really* upped the dosage,' he complained.

'Why didn't it kill you?' asked Gwen. Hudson and Liam both looked down at Ahren lying on the floor.

'The older we get, the stronger we become,' Hudson revealed. 'My brother is five-thousand- years-old, Mrs. Rhys.'

'Thousand?' Gwen repeated in disbelief.

'Give or take a few centuries,' Liam inserted as though embarrassed by his age.

'I thought we were surrounded?' Charlotte reminded them nervously.

'We took care of that,' Liam assured her, and she sighed in relief before sagging more comfortably against the floor.

'Does anyone know if my husband is okay?' she asked.

'Derek is fine,' said Hudson. 'Miguel and his sister got to him.'

'They went after Derek?' Charlotte snarled.

Gwen stood glancing back and forth between all the vampires in the room. They supposed to be monsters, but they'd just risked their lives to come to her rescue. She glanced down at the bodies of the two humans who had been trying to kill her, and she felt sick. It was confusing to suddenly find herself on the wrong side of humanity. Like the entire world had flipped on its end.

'I need to see Miguel,' she said shamefully.

'I was told to take you to a Sanctuary,' Liam informed her firmly. 'It was created for you and other women like you. Vampires are not allowed to go there. You would be safe.'

'She will be safe with me,' Jacqueline cut in. 'We talked about this,' she reminded Hudson angrily.

'I'm sorry, Jacqueline. I answer to Miguel on this one,' he confessed, and she rolled her eyes.

'I've heard of the Sanctuaries,' Charlotte acknowledged. 'Miguel said my husband is welcome?' she verified worriedly.

'Yes, of course,' said Liam.

'Why can't I see Miguel?' Gwen demanded anxiously, and Hudson shared a look with his brother Gwen didn't trust.

'Perhaps we should speak alone,' Hudson suggested. 'If you feel comfortable,' he amended quickly, and Gwen immediately understood.

'You think I'm still afraid of him,' she realized aloud.

'You're not the first, nor will you be the last Dowrra to suddenly find yourself in this situation,' Liam explained. 'Years ago, Miguel— ... *We* created a place for you beyond human threat and vampire manipulation.'

Everything suddenly became clear to Gwen.

'Those charities Miguel hosts are for the Dowrra. To ensure they are safe?' she confirmed, and Hudson looked incredibly uncomfortable. He and Liam seemed to consider what to tell her.

'There are very few Dowrra convents around the world, and they are mostly concerned with their own internal struggles. They are not able to provide much support for women who find themselves outside their walls. Miguel's mother was one of those women, and she was murdered by her brother after giving birth to a vampire. Miguel and his father have spent centuries trying to find a way to be the unique support Dowrra need,' Hudson admitted finally. 'I didn't tell you that,' he added seriously.

A. A. G O R D O N

'Why not? That's amazing!' Charlotte exclaimed as Gwen's stomach twisted guiltily.

'We are not supposed to interfere with your decision,' Liam revealed. 'Once a Dowrra decides to seek Sanctuary, no vampire can obstruct her wishes.'

'It is your opportunity to seek refuge without questions asked,' Hudson clarified.

'I… can't make a decision until I talk to Miguel. I don't know what my other options are,' Gwen admitted a little awkwardly. She glanced back at Charlotte, who seemed pleased she was considering there might be other options.

'We really don't have much time,' Liam broke in anxiously. 'It might take more than a little werewolf venom to bring me down, but even I can't stand up to a full dosage. They'll be back with one.'

'Werewolf venom?' verified Gwen.

'Long story!' exclaimed Charlotte. 'Let's see Derek and Miguel. Can we do that?' she asked Hudson earnestly, and he grimaced as he looked at Gwen.

'It is not the way it is supposed to be, but if that's what you want, I will take you,' he acknowledged. Gwen nodded eagerly even though her heart was pounding at the idea of confronting Miguel after everything that had happened.

Christ, Jon was dead, and Miguel was a vampire! She was Dowrra, and humans wanted to kill her. Her mother had Chosen a vampire over her, and she had a half-sister who was a vampiress. Now, it seemed as though her life as she knew it was over.

'We must go,' Jacqueline broke in reluctantly. 'Please call me if you need anything,' the vampiress told Gwen sincerely, and she reached out. Gwen felt her cold fingers slide a card into her hand while Matthew went to collect their dead companion. Jacqueline turned to approach Hudson near the door.

'See you soon?' she asked him, and Gwen was impressed to see just the hint of a smile tug at the corner of his lips. Gwen became suspicious he was sleeping with her half-sister.

'Not soon enough,' he assured her before Jackie left.

'Do we have time to change?' Charlotte asked, and Gwen glanced down at her ruined dress.

'Make it quick,' Liam agreed.

'Go with them,' Hudson insisted seriously, and he dialled a number on his phone. Gwen assumed it would be Miguel, so she lingered a little in the hallway.

'Yah, I'm here with Liam. She's safe,' he said as she stepped into her bathroom to wash her bloody face. Then she went to her bedroom.

Liam came with them and went to stand by the wall that had been partially blown apart. He kindly gave the women his back while Gwen found Charlotte a pair of sweatpants and a sweater. She also took an opportunity to cram a few things into a bag.

'So... five-thousand-years, hmm?' asked Charlotte with her typical, helpless curiosity.

'Give or take,' Liam insisted. He kept his back to them.

'I know who you are,' Charlotte declared. 'All Dowrra know who you are.'

'I know,' he assured her impatiently.

'Was it true about Aphrodite?' she pressed, and Gwen glanced at her skeptically. Liam laughed softly.

'Not even my twin brother knows all the truths of that affair,' Liam revealed. He turned back toward them when Gwen zipped up her overnight bag. 'What makes you think I'd tell you?' he demanded before wordlessly taking Gwen's bag for her.

He jerked his head toward the door, and Charlotte grudgingly led the way back into the living room where Hudson was waiting.

Miguel

Chapter Twenty-Six

I didn't know where I was going or what I was going to do with all the raging emotions at war within me. I'd never felt such turmoil even after my mother had been killed.

Drunken people walked by me in their costumes as they meandered from bar to bar. A couple of girls gave me the thumbs up.

'Nice vampire costume,' they congratulated me, and I glanced down. My masquerade suit was splattered in Jon's blood.

'You look like you've had a rough night,' observed a familiar voice. I turned, fighting a fierce glare, to see my sister on the street in front of me.

'I told you not to come. It's too dangerous,' I chastised her, and she snorted dismissively.

Mackayla and I had always been very close, but it had been a year since we'd seen one another. Her dark hair spiralled into thick curls that hung to her slender waist. She was wearing black leather pants, tall wedged boots, and a cropped lace top that exposed her toned belly. Her long black coat was open and flapping behind her in the wind.

If I were wearing the classic vampire costume, my sister was wearing the modern Goth version.

She reached me, and she wrapped her arms around me

to give me a quick squeeze. I grunted in pain. She was older than I was, and she liked to remind me her strength was greater than mine.

'I missed you, Miguel,' she assured me sincerely. 'I've been worried.'

I opened my mouth to respond, but my phone rang, and I reached for it grudgingly. When I saw Derek's number, I almost put it back in my pocket. Thankfully, I didn't.

I lifted my hand to my sister, who nodded, and I stepped away from her. The distance wouldn't make a difference to her superior hearing, but it was still polite.

'Miguel!' Derek cried into the phone, and I heard tires squealing in the background. 'They're chasing us on Bay Street! We just passed Edward.'

'Who is chasing you?' I demanded as my heart slammed immediately into my throat.

'Humans,' Derek assured me. 'They look like some military guys!'

I realized we were out of time. Mackayla stepped a little closer to me, and I could see her glancing around us protectively.

'I'll be right there,' I told him.

'No! The women stayed at the apartment. You have to protect them first, Miguel!' Derek shouted. 'If they're coming for me, they must know about Charlotte.'

Those words resonated with me, and I hung up instantly. I was about to ask for my sister's help, but my phone rang again. When I looked down and saw Gwen's number, I immediately answered.

'Are you al—'

'Jacqueline Iscariot, you said your name was?' asked Charlotte on the other end of the phone. 'Your father's name is Judas, and the humans have werewolf venom darts?' she continued, and my stomach twisted in dread.

'That is what I said,' said a familiar voice. I remembered the dark-haired vampiress I'd sent to Hudson after she'd tried to seduce me weeks before. She was

Judas's daughter!

'Werewolf venom,' hissed Mackayla resentfully, and she pushed me into the shadow of the building.

Thinking fast, I hung up and called the only vampire I'd ever known to survive werewolf venom.

'Liam, I need help,' I said when he answered.

'I'm currently in the middle of something,' he admitted with feigned delicacy. I heard feminine laughter on the other end.

'Liam, they have werewolf venom, and they're coming for my mate. I *need* your help,' I repeated through my teeth.

There was just a brief hesitation on his end before he cleared his voice a little awkwardly. I could hear several disappointed sighs from the vampiresses with him, and I knew he'd pried himself loose of them.

'Where is she?' he asked, and I gave him Gwen's address.

'Liam, you need to offer her Sanctuary from me,' I added before he could hang up. 'She knows.'

There was another momentary silence on the other end. We didn't have time even for the briefest of pauses, but I needed to hear him confirm.

'I'm sorry,' he said with reservation. 'I will.'

I hung up feeling certain that even if I were not able to save Derek, at least Gwen would be safe with Liam protecting her. I saw Mackayla gazing at me in remorse, but she knew better than to try and console me.

We melted into the shadows and took to the roof while I dialled my butler.

'Ainsley, code black,' I said when he answered.

'I just sorted that out, Sir. They came to the penthouse, but I was ready for them,' my butler revealed proudly. 'See you soon, Miguel,' he added. It was the first time he'd ever used my first name, and I was abruptly very pleased he'd gotten out alive.

I hung up with him and immediately called Derek again.

'You go to Charlotte first, Miguel!' he shouted before I could even say anything.

'Liam will get to them first,' I assured him with a calmness I didn't feel. 'Where are you?'

He was silent, and I imagined he was genuinely surprised to know I'd bother to come for him at all. I'd spent the entirety of my relationship with Gwen keeping him at a distance. I'd repetitively declared any protection I'd provided to him was for her benefit. Now, with her life in the balance, I could no longer pretend his life didn't mean *something* to me.

'Wellesley,' he said finally. 'Miguel, are you sure Char—?'

I hung up, and before long, my sister and I reached Wellesley Street West. From there, I easily spotted the limo several blocks north as it raced recklessly down the crowded street with the horn blaring. There were several police and armoured cars behind.

'What's the plan?' asked Mackayla.

'Element of surprise and *not* getting hit,' I explained. She snickered at my warning.

'As if they will see me coming,' she responded in her typically cocky way, and I laughed. I returned my attention to the scene below us as army trucks parked on the street to block the limo.

Mackayla followed my lead as we raced ahead so we were behind the blockade. I saw men in black combat gear peering around the edges of the vehicles with automatic weapons at the ready.

We hit them hard and too fast for them to react. Bullets tore the buildings apart around us, and human pedestrians screamed out in fear.

Once the soldiers were dead, I grabbed the truck by the front bumper and flipped it out of Anthony's path. I waved to my driver, who saluted me back as he roared by us.

My sister stepped into the road behind the limo and deliberately into the path of a following cruiser. The brakes squealed, and the car fishtailed as it hit ice. When the tires met dry pavement again, the vehicle flipped and rolled quickly toward us. Mackayla crouched under it as it came at her so she could get her hands under it. Her palms dented the roof when she rose and pitched it across the lane into the next cruiser. The wreck cut off road access for the entire fleet of police cars, which came to a screeching halt. I applauded her, and she preened with pride.

Gunshots suddenly rang out, and we both ducked into the shadows. I checked the bricks near where my head had been and saw rivulets of a clear solution running down the wall. I could smell it.

Werewolf venom…

My sister met my eyes knowingly. We kept to the shadows and never paused for more than a couple of seconds. No human sniper would have ever been able to hit us.

We regrouped a couple of blocks north, and Mackayla was on the phone. I didn't have to hear his voice to know Hudson was on the other end. They might have separated over six hundred years ago, but there was still a certain way my sister behaved around him. I knew she was still in love with him, but I wasn't stupid enough to bring it up to her.

I saw the limo had been ditched on the side of the road with all the doors open. Following the scent of Sandra's blood, we caught up to them in an alleyway far away from the city lights. Anthony was carrying Sandra, who was still unconscious. Derek had a gun levelled toward the alley opening, but he lowered it instantly when he recognized me.

'Miguel,' he said in relief.

'Mackayla, take Sandra to the nearest hospital,' I said quickly. 'Meet us at Highberry Park.'

She nodded wordlessly and stepped forward to accept Sandra's limp body from Anthony. 'See you soon, brother,' she said, and she left as my phone rang. It was

Hudson, so I picked up immediately.

'Hudson!'

'Yah, I'm here with Liam. She's safe,' he assured me, and I felt an immense relief consume me. 'I spoke to Mackayla—'

'I know. Meet us in Highberry Park,' I advised him. I knew he would recognize the remote estate just north of the city where I'd set up a halfway house for vampires.

'Miguel, she wants to see you. It's not customary, but I think you should speak with her,' he informed me.

I had started enforcing the notion of Sanctuary for Dowrra to protect them from the fate of my mother. She had had nowhere to go, no one to turn to, and as a result, her brother had murdered her. Separating a Dowrra from her mate and family during her transition to the Sanctuary was done to avoid coercion, duress, and violence.

'She wants to see me?' I said and was unable to help the painful resurgence of hope. I'd mentally and emotionally crushed all aspirations for our future after leaving her a short hour ago. Now, those hopeful seeds were germinating again.

I saw Derek lift a hand toward my shoulder and was reminded of my audience. Lucky for him, he stopped short of offering me a consoling touch, and his hand returned to his side.

'She's adamant, but I can't tell you what she's thinking. I can't even promise she won't give you more hell, but I do think you should talk to her,' Hudson admitted.

'I'll see her at Highberry,' I told him, and I hung up before I lost control of my tone.

xxx

Gwendolyn

They walked to a part of town where all the building faces were terribly dark and dingy. Hudson insisted Gwen and Charlotte walk between him and his brother, who acted like their invincible shields against attack. It amazed Gwen that the humans walking by them in their costumes had no idea they were so close to predators.

Liam stepped up to a metal door covered in graffiti, and he exerted enough strength to break the lock. They stepped inside, and Liam clicked on the light. It flickered as they descended a dark set of stairs.

'How do we know you aren't going to kill us?' Charlotte muttered, and Gwen squeezed her hand. She wasn't sure when they'd started holding hands, but it felt really good just then.

'I suppose you don't,' Hudson admitted as they entered an underground parking garage.

'My personal stash,' Liam advised them as he indicated the rows of vehicles. There were beautiful cars that looked like Miguel's, but there were also military trucks and even a couple of transport trucks.

Liam led them to the back, and Gwen's eyebrows rose at the sight of a plain black Mazda hatchback with tinted windows.

'Most valuable car in my collection,' Liam boasted.

'Inconspicuous, you mean,' Charlotte acknowledged as the vampire opened the back door for her and Gwen.

'Exactly,' he acknowledged with a deceptively angelic smile. If he were anything like Miguel, Gwen knew his face was capable of betraying true savagery. She closed her eyes when she remembered Miguel's bruised eyes that had become black as coal.

They drove out of the city, and though it was the early hours of the morning, Gwen couldn't fall asleep. The city lights faded around them, and Charlotte passed out on her shoulder, but she stayed awake with her eyes closed.

'Will they awaken him now, do you think?' asked Hudson reluctantly. Gwen realized they must think she was sleeping.

Liam, who was driving, sighed. 'I don't believe anyone will see him as necessary until the Angeli Mortis are actually recreated,' he responded.

'You told Miguel about Serena and the Aegian?' verified Hudson.

'I told him about Attula,' Liam informed him. 'He was angry.'

'Of course, he was angry,' snarled Hudson.

'I've already sent envoys to the convent in Ur. They will be meeting with the Dowrra Matrons within the month to put pressure on them. If they still will not awaken Quinn, my agents will awaken him for them,' Liam revealed grimly.

'Liam,' said Hudson in concern, 'What if he—?'

'I will take whatever blame he imagines we deserve. I will bear the burden of his wrath,' Liam assured his brother, and Gwen was touched by the tenderness in his voice.

'You were never his favourite,' Hudson teased, his tone lightening. 'Perhaps I'm the one who should confront him.'

'He is familiar enough with my foolishness to forgive me. He would be dreadfully disappointed to know you had a hand in any of this,' Liam returned seriously.

'He is going to know, Liam. He knows *everything*.'

There was silence for some time as the brothers mulled over their problem.

'Does anyone know about him?' asked Hudson a little anxiously. Gwen saw Liam shake his head through her lashes. 'Perhaps we should tell them,' Hudson suggested. 'They will all find out once Quinn awakens. He rarely does anything sensitively,' he muttered.

'We need to wait, Hudson. I'm not ready for them to know,' Liam insisted.

'Fine,' Hudson hissed.

Chapter Twenty-Seven

Gwen woke after not meaning to fall asleep when the car came to a stop, and the vampires got out. Charlotte yawned and stretched contentedly, but Gwen was glancing around them nervously at the darkness. They appeared to be in a forest on some dirt road covered in snow.

Liam opened her door and offered her his hand. With a small hesitation, she took it, and he pulled her out of the car. He had her overnight bag already in hand as he guided her to where Hudson stood with Charlotte.

There was a sign, covered in snow, but she immediately recognized the name glinting in the headlights. They were back in her hometown of Silver Springs.

Liam tossed the keys in his hand, and Gwen glanced aside to see Anthony was standing at the front of the car. He smiled at her when she saw him.

'Hopefully, I'll see you soon, Miss Rhys,' he said before he went around the car and got into the driver's seat. The hatchback drove away, which left them in almost complete darkness.

It was snowing, and Gwen shivered under her coat as she stood in the snowbank wondering why they were in her hometown. She had not been back there in almost ten years.

Liam offered her his arm, and he steered her toward the ditch and the dark treeline. She found the trail

Anthony must have made through the snow. She stumbled, but Liam seemed to be able to see, and he helped her along. They entered the trees, and Gwen couldn't help but sidle a little closer to her vampire protector. It seemed ridiculous, but she was more afraid of the dark than she was of him.

They walked for several moments, and Liam was kind enough to hold the branches out of her way. She could hear them snapping under his fingers as he bent them back. She imagined those fingers had snapped a lot of human bones too.

Finally, she saw a small, snowy cabin with a warm light glowing from the small windows. Feeling emotionally weary, Gwen stumbled toward it gratefully, and Liam opened the door for her. Warmth thawed her frozen hands as she glanced quickly around the small living room.

There was a fire glowing in the hearth, which was surrounded by leather couches. A woman with long black hair was sitting in front of it with a mug in her hand. She wasn't surprised by their sudden appearance.

'It's about time,' she advised Liam familiarly as she rose from her seat. Gwen knew right away she was Miguel's sister. The resemblance between them was unmistakable.

Hudson walked into the cabin with Charlotte, and Mackayla's brows rose at him. She set down her mug before crossing her arms over her chest. 'Hudson,' she acknowledged him frostily.

'Mackayla,' he returned drolly.

'Where is Miguel?' asked Liam impatiently.

'Scouting,' Mackayla answered. 'He'll be back soon.'

'I have my own people to worry about now so, if you'll excuse me, this is where I leave you,' Liam admitted. He handed Gwen's bag to Hudson and turned toward the cabin door.

'Thank you,' said Charlotte, which stopped the vampire in his tracks. He glanced back at her, looking incredulous, but then he smiled that breathtakingly gorgeous smile.

'My pleasure,' he responded, and he bowed briefly before taking his leave.

Gwen turned toward Miguel's sister, and she saw Mackayla was already looking at her speculatively.

'You're probably tired,' Mackayla assumed. 'I have prepared a bed for both of you. You may leave your wet things at the door.'

The expression in Mackayla's eyes betrayed distrust, and Gwen felt a little nauseated wondering how Miguel was.

She took off her boots and then took her overnight bag from Hudson. The women left him by the door as they followed Mackayla down a hallway with several rooms behind the kitchen.

'One bed here,' said Mackayla, and she indicated Charlotte. 'Your husband will be back with my brother presently.'

Charlotte seemed absurdly comfortable despite everything that had happened, and she squeezed Gwen's hand before retiring. Gwen followed Mackayla, who indicated the next room on the same side of the hall at the end.

'This is you, Gwen,' she said, and Gwen smiled half-heartedly as she stepped into the room. Mackayla turned to go.

'How long will it be before Miguel comes back?' asked Gwen. Mackayla frowned as she considered.

'Soon,' she promised enigmatically. 'I suggest you sleep, Gwen. It's a long way to the Sanctuary,' she informed her with unmistakable antipathy. Gwen opened her mouth, but Mackayla turned away.

Gwen crawled into the bed, still fully clothed, and she fell asleep almost immediately. She didn't wake until the heavy drapes in her window were fully lit by the sunlight in the forest. She sat up as the scent of pancakes and bacon came to her. She could hear laughter coming from the front room so she got up and crept silently out of her room.

To her surprise, she saw Ainsley in the kitchen. Miguel's butler was making pancakes, which Charlotte was eating at the counter. Next to her, Derek was finishing up the dishes, and they both looked incredibly happy to be back together. Mackayla was leaning over the couch so she and Charlotte could speak across the kitchen counter. Hudson was sitting at the end of another couch next to Miguel, who was standing at the window with his back to the room. The two men were talking quietly.

Charlotte laughed loudly at something Mackayla had said, and Gwen looked back at them.

'That is my favourite store! They have everything an unmated Dowrra could ever possibly need,' her friend gushed. 'I even found that *Venom* brand there.'

'Bloody hell,' grumbled Derek, who was blushing. He kept glancing guiltily toward the men at the other side of the room to make sure they were not listening.

'I'd never thought of that!' Mackayla admitted, and Gwen saw she looked much less severe than before. 'Having a human mate would be problematic for you. Intimately speaking,' she acknowledged.

'Many thanks to the vampire who was kind enough to lend us his venom,' said Charlotte as she ate a mouthful of pancakes.

Gwen must have made the softest sound of confusion because Mackayla's eyes flickered up to meet her eyes. Miguel's sister sobered, and her grin faded.

'Morning,' she said coolly, and Charlotte turned quickly.

'Gwen!' she cried, but Gwen wasn't looking at her. She'd lifted her gaze toward the other side of the room, and her eyes met Miguel's when he turned toward her.

Seeing his face, after everything that had happened, was the single greatest relief she'd ever felt. The emotion that tore through her was ruthless, and she tried to control it, but tears began to sting her eyes. There was a pregnant silence, and Charlotte looked embarrassed by her excited outcry.

Miguel glanced to Hudson before he came across the room toward Gwen. She'd always noticed how silent and gracefully he moved, but she'd never once imagined it was because he was a *vampire*. Watching him now, she berated herself for ignoring the little voice that had suggested there was something off about him all along.

He reached her, but he kept a good deal of space between them, and he didn't touch her.

'Do you want to speak privately, or should Charlotte join us?' he asked her. Despite the detachment in his tone, she could see he was exerting a lot of effort into maintaining his expression. He was hurting, and she felt awful.

'Privately,' she assured him, and he nodded before indicating the hallway behind her with an incline of his head. She glanced at Charlotte, whose hopeful smile was heartening, before she led him back to her room where she closed the door. He went to the window and opened the blinds, so the room was filled with the gleam of sunlight reflecting off the snow.

'I'm sorry,' Gwen began, and he turned back toward her. He seemed surprised by her words.

'You have nothing to be sorry for,' he said. 'I'm the one who deceived you.'

'I should have trusted you, and I should have trusted myself,' she insisted. 'I *knew* I wasn't normal. I knew *you* weren't normal.'

'Gwen—'

'I'm also sorry because I'm still afraid of you and of myself,' Gwen continued determinedly. 'It's scary wanting to be with someone who kills,' she tried to explain, and Miguel looked down as his jaw clenched. 'Isn't there a way... not to?' she asked him hesitantly, and he looked surprised.

'Do you mean... is there a way to *not* be what I am?' he confirmed, and when she sighed guiltily, he seemed upset. 'You make it sound like a lifestyle choice! Gwen, it's not something I can quit or reverse. It's who I am!'

'I know—' she began as her cheeks flushed with shame.

'Humans have this notion their lives are sacred while they freely kill and maim nonhumans. They are not above the laws of nature!' Miguel scowled furiously. Gwen was horrified by this revelation.

'They kill nonhumans?' she verified.

'They nearly eradicated my race,' Miguel told her bitterly. 'Now, they're overpopulated and slowly killing this planet.'

Gwen decided they would come back to the topic of taking human life. He was more sensitive about it than she'd anticipated, and he'd made some startling points.

'Can we talk about you?' she redirected him. 'How... old are you?'

Miguel's defensive tension melted a little, and he seemed to regain his composure.

'I was born in 1501,' he told her, and her eyes widened. So much about him made sense.

'How long will you live?' she asked worriedly as she recalled Anita's presentation about the longevity of vampires. Hudson's brother was five-thousand-years-old!

'We seem to have the potential for immortality if we are not killed,' he revealed.

'What about me?' Gwen asked him worriedly.

'Dowrra live as long as their mate does,' Miguel informed her. 'My venom in your blood would keep you young,' he explained.

'You mean... if you bite me,' Gwen guessed. She remembered the way Jon had spasmed helplessly, and she felt ill.

'It wouldn't be like that,' he said knowingly when he saw her expression. Gwen took a moment to let this frightening new tidbit sink in.

'So your mother was like me,' she acknowledged, and he nodded.

'She met my father in Castile. He was her favourite artist of the time,' he said softly.

'What was his name?' Gwen asked eagerly, and she saw Miguel's mouth tense as he looked away from her eyes.

'Giovanni de los Santos,' he confessed, and her eyes opened wide.

'Your *father* is Giovanni de los Santos?' she demanded, and then she sobered as she realized something even more incredible. 'Giovanni de los Santos was a *vampire*.'

'Many famous people have been,' Miguel revealed.

'Who was your mother?' Gwen asked. 'I know you don't like to speak about her. You don't have to,' she assured him when his lips pressed together with familiar reluctance. This time, however, he finally agreed to indulge her.

'Her name was Francis, of the House of Habsburg. Her father was Maximilian I. The Holy Roman Emperor,' he admitted.

There was a long moment when Gwen had no idea what to say to him, and she merely stood staring up at him in astonishment. Just twelve short hours before, he'd been her boyfriend, who'd come suddenly into her life and changed everything. Then he'd abruptly become a monster far darker than anything she'd ever imagined. Now, he was the five-hundred-year-old vampire grandson of one of the most famous Holy Roman Emperors in history.

'What happened to her?' Gwen asked, and he was silent for a long time.

'I already told you they met in Toledo. My mother knew what my father was almost immediately, but she loved him anyway,' Miguel began. 'She found out she was pregnant when my father went to Rome to complete a commissioned piece for Pope Alexander VI.'

'*Il dono di Cristo,*' Gwen recalled, and he nodded.

'When my mother's family learned of her pregnancy,

they sent her to Romsey Abbey in England,' he continued. 'The nuns learned it was no human child my mother carried, and the Abbess threw her out. That's where I was born,' he said, and Gwen wanted to reach out to him, but she could tell he didn't want to be touched. 'The Dowrra bloodlines are an ancient secret many noble families have tried to cleanse themselves of. My uncle came after us, and my mother tried to get us across the English Channel. They fought, and he threw her from the White Cliffs of Dover. He meant only for me to fall into the ocean,' he confessed, and Gwen could see there was a great deal of shame in his eyes. 'She wouldn't let me go and, in the struggle, he deemed it best to release us both. Better to sacrifice her life than to allow me to live. I survived the fall, and she did not,' he finished.

Gwen couldn't draw breath as she looked up at his tortured expression. She stepped forward in spite of his aversion, and she wrapped her arms around him. At first, he was very stiff, but eventually, he wrapped his arms around her too. She pressed her head against his chest and closed her eyes.

'I want to be with you. Tell me what that looks like,' she bade.

He was silent, and she felt his breath still in his chest beneath her cheek. Slowly, he extracted himself from her grip, and she saw his expression was unexpectedly hard before he faced the window. He leaned with his palms against the frame, and she couldn't help noticing how sexy he looked in a long-sleeved sweater and jeans. She began to wonder what Charlotte had been hinting at when she'd mentioned the use of vampire venom during intimacy.

'It's not enough,' he said finally, shocking her. At first, she thought she must have heard wrong.

'What?'

'I said it is not enough,' he spoke more loudly, and he turned to face her with firm resolve. 'Gwen, I think you should go to the Sanctuary with Charlotte and Derek.'

Gwen stared at him in shock. 'I don't understand,' she admitted.

'The bond between us is strong,' Miguel explained, his mouth twisting in his attempts to keep his composure. 'It's even strong enough to make you want me against your own wishes. That's not what I want.'

'That's not what I said—'

'It's what you meant,' Miguel interrupted roughly. 'To be with me, you will need to accept what I am *completely* because nothing about me is changing. I don't want you to hate me.'

'I don't think you—'

'Every moment I'm with you, I fall so much harder for you,' he told her softly. Tears suddenly stung her eyes when she saw the love and heartache in his eyes as he confessed this. 'There is nothing about you that makes me wish you were different. The longer I'm with you, the more difficult it will be to know you dislike who I am. And...' he hesitated as his eyes lowered to the floor. 'Someday I hope to be a father,' he told her even more softly, and Gwen's eyes opened in shock. 'You might be able to love me, despite hating what I am, but could you love my child? A vampire child,' he elaborated firmly.

'Talking about children seems—'

'Realistic,' he insisted. 'You would be surrounded by vampires all the time,' he illustrated. 'The Sanctuary is inhabited entirely by Dowrra and humans.'

The enormity of what he was saying took her completely unawares, but she knew in her heart he was right. She couldn't make her decision to stay with him based only on how she felt about him. His surviving family was composed of vampires. Charlotte had said he was a prince with responsibilities to protect his people and their way of life. If they had children, she had to be certain she wanted vampire babies.

She lifted her hand to her face and rubbed at a tension headache in her forehead.

'The last twelve hours have been a lot,' she reminded

him, and he nodded in understanding. 'If there's something I've learned, it's that I don't know everything. I think I deserve that before we make any formal decision,' she insisted. 'I *want* to try, Miguel. I want to promise you nothing is going to scare me away, but I can't make that promise right now. What I *can* say is… I love you, and I'm willing to try.'

He considered her words for a moment before he began to nod. Her gut eased a little, and she realized she was nauseous with worry.

'Very well,' he said as his expression became smug. 'Prove it.'

'Prove it?' she repeated in confusion as he moved closer, and his eyes swept her thoughtfully. She felt her thighs warming automatically at the hot look her body had become so conditioned for. 'How?' she asked as he brushed a red curl behind her ear.

'Let me show you what it's like,' he proposed. 'You put your trust in me, in what I do, and we will see if you can be in a relationship with a vampire.'

Gwen's eyes widened up at him.

'What are you going to do?' she asked slowly, and he smiled at the way her voice shook a little.

'Do you trust me?' he asked.

'Are you going to bite me?' she blurted, and her heart leaped into her throat when he simply nodded. 'Is it going to hurt?'

'I suspect it will feel very much like when I took your virginity,' he admitted. 'There will be some initial discomfort.'

When he brought up that night, and the gentle patience he'd shown her, she was reassured. She'd been nervous to experience something new, but since then, she'd learned to trust Miguel's guidance. She needed to trust him now if she wanted to stay with him.

Her eyes wandered down to his full lips behind which he was hiding those fangs. 'Okay,' she agreed.

He smiled before he leaned down, very slowly, to kiss

her and she instantly forgot everything uncomfortable between them. There was nothing more compelling than the perfectly simple chemistry between them. Whatever turmoil was ahead, she felt confident they would deal with it.

Miguel broke the kiss to peel her sweater over her head, and Gwen took the opportunity to pull off his shirt too. The familiar sight of his body was comforting.

She laughed when he picked her up, and she wrapped her legs around him as he carried her to the bed. She remembered Liam busting through her door, and she wondered how strong Miguel really was as he tossed her on the mattress. Before she'd gotten her elbows under her, he'd crawled over her, and she gasped again. He wasn't pretending with her anymore.

'Holy, you're fast,' she hissed. The other vampires had moved from one side of the room to the other in the blink of an eye.

'Very,' he growled in confirmation before she pulled his unshaven jaw down for another kiss. Holding himself over her with one hand, he unbuttoned both of their jeans, and she pushed his down his legs. Her fingers skimmed back up his thigh to his hardened cock, which she gave a firm stroke. He groaned into her mouth and continued to kiss her a little more viciously.

It was hard to reconcile him with the creature that had come through her bedroom window to kill Jon, but she would have to. If she wanted to love him, she would need to accept that her lover had two sides and she'd only gotten to know one of them. As he began to make love to her, more demanding than ever, she got the impression she was about to meet the other.

'Are you ready?' he whispered, and she froze.

'I trust you,' she promised even though she was afraid as his lips trailed along her collarbone and up to her throat.

Gwen closed her eyes as he laced their fingers and crossed his forelegs over hers. His weight pressed her into the bed a little more firmly, and she realized he was restraining her. Panic and adrenaline coursed through her, but she remained as still as she could with his hips still thrusting against her. It was almost impossible not to respond to his cock inside her.

She tensed beneath him when his mouth opened, but he merely sucked gently on her skin. She shivered, and her flesh began to tingle a little.

His strokes between her legs slowed until she was aching for him desperately, and she forgot about his impending bite. Then he sunk against her suddenly hard, and she cried out as her head fell back. Before she knew it, his teeth had sliced through her skin.

It was a split second before she felt the pain of the intrusion, and she jerked impulsively against his hold on her arms. Immediately after registering the agony, however, she was suddenly arching against him in ecstasy. It was far more potent than anything she'd ever known before, and she cried out. Her sex spasmed hard in a ruthless orgasm so intense it was almost painful.

She recognized it immediately. It was the same sensation she'd had in the limo the night they'd first had sex. She wondered if he'd bitten her somehow.

He pulled his teeth away from her, and she was reminded briefly of the pain in her neck. He began to kiss and suck at her skin, and the rawness of the bite lessened.

Then, something truly horrifying happened she hadn't expected.

He began to thrust into her again, and she thought she'd climax all over again from the sensitivity of her first orgasm. Instead, her throat began to burn with a distracting thirst, and she felt a terrible ache in her eyeteeth. She tried hard to focus on Miguel as he began to groan more loudly. She knew he was close, but she couldn't ignore it when she felt her teeth begin to move in her gums. Her tongue flickered forward, and she felt both incisors lengthening.

Something wildly instinctual overcame her, and she

had no time to think about her actions. She simply sat up and abruptly sank elongated teeth into Miguel's shoulder.

She'd bitten him lots of times during sex, sometimes even hard, but she'd never broken the skin and never tasted his blood. She wasn't prepared for it to overwhelm her senses.

Miguel cried out, and he held her hips as he came undone in a way Gwen had never seen him do before. She could feel the orgasm shuddering through him so powerfully it overcame every wall of composure.

She sank into the mattress beneath him, feeling stunned and horrified at the same time. She was suddenly staring up into black eyes that looked bruised around the edges. His mouth was swollen, and her blood was staining his lips. She was caught someplace between awe and terror looking up into the face of something very inhuman.

Then he tenderly brushed the hair back from her forehead, and all fear was gone.

She felt a drop fall onto her chest, and she looked down. A drop of blood had landed on her breast, and she looked up. There were deep and painful looking teeth marks in his skin, and he was bleeding!

She reached up to touch her neck, and it took her a moment to even find the neat little holes he'd put in her skin. In comparison with the terrible wound she'd given him, they were inconsequential.

Her mouth opened in horror, and she looked up at him apologetically. Before she could stutter over an apology, he leaned down and licked up the drops of blood on her skin. She met his dark eyes again, and she felt reassured.

'I guess this means I'm staying with you' she pointed out, and he smiled with a nod.

'You're coming with me to The Wayside.'

Epilogue

Gwendolyn Rhys had decided to stay with me.

It seemed extraordinary, but I continued to wake each morning with her still nestled safely against me. I kept expecting her to bolt over the next couple of days as she was gradually introduced to my world. I was sure something would push her over the edge and she'd leave, but it was day four, and she was still there with me.

The weather was warmer, and the snow had melted since Halloween night. The forest was truly beautiful with the sun shining warmly and the autumn leaves frozen from the sudden onslaught of winter. So, we each strapped on a pair of snowshoes and walked down to the river bordering the property. It was an hour hike but worth it.

The cabin was a perfect haven in which to educate my mate, but it was a little stuffy with two couples trying to find privacy. Mackayla and Hudson had moved on quickly, which was not surprising. They didn't like to be in each other's company for more than a few hours at a time.

'You're really not cold at all, are you?' Gwen asked in amazement.

'Not at all,' I admitted with my hands tucked into my jean pockets. There was no need to fool her anymore, so I was dressed comfortably in a long-sleeved shirt and jeans. She'd donned a jacket, mittens, and a hat.

She peeled off her glove, and she touched me. Her

cool fingers tingled against my neck. 'You feel warm,' she insisted appreciatively, and I unhooked my thumbs from my jean pockets to wrap my hands around her frozen fingers.

'That is vampire myth number twenty-three. We are not always cold,' I said sarcastically. 'We can feel as warm as a human if we feed regularly.'

'You've been well fed,' she acknowledged, and she lowered her eyes as her cheeks flushed. There was a smile on her lips as I laughed and nodded.

After our initial test run, Gwen had decided she rather liked my bite. It was a high unlike any other, and it was what she'd been craving since the beginning.

We reached the river where there was a bridge across the narrowest part of it. Gwen seemed to become immediately enraptured by the scenic atmosphere. She quickly struggled out of her snowshoes so she could walk across to stand at the middle of the slightly arched bridge. She looked back at me and smiled enormously.

'This is beautiful!' she gushed.

I reached her and gently touched her cheek, which drew her attention. She went to her toes to kiss me, and I pressed her against the railing of the bridge as I instantly deepened the kiss. I was thinking her coat would make a good blanket to lay over the snowbank when I heard something moving through the trees.

I stopped kissing Gwen and turned, pressing her behind me, as I prepared to defend us.

A clumsy teenage girl stumbled out of the bush cursing softly and shaking her hand as though she'd hurt it. She had wildly curly dark hair that had been cropped to the nape of her neck and a faint spattering of freckles. She had unique green-amber eyes, and she came to a halt when she saw us standing there staring at her.

'What are you doing here?' I demanded and scented the air to determine her race. I detected a strange buzz in the air, but she seemed human.

'I'm walking home from school,' she said as if this

should have been obvious to me.

'*School*' I repeated in disdain. 'What damned school?'

'The high school,' she answered with that teenaged tone of impertinence. I glared at her, estimating her to be somewhere around seventeen or eighteen. She was old enough to know better than to trespass.

'This is private property,' I reproached her, and I felt Gwen touch my shoulder before she squeezed out from behind me.

'I'm Gwen,' she said. 'What's your name?'

'Emily. William,' the child added as an afterthought.

'William. Liv William must be your mom,' Gwen guessed, and I remembered we were near Gwen's hometown.

'That's right,' Emily acknowledged suspiciously. She glanced back at me in uncertainty.

'I'm Gwen Rhys. You might know my father, Arthur Rhys.'

'He's the mechanic in town,' Emily acknowledged, and her face brightened as she recognized another person from Silver Springs.

I heard someone approaching behind the girl before either of the women. I was prepared for it when a young man with ebony hair stepped out of the trees.

I was *not* prepared for what he was, though…

I couldn't see it, of course, but I could *feel* the immensity of his aura charging the air. I'd never met one of them before, since they were supposed to have gone to another world, but I'd heard plenty of stories. He smelled just as the legends had said he would of fire and ash.

'Emily, what are you doing?' the stranger asked softly with the hint of a stern reprimand in his accented voice.

'Just talking,' she defended herself impatiently, and she rolled her green eyes. I was shocked he would put up with the insolence, but I wondered if perhaps she wasn't what she appeared either.

He put his shoulder in front of hers as he reached her side, and he faced me directly with cold blue eyes. It was not overtly protective, but I understood he was challenging me. I anticipated he would know what I was just as easily as I had sensed his true form. He wanted me to move away from the bridge so the girl he was shielding could cross over safely.

'It's going to be dark soon,' the stranger commented, and Emily sighed in irritation with him.

'Fine,' she relented sharply. She was clearly not aware of the destruction of which he was capable. Otherwise, I was sure she'd have treated him far more gently.

I took Gwen's arm to pull her across the bridge away from them. She looked at me in confusion, but I discreetly shook my head as the girl and her guardian followed us. He ensured there was plenty of space between us, and he always remained between me and his companion.

'See you later, Gwen,' Emily called over her shoulder as they continued on their way. Her male companion's last dark glance at me suggested this was very unlikely. They rounded a bend in the trees, and I sighed in relief.

'I didn't realize your little hometown was such a hotbed for paranormal activity,' I advised Gwen distractedly.

'What?' she asked in bewilderment.

'The man is not human,' I informed her.

'He isn't?' she demanded in shock. 'Is he a vampire?'

'No,' I laughed as we walked across the bridge to where our snowshoes were sitting in the snow. 'He is something far more terrifying.'

'What is that?' asked Gwen in fascination.

'That would be a dragon,' I answered.

'A *dragon*?' she gasped in disbelief. She glanced back over her shoulder in amazement. 'He looked human.'

'He is a shifter,' I explained.

'Like a werewolf?' she verified, and I nodded.

'There are many breeds of were, but his kind do not live in this world anymore. I don't know why he is here, but I'm certain it has something to do with the girl.'

'What do you think he wants with Emily William?' she asked apprehensively, and I shrugged.

'A story for another time, perhaps...'

THE END

Coming Soon!

BLOODLINE

REDEMPTION

WOLFSBANE

INCUBUS

Visit **authoraagordon.com** or
facebook.com/authorAAGordon

(Spoilers Alert!)

INDEX

Characters
MAIN:

Miguel Santos (*mig-el*)**:** the Ambassador of Human Affairs and a five-hundred-year-old coven prince who falls in love with Gwen Rhys. His father is the Lord of the Wayside Coven and a famous artist who met Miguel's Dowrra mother, Francis, in 1501. She was murdered by her brother after giving birth to a vampire, and this shaped Miguel's life. He and his father have spent centuries trying to help the Dowrra who live outside convent walls. Miguel is wealthy and powerful but very afraid Gwen will leave him if she learns he is a vampire. He protects her ardently after she Choses him.

Gwendolyn Rhys: a redheaded waitress who falls in love with Miguel Santos. She doesn't know he is a vampire or that she is Tatamora Dowrra and has Chosen him as her mate. She was born in the town of Silver Springs, which is run by a Dowrra cult. After her mother left, her father became estranged from the cult, which is why Gwen doesn't know anything about her heritage. She believes her mother died when she was seven, but Maria Chose a vampire mate and left. Gwen's half-sister is Jacqueline Iscariot.

Charlotte Wells: was also born and raised in Silver Springs. She is a Nasaru, which is a lower class of Dowrra, who was sent to watch over Gwen in Toronto. She works in a bank, and she is Gwen's obnoxious best friend. She is married to PSA Agent Derek Wells. She knows what Miguel is almost as soon as she meets him, and she encourages Gwen's relationship with him.

Derek Wells: was also born and raised in Silver Springs. He is considered Nasaru as are all male members of the Dowrra cult. He came to Toronto to watch over Gwen, and he is married to

Charlotte. He works for the PSA, so he recognizes Miguel. At first the two men dislike one another, but they gradually develop a friendship based on mutual respect.

Ainsley Westin: one of many humans who works for the Tribunal as an agent. He came from London originally to work with the Ambassador before Miguel and was highly recommended. He is trained as an assassin, but he also functions as Miguel's trusted butler. Gwen develops a fondness for his gentlemanly demeanour, but she doesn't know what he does.

Jonathon Welford: Gwen's violent ex-boyfriend with a grudge.

LAMIA:

Hudson of the Wendat: a twenty-five-hundred-year-old Etruscan vampire who is the youngest of the Lamia brothers. He is Miguel's friend, and he agrees to act as Gwen's bodyguard after Miguel uncovers a photographer taking pictures of her for her ex. His parentage is unknown.

Liam Demetrius: Hudson's five-thousand-year-old brother, who also protects Gwen when she needs it. He was originally born as Anatolius Liakos of Demeter and was the lover of Aphrodite, who cursed him with insatiable lust. He shares Lordship of the Redemption Coven with his twin but rarely plays an active role. His parentage is unknown.

Tyler Demetrius: Liam's reclusive twin brother who acts as the primary Lord of the Redemption Coven. He was originally born Thanos Vasilios of Demeter. He is known as a harbinger of death. His parentage is unknown.

The Destroyer: possibly an eight-thousand-year-old Sumerian and eldest of the Lamia brothers. Miguel thinks he might be older. He is feared by all the gods and has a reputation for ending civilizations. He is also known as Quinn O'Connor but was born Nirgal Enkara. His parentage is unknown.

OTHERS:

Agent Samuel Benet: Miguel's human contact, who was

supposed to date Gwen but never did.

Ahren Schmidt: Jacqueline Iscariot's bodyguard. He sacrifices his life to protect Gwen.

Alexios Kokinos: an unruly four-hundred-year-old vampire from Larissa, Greece, whom Miguel cannot free from PSA prison.

Angjelko: a Macedonian vampire whose castle Miguel and Boerio burned down.

Anthony: one of many humans working for the Tribunal. His widower father was a human aide who was killed in a car crash twenty years ago. Miguel took guardianship of Anthony, and now he is Miguel's driver.

Arthur Rhys: Gwen's father whom her mother left for a vampire. He became estranged from the Dowrra cult after they supported his wife's decision. He secluded Gwen from the cult, which is why she doesn't know what she is.

Attula (*at-oo-la*): an Aegian alien who was entombed by Quinn O'Connor after his people were destroyed.

Carlton: the doorman at the Royal Alton.

Darius of Gilan: Miguel's four-hundred-year-old Persian agent.

Director Donaldson: the head of the PSA.

Dr. Anita Johansson: an anthologist with an obsession with vampires who seeks to unmask them and is killed for it.

Dr. Michael Turner: Johansson's colleague in the Ur excavation.

Francis of the House of Habsburg: Miguel's Dowrra mother. She became pregnant out of wedlock and her family sent her to Romsey Abbey. When her brother learned she'd been thrown out and given birth to a vampire, he murdered her. Her death is the reason Miguel became a philanthropist.

Giovanni Jaevus de los Santos (*gee-O-van-E / jay-vus*): Miguel's father who is a famous artist. He is the Lord of the Wayside Coven.

Jacqueline Iscariot: Gwen's younger vampire half-sister who comes to warn her about the PSA. She is nicknamed Jackie.

James McNeil: a three-hundred-year-old vampire from Barra, Scotland. Miguel steps in while he is accosting Gwen.

Judas Iscariot: Lord of the Aura Coven and Jacqueline's father. He was the vampire Gwen's mother Chose.

Luka Menshikov: Miguel's five-hundred-year-old Russian agent with a twin sister called Natalia.

Mackayla Santos: Miguel's sister. She has an on and off relationship with Hudson with whom she is still in love.

Madame Rosetta: the designer who dresses Gwen in the red dress for the charity ball. She is also known as la Madame.

Maria Rhys: Gwen's mother who left her after Choosing Judas. She is murdered when she comes to warn Gwen about the PSA.

Matthew Dentz: Jacqueline Iscariot's bodyguard.

Melisandre Moore: Gwen's artistic roommate. She is also known as Sandra.

Natalia Menshikov: Miguel's five-hundred-year-old Russian agent with a twin brother called Luka.

Niccolò Boerio: a four-hundred-year-old Italian vampire who is an old friend of Miguel's. Boerio is a businessman and prominent source of power outside the covens. He was exiled, by Miguel, for trafficking werewolf slaves and dealing with the Dominus.

Olivia Trolley: the CEO of Trolley Accounting who hires Gwen.

Rosalina Armando: a two-hundred-year-old vampiress from

Évora, Portugal, whom Miguel releases from PSA prison.

Sonia: Gwen's waitress co-worker.

Locations/Events:

Aegea (*a-gee-a*): the world from which the Aegian aliens originated.

Annual Toledo Charity Ball: Miguel's charity event at which Jon nearly drags Gwen into the street. Miguel purchases *La Dame en Rouge*.

Atlantis: an advanced civilization destroyed by Quinn O'Connor.

Diner (The): where Gwen works as a waitress and meets Miguel.

Highberry Park: an estate owned by the Wayside Coven on which Miguel built a halfway house.

King's Court Steak House (The): a restaurant owned by Boerio which is famous for its medieval embellishments. Miguel takes Gwen there for the Wells' anniversary.

Madame Rosetta's Boutique: la Madame's designer shop.

NTM: The National Toronto Museum where Miguel takes Gwen on their first date. Gwen learns about vampires and the Dowrra.

Palazzo di Giustiniani: another establishment owned by Boerio where Gwen and Miguel go to the masquerade ball.

Redemption Coven: the coven of which Liam and Tyler share lordship.

Royal Alton (The): the lavish hotel where Miguel resides in the presidential suite.

Silver Springs: a paranormal little town north of Toronto where Gwen was born. It is run by a Dowrra cult.

Trolley Accounting: the new company Gwen begins to work

for.

Warm Blooded: a vampire nightclub.

Wayside Coven: the coven to which Miguel belongs. His father is the presiding coven lord.

Welford Accounting: Gwen's old place of employment from which she was fired after her ex tried to assault her.

Terminology:

Aegian Crystals (*age-E-in*)**:** powerful source of magic the gods tried to steal and use against the Destroyer.

Accords: vampire law signed two hundred years ago. It outlines the relationships, rights, and privileges of all races including humans.

Akaharu (*ah-ka-har-oo*): ancient Sumerian for "vampire."

Ambassador of Human Affairs: Miguel is the mediator between the Tribunal and the PSA.

Bloodlust: the passionate desire that overcomes vampires when they need to feed.

Bond (The): a biological connection formed between a Dowrra and her Chosen mate.

Chose/Choose: the act of a Dowrra subconsciously forming a bond with a mate.

Convent: a fortified community of Dowrra.

Coven: a group of vampires living together under a coven lord.

Cult: the followers of a particular religion. The Dowrra worship Inanna, so they are her cult.

Donor: a human who is licenced to partake of vampire lifestyle despite the risks.

Halfway House: a place where vampires can be reintegrated into society after time spent imprisoned.

Hul Gil: an opium tea still ingested by some Donors to make the bite of a vampire less painful.

Matrons: the elderly council overseeing a Dowrra convent.

Nasaru (*nas-are-oo*)**:** the lower class of Dowrra. They can no longer form the bond with a vampire.

Neutral Zones: areas where no coven presides. They are almost entirely without law and order.

***Sanguinem furoris*:** "blood madness" resulting from humans consuming vampire blood. They often do this under the illusion it will make him immortal, but it slowly poisons them.

Summons: a meeting of all the coven lords.

Syphoning: is the act of taking energy from another living creature. There are many ways it can be done. Empaths feed on emotional energy while incubus feed on sexual energy.

Tatamora (*tata-more-a*)**:** the upper class of Dowrra who can still trace their lineage back to Inanna. They can form the bond with a vampire.

Venom: erotic brand used by unmated Dowrra to stimulate sex drives.

Races:

Aegian (*age-E-in*)**:** aliens who founded Atlantis. They have human ancestors called empaths. Plural: Aegiani (*age-E-in-E*).

Angeli Mortis (*an-gel-E   more-tis*)**:** vampire-like creatures which were originally created by the Church with the use of vampire and empath DNA. They feed on vampires, and they almost drove the species to extinction a thousand years ago. They were defeated.

Dowrra (*d-ow-rr-a*)**:** women who have the ability to bond to a Chosen mate. Most often they Chose vampires, but they can also bond with werewolves or Aegiani. They trace their lineage back to the goddess Inanna, whom they worship.

Dragons: shifters who can take the shape of a human or dragon. They upset the Destroyer and had to flee this world.

Empaths: human descendants of the Aegian aliens with empathic powers. They were used by the Church to create the Angeli Mortis, and vampires hunted them all down. Not many of them remain.

Murhyaeli (*mur-rail-E*): a type of dragon shifter. There are five.

Ulfur Wolf: a Viking werewolf.

Vampires: a predator which feeds on humans. They were almost driven to extinction by the Angeli Mortis during the crusade of the Church to eradicate nonhumans. They are the unofficial rulers of the paranormal world and mediate between nonhumans and humans via the Ambassador.

Werewolves: shifters who can take the form of a wolf. There are many kinds.

Mythology:

Anu (*a-new*): the Sumerian King of the Gods. He stopped the feuding between goddess sisters, Ereshkigal and Inanna, by connecting their children together forever. This is the Dowrra bond.

Ereshkigal (*er-esh-ki-gal*): the Queen of Irkalla, the Sumerian Underworld. She is Lilith's mother.

Inanna (*in-an-na*): Goddess of Love and the Mother of the Dowrra. She cursed Lilith to make her infertile.

Lilith: Ereshkigal's daughter whom Inanna cursed infertile. She is credited as the mother of vampires although it was her brothers from whom the race truly descended. Her curse is the reason vampiresses are still infertile.

Organizations:

Church (The): the Catholic Church became a platform from which the Iscariot humans targeted vampires. It waged a holy war on all nonhumans for centuries. The Lamia finally put an end to it after the Church created the Angeli Mortis.

Iscariots (The): a family that has been entrenched in a blood feud between the vampire and human halves for centuries. It began with the birth of Judas Iscariot and a subsequent endeavour to kill him. The Iscariot family was wealthy and influential. Many of the men were cardinals and bishops, which brought their family's war to the doors of the Catholic Church. They funded the creation of the Angeli Mortis. Their family is thought to have been destroyed.

PSA: The Protection Services Agency is a human bureau for mediating with vampires. They dictate expectations for paranormal behaviour, some of which is enforced by the Ambassador. Miguel finds out they are just the front for a much larger organization that may be gearing up for war.

Tribunal: a council of vampires that make all the decisions regarding breeches of the Accords. They also interpret the Accords and dispense Orders of execution, exile, or pardon for all nonhumans.

A Sneak Peek at…

BLOODLINE

Serena

Chapter One

I was never normal, but then, I'm from Silver Springs, so I guess that goes without saying.

I have no idea why I imagined I could go off to university, leave that little paranormal hometown in rural Ontario behind, and carve out an existence of normalcy. In a world shaped by humans, who vehemently believed it belonged only to them, this would always be impossible. I can't say why I even felt it was remotely desirable.

Maybe I sort of envied them their blissful ignorance.

In any case, it didn't matter how hard I tried to become part of their pretty world of lies in that first year at McGill. Either they sensed I wasn't really one of them, or it inevitably became too difficult for me to be around them. Humans feel erratic to empaths. Their unchecked auras spark around them like electricity.

So, there I was in Montreal. It was one of the most beautiful cities and top tourist destinations in all of Canada, but I was more alone than ever.

By second year, I'd more or less accepted my lot in life and began to focus all my efforts on school. I attained a degree in Biology from McGill and a degree in Medical

Genetics from the University of British Columbia. It took me just five years of summer classes, online courses, and two and a half years in Vancouver. I worked for two years at The Ottawa Hospital to obtain my certificate as a medical geneticist whilst I was getting my masters in Genetics.

At this point, I was approached by a multitude of Canadian and American universities. I was even treated to an incredibly expensive dinner by Trevor Kirkland, who was the CEO of First Genesis Labs Inc. His research facility was the biggest and most prestigious in all of North America, and he offered me a job starting at six figures. I was only twenty-four.

My education wasn't finished, however, although it did switch gears dramatically.

It took me just a year of intensive studies to get a degree in ancient history. In another two years, I'd gotten my doctorate in anthropology with a focus in linguistics and mythology. Many of my professional suitors from the world of science didn't like competing with anthropologists, archaeologists, and linguists for my attention.

Now, I was twenty-seven and one of the most highly educated people in North America. Articles had been written about me in *Discover Magazine* and the *American Journal of Human Genetics*. I'd been featured multiple times in both the *Toronto Star* and the *New York Times*.

'Serena?'

I caught Mrs. Durand's eyes on me and realized I'd momentarily zoned out at my desk. I blinked blurry eyes before lowering my gaze back to the stack of paper in front of me. I'd been hunched over it so long my back was starting to ache, and my shoulders popped as I stretched. I quickly reread the simple essay question I'd answered on possible causes for the Dark Age in early Mediterranean civilizations one last time.

Obviously, I couldn't write the truth. The Dark Age was the result of the destruction of Atlantis. The highly advanced civilization had been founded by an empathic alien race. It had been the centre of Mediterranean trade before it was sunk by a Sumerian demigod known as the Destroyer.

I set my pen down decisively on my desk. I was functioning on the borrowed energy of another student, who was operating on an hour nap, and it was about time to call it quits.

I had finished the last final exam of my doctorate, and I should have felt like celebrating! A couple of my classmates had given obnoxious whoops of joy as they'd left the exam room. I couldn't imagine mustering the vigour. I felt lost now that it was over after so many years of determined drive.

I pulled myself up from my seat and handed in my paper. I collected my things and left the room feeling light-headed.

I probably should have gone directly home to bed, but I started to walk down Doctor Penfield Avenue toward Gerts. I had finished my doctorate! A drink at the campus pub was in order whether I felt like it or not.

It was a mid-April night and still quite cool, so I snuggled into my woollen scarf and tucked my hands into my coat pockets. The sun had gone down, and the street, bathed in artificial light, seemed unnaturally quiet. I wasn't worried, though. I was by far the most dangerous thing I'd ever encountered walking the streets of Montreal.

It didn't take me long to realize someone was following me.

Most women feel anxiety at the possibility of an attack on a dark street. I've heard them tell their tales with friends around a bar table.

I'm not "most women," and I wasn't afraid.

Without turning, I expanded my aura to him and felt a sphere of unfathomable hatred bubbling around him. It was angry and violent, and I knew he wanted to hurt me. I savoured the taste of those rich emotions, and then I withdrew from him. I fell into the familiar ruse of damsel in distress, which was sure to lure him in. I picked up the pace, and felt a fissure of excitement sizzle through the air. He thought I'd noticed I was being followed and that I was afraid. My fear excited him, and his excitement was delicious.

I lowered my head further into my scarf as my empathic hunger began to flex in eager anticipation inside me. It felt the way I imagine the coils of an enormous anaconda moving within me would feel.

Usually siphoning is done between consenting empaths. Unfortunately, I had yet to meet a male member of my race who wasn't my brother or my father because we were almost extinct. Most often, I'm forced to take what I need from strangers instead of sharing what I have with a lover. I don't need to be intimate with them, but sometimes I choose to be. Empaths have insane sex drives. I can always make them forget if I want.

I'd been on McGill campus for nine years, and I knew when certain entrances are locked. I darted off the sidewalk and headed for one of them. At this time, it was dark and secluded as I pressed against the doors in feigned earnest. The doors jiggled hopelessly.

As I'd hoped, my stalker loomed up behind me. I could tell, from his perverse energy, he thought he'd cornered his prey. I had to clamp down viciously on my appetites so they didn't flicker tellingly in my eyes as I turned toward him. I didn't want him running away.

I saw he was a handsome man in his late twenties. He had a cruel smile.

'It's awfully late for a pretty little thing like you to be out here all by herself,' he commented. He didn't have a Quebec accent.

'It's safe enough on campus,' I respond and glanced past him toward the street. He thought I was looking for help but I was looking for witnesses to what I was about to do to him.

'There's no one there,' he told me smugly, and he lunged suddenly toward me. He grabbed my bag and threw it to the ground in an aggressive demonstration meant to frighten me. I could see the heat of his expectation rising in his eyes, and I couldn't help it. I smirked.

It slipped out unintentionally, and my eyes widened up at him in embarrassment. He stared at me in confusion with my reaction to his violence.

'You think this is *funny*, bitch?' he snarled.

'No,' I told him guardedly. The hostility of his emotions was making it difficult to reign in my hunger. The taste of it on the air was making my skin tingle with anticipation.

I could tell when he realized something was very wrong. Probably my eyes had begun to change colour. I could feel my skin rippling, and he could probably see the waves of energy flexing inside me.

He began to back away, and I reached up to grab him around the head. I exerted my empathic power over him, so he stopped screaming and went compliantly to his knees.

He's from a wealthy family in Vermont. He comes over the border to hunt young women in Montreal, and he's been doing it a long time. He's an abusive boyfriend, an arrogant friend, and an irresponsible son. His stepfather used to beat him, and he blames his mother for letting it happen...

I sucked in all the pain, the grief, the horror, and even the brief moments of satisfaction that are all he had from hurting others. Some empaths kill when they feed this heavily, but I never had.

Once I'd finished with him, my flesh was pulsing, and I would feel twice my usual size until I'd properly absorbed the influx.

Benjamin Fredrick Mallory, aged 27, fell to the pavement, and he lay very still with his eyes rolling into his head.

I stretched, and the crack in my neck was particularly satisfying. I felt awake now. I felt energized and ready to close the bar.

After a moment, I picked up my bag and considered his body on the ground. I'm not really a callous person, but I do find it hard to feel bad for the type of people I choose to feed on this much. Usually, I only take enough of their strength to leave a human with a slight headache that a good nap will fix. The ones I decide to hurt are *never* nice people, and most often they have tried to hurt me first. It's why I can do what I do to them.

He'd be fine in a couple weeks. He'd never remember what happened, but the sudden illness and brush with mortality might scare him. Maybe he'd think twice about hurting someone else.

I straightened my jacket, and I stepped neatly over him to resume my way seamlessly toward Gerts.

'You're just going to leave him there?' asked an incredulous voice in an accent I'd never heard before.

I whirled around and spotted my unwanted audience of one where he was leaning against the building in the darkness. I couldn't see much except he was very tall and quite wide through the shoulders.

I didn't even hesitate to ask questions because chances were he was a vampire who'd sensed my aura, and he was there to kill me. I lashed out with all the power I'd just acquired, and I expected to strike him instantly dead. Instead, when the invisible fissure touched him, it flashed green and then was utterly extinguished.

I was stunned.

'What the hell are you?' I snarled at him.

'A friend, I hope,' he advised me as he pushed away from the wall against which he was leaning and walked toward me. He glanced down at the unconscious man, and then stepped into the light of the streetlamps.

He was strikingly attractive but in a strangely savage way. I'd never seen someone who looked like him, and I would have known he wasn't human even before he'd absorbed my power. Thick, wavy auburn hair fell to his broad shoulders. There were tiny braids strewn through its length, which made me think of another time and a long forgotten culture. He had prominent cheekbones and a stern square jaw dusted in a dark auburn shadow extending down his neck. His eyes were a fierce emerald green unlike anything I'd ever seen before. His nose was just a little crooked, like it had been broken, and his sensual lips were the only part of him that seemed remotely soft. He moved commandingly with a body that seemed to be cut from rock in jeans and a long-sleeved shirt. He was the kind of man who could instantly bring any woman to sexual alert, and I was definitely no exception.

He came to a stop a couple of feet from me, and I felt my neck straining as I looked up at him. I'm taller than the average woman, but he was six-four.

'How do you know we are friends?' I challenged him distrustfully.

'I don't,' he said deeply, and I recognized his accent was Scottish or Irish. That seemed about right. He certainly looked like a Celtic warrior to me. 'I hoped to establish an alliance.'

'Who are you?' I demanded suspiciously.

'My name is Cian O'Duinn,' he said very quietly, as though the name might draw unwanted attention. 'You would be wise not to repeat it.'

'You have enemies, Cian O'Duinn?' I asked tauntingly.

'The same ones you do, empath,' he informed me calmly, and my amusement faded almost immediately. 'Anatolius and Thanos of Demeter and Natula of Alalia,' he confirmed.

I found it hard to breathe as I gazed up at him in deep suspicion.

'They haven't been known by those names in a thousand years,' I hissed. 'You mean Tyler and Liam Demetrius and Hudson of the Wendat. Brothers of Quinn

O'Connor, *the Destroyer,'* I whispered pointedly. He wasn't intimidated.

'If that is what they call themselves now,' he dismissed. 'The names matter not. Only that they suffer,' he assured me with absolute confidence.

'*Them* suffer?' I snorted with laughter. 'You cannot hurt demigods! Don't you think my people have tried?'

'I'm not an Atlantean. I can hurt them, and I *will,'* he promised. 'Your kind may thrive again if you help me deliver retribution.'

Retribution...

Justice for the last two thousand years the Lamia had spent hunting down my kind and exterminating them. Vengeance for the life I'd lived in terror that vampires would come for me as they had come for so many of my father's relatives. It sounded like a fantasy, and I was no fool.

'You will get me killed!' I chastised him.

I meant to walk away from him, but he grabbed me with reflexes even more impressive than my own. I reacted viciously and was satisfied at least when he physically touched my skin, I could still burn him with my power. He hissed, releasing me in surprise, and then he looked furious.

'You're so afraid of them you will ignore a chance to return your people to the glory of Atlantis?' he demanded.

'We do *not* speak that name!' I snarled immediately. 'There is only one who can return us to that glory, and he's been imprisoned by the Lamia.'

Cian stepped nearer, and I saw excitement in his eyes even though I couldn't feel it in the air around him. It was the first time I'd been unable to sense the aura of another living creature.

'What if I told you I intend to help you raise Attula so, together, he and I can seek vengeance?' Cian asked me eagerly. I was intrigued.

'What do you want from me?' I asked reluctantly.

'You're an empath and an expert in your field. With my power and your research, we can find Attula's tomb,' Cian reasoned.

'What if *they* find us first?' I wanted to know.

'The less you know of me the better, but I hope they *do* find us,' Cian informed me. 'Once they are dead, I will find O'Connor wherever he sleeps. And I'll be coming for him too...'

About the Author

A.A. Gordon is the author of *The Dowrra Series*. She grew up on a farm in Markdale, Ontario, which is a very small town north of Toronto. She started writing at an early age. As a young adult, she moved to downtown Toronto to study history at Ryerson University where she earned her Bachelor of Arts.

She now lives happily in Southampton with her wonderful partner, Daniel, and their dogs, Tadhg and Fionn. She is looking forward to sharing more of her writing soon.

Please enjoy!

authoraagordon.com
www.facebook.com/authorAAGordon

Made in the USA
Monee, IL
07 November 2019

16464635R00182